LADELLE & JUBILANT

ENDORSEMENTS

I am writing to express my full endorsement for Cathy McIlvoy's novel, *LaDelle & Jubilant*. Set in 1930s Tuskegee, Alabama, the story revolves around George Washington Carver and other characters in a fresh and historically accurate portrayal of the people and events in that difficult time. Well-researched with great insight and integrity, McIlvoy's work tells a story that is compellingly simple and clear. *LaDelle & Jubilant* goes beyond some of the recent fictional works that have George Washington Carver as a central character but are written for younger audiences. It is my hope that this manuscript will be made available to audiences around the world.

—**Dana R. Chandler**, University Archivist/Associate Professor, Tuskegee University.

LaDelle & Jubilant is an authentic, deeply engrossing story that will take you on a relatable journey of emotions. Cathy McIlvoy's storytelling thoroughly captures the essence of family dynamics and history. This book will stay with me for a long time.

—**Brendan Slocumb**, author of *The Violin Conspiracy* and *Symphony of Secrets*

With humor and history, McIlvoy's *LaDelle & Jubilant* takes us to Tuskegee in the 1930s and invites us to journey

with some endearing characters, including the amazing George Washington Carver. As a child of Mother Tuskegee (both my parents and grandparents are graduates), this novel was a delight to read.
—**Jewel Burks Solomon**, Managing Partner, Collab Capital

Heartwarming, humorous, and inspirational, *LaDelle & Jubilant* is a well written, multi-generational story that left me wanting to know more about George Washington Carver and the community around the Tuskegee Institute.
—**Angela Correll,** author of *Grounded*

LaDelle & Jubilant by debut author Cathy McIlvoy is an insightful look at the life and times of George Washington Carver through the eyes of a twelve-year old boy named Jubilant and his aunt LaDelle. Full of heartwarming moments and a pinch of boyhood mischief, this book will keep you turning pages. The characters were relatable and came alive through McIlvoy's description and dialogue. I'm so glad I met LaDelle and Jubilant!
—**Karen deBlieck**, author and poet

LADELLE & JUBILANT

CATHY MCILVOY

A Christian Company
ElkLakePublishingInc.com

COPYRIGHT NOTICE

Cover and Interior Design: Derinda Babcock, Deb Haggerty
Editor(s): Peggy Ellis, Cristel Phelps, Deb Haggerty
Author Represented by Pape Commons, Don Pape

PUBLISHED BY: Elk Lake Publishing, Inc., 35 Dogwood Drive, Plymouth, MA 02360, 2023

Library Cataloging Data
Names: McIlvoy, Cathy (Cathy McIlvoy)
LaDelle & Jubilant / Cathy McIlvoy
260 p. 23cm × 15cm (9in × 6 in.)

ISBN-13: 9798891340121 (paperback) | 9798891340138 (trade hardcover) | 9798891340145 (trade paperback) | 9798891340152 (e-book)

Key Words: Historical fiction; Christian; Women's, Southern; African American/Black; Tuskegee; George Washington Carver

Library of Congress Control Number: 2023944907 Fiction

DEDICATION

To Ian and Noah. Teaching you about George Washington Carver all those years ago planted the seed in me to make him a character in a story which grew into this book.

TABLE OF CONTENTS

ACKNOWLEDGMENTS

George Washington Carver—what a gift you were to many when you lived on earth, and a gift you continue to be to me and others in the legacy you left behind. Though LaDelle and Jubilant take center stage in my story, the impetus for writing this book was you. Writing and getting the story published was a long journey filled with detours. Your life—with its greater detours and challenges—helped inspire me to keep going. Your accomplishments and the virtues you exemplified captivated me from the get-go and still do.

Thank you, Kyle Negrete, for introducing me to my agent, Don Pape. Don, thank you for being in my corner and taking me on as one of your Pape Commons writers.

Thank you to Dana Chandler, the archivist at Tuskegee University, for generously sharing your insight and knowledge about GWC and Tuskegee University.

Thank you to Deb Haggerty and Cristel Phelps at Elk Lake Publishing. You took a chance on me and on *LaDelle & Jubilant*. You evaluated my work and didn't focus on my skin color. That was brave of you.

A special thank you to Peggy Ellis, my editor. You are knowledgeable and straightforward, but you're also open and willing to consider my pushbacks! I learned a lot working with you and appreciate how you helped make this a better read. You are a pleasure to work with. Let's do it again!

Thank you to Jennifer Garrity. No matter how many years go by, and projects get written, I will always consider you my first and best writing mentor! Thank you for what you taught me in my early days of writing when we lived in Germany. I appreciate your continued friendship and input more than you know.

Thank you to Ruth, John, and Nancy Brandon for getting me to Tuskegee University to do the research, walk where Professor Carver walked, and have my first taste of legit southern grits, sweet tea, and catfish. That trip was a huge help to me, and I still smile when I think of it.

And finally, to my family: Thank you to my sister Arlene for being my cheerleader since birth. Your encouragement all these years has been a buoy and a blessing. Thank you to all my sons—Erik, Isaac, Ian, and Noah. I hope "the Jubilant story" makes you proud. And, to the highest of heights, I thank my husband, Rob. I would have given up on writing fiction long ago if it weren't for you. Seriously. I love you.

To God be the glory.

CHAPTER ONE—LADELLE

An inconvenience is an adventure wrongly considered.
(Gilbert K. Chesterton)

TUSKEGEE, ALABAMA—1937

Today is the day. LaDelle Harris sighed, stretched her arm out of the covers and blindly reached for her alarm. She made contact with the button and slapped it with her palm.

"Beat you to it," she mumbled. LaDelle remained lying on her back, gazing at the ceiling before adding a final point in this imaginary competition she held with her alarm clock. "What purpose do you have when every morning I rise and shine before you ever have a chance to jolt me awake?"

It was true—an alarm clock was an unnecessary fixture on her nightstand, but there it was—placed at just the right angle. Always dust-free. LaDelle's inner body clock was just as reliable as any alarm. Perhaps more so. Besides, she resented the shrill of the bell. *Would it kill a clock company to produce one with a gentle sound? We don't all need to be rattled awake, for goodness' sake.*

She yawned, sat up in bed, and moved her head from side to side, up and down. The cracks and pops in her neck caused her to grimace but also gave her a sense of satisfaction and productivity. LaDelle perched her specs on her nose and snatched the Western Union telegram off her nightstand to reread it for the tenth time. Afterward, she uttered another sigh punctuated with "Today is the day." She said it out loud this time as if it would help her accept the reality of the words and then tucked the telegram inside the drawer. She slipped her Timex onto her wrist before touching feet to floor. Letting out a full-mouth yawn, LaDelle stood, bent over, and reached for her toes. Touching them in this position had been beyond her reach for the past twenty years or so, but at least she tried. The groans that involuntarily escaped her lips every single morning during this ritual testified that her effort was an honest one.

Fully awake, she pulled and tugged at the sheets, making her side of the bed nice and tight. No need to make the entire bed—the right side was left unused, her husband Garvin gone now. He'd been killed nine years earlier. Since then, she kept to her own side while his remained barely ruffled, ever vacant, and cold to the touch. Each morning (except Saturdays when she did laundry), she simply gave the corner of his side of the bedspread a hearty tug and gently smoothed the surface with her hand. "There," she'd whisper, setting things to right in the only way she could.

Bed made and pillows in place, she moved on to her closet and took the day's dress off the hanger. She owned nine of them—ten if you counted the plain black one reserved for funerals stored in the back of her closet. Five dresses she sewed from one McCall's pattern, four from another. With each pattern, she used an assortment of fabrics, sleeve lengths, and collars to give her reasonable yet unpretentious variety. One dress was store-bought.

The one purchased from Daisy's Dresses and Fashion Accessories was not just a dress but a suit made of ivory and gold brocade fabric. She'd worn it only once—at the intimate wedding ceremony the day she and her Garvin were married. LaDelle was no small woman. She was big-boned—some would say "solid"—and taller than the average female, which caused people to take notice. Her perfect soldier-like posture made her presence even more commanding. On her wedding day, that ivory and gold suit, in contrast with her espresso skin tone, and a pillbox hat with a short veil adorning her black hair like a crown turned her into a regal sight. Her carefully applied red lipstick made her face glow and illuminated her unrelenting grin. She purchased the tube of Ravishing Red just for this occasion, but never wore the color again.

Garvin, not quite a full inch taller than his bride and half the weight, stood tall as well. His face beamed more than usual that day. He wore a simple gray suit with a white rosebud fastened to his lapel. He later confessed to her that he'd plucked it from a neighbor's garden. He was a sentimental man, at times too trusting according to LaDelle, with a ready-smile and good-natured confidence. He had a playfulness about him that drew others in and offset her more serious and sometimes cynical nature.

Both in the latter half of their thirties, they were ready for matrimony after two years of friendship and a purposeful year of courting. The couple had a five-week engagement before ushering themselves to the chapel. Some commented in secret that LaDelle Bartley and Garvin Harris were an unlikely, if not irregular, couple. Yet something about them standing there that afternoon, hand in hand as they pledged their love and commitment to each other, closed the mouths of covert naysayers.

"Marriage is made up of two flawed people," the minister conducting the ceremony reminded them as bride and groom faced him at the altar. "You must daily bestow grace and forgiveness unto one another."

Some "amens" could be heard from several of the forty-seven people in attendance. This seemed to encourage the minister, and thirty minutes later with escalating zeal, he was still on a roll and well into a full-blown sermon until LaDelle shot him a look. He cleared his throat and wrapped things up with the passage about wives submitting to their husbands. Then, he moved on to their vows.

LaDelle and Garvin's relationship may not have been perfect, but the virtuous nature of their union was recognized and audibly cheered when they vowed, "I do." Afterward, a bounty of food, drinks, and desserts were set out on tables covered in checkered tablecloths. The celebration lasted for hours as no one seemed in a hurry to leave.

Garvin and LaDelle had reminisced about their wedding day from time to time, commenting to each other how perfect the day had been.

LaDelle allowed herself a quick glance at her never-again-worn suit before returning her eyes and mind to the more mundane attire in her closet. Six of her frocks were work dresses. She rotated them each day except for the black one. The remaining two were reserved as housedresses to be worn after work and on weekends. For church, she wore whatever work dress hadn't been rotated in during the week. This system of hers gave her peace of mind if not genuine pleasure. Today was Friday, a workday, so she'd wear the solid forest green dress with the right breast pocket and buttons on the bodice because yesterday she wore the navy cotton one with small white polka dots and lace collar. *Organization and routine save time and trouble. Why don't more people recognize this wisdom and discipline themselves to put it into practice?*

Dressed now, LaDelle made her way through the kitchen to the back door.

"Come on in, boy!" She said after opening the back door just wide enough for her beloved dog to fit through. She spoke with affection but in a hushed tone. There was no reason to whistle or holler for him—there he sat on the back porch as usual, staring up at the doorknob, waiting to be let in. Dewey wagged his tail with such intensity it looked as if his whole body might be set in motion and take off in flight. He entered the kitchen and galloped around the table before nudging LaDelle with his nose as she filled his food dish.

This was their routine from May to the end of October. In the winter, she'd allow him to sleep inside on his designated rug, but Alabama summers were hot and muggy, and outside, though still humid and sticky, was where a canine should be this time of year. If left inside at night, his panting and drinking from his water bowl kept her awake, even from the kitchen. Some nights would provide a degree or two of cooler air. At those times, she thought to join him outside, especially as the change of life invaded her, heating up her insides like a lobster plopped mercilessly into boiling water. *A result of the fall of man, no doubt.* One of these days she'd have a screened in sleeping porch built onto the kitchen. *One of these days.*

"Well, company's coming, Dewey," she told him matter-of-factly, refocusing her attention on her dog, her voice flat if not annoyed. She set his dish in front of him and patted his head, almost cool from the morning air. She scratched him behind his ears and checked for ticks while he devoured his morning meal.

"And it looks like he might have to stay here for quite some time. How are we going to cope with this, Dewey? Huh, boy? What are your thoughts?"

Dewey looked up from his bowl, wagged his tail, and let out a joyful bark as if, somehow, he believed he'd been told good news.

"Glad *you're* happy about the prospect." She gave his head a playful tussle. "Sure wish I shared your enthusiasm."

Garvin had wanted a dog. LaDelle argued that having an animal around would just make the house dirty and a dog would be annoying with all the inevitable barking and fleas.

"We ain't gonna be blessed with no children, Delle," his tone gentle as he put his arm around her and gave her shoulder a tender rub. "We might as well put a speck of energy into loving a pup together. Dogs are great fun! Didn't you always want one as a child? In a small way, a pup could fill a hole for us."

With that last comment, LaDelle stepped away from Garvin. She shook her head and shoved her hands on her hips. Through pursed lips she retorted, "A pup won't fill any such hole—just create a mess of holes in our backyard!" She turned on her heels after giving what she considered a clever comeback and exited the room.

Garvin was no milquetoast—LaDelle would never have married him if he were. He was strong when he needed to be, but secure and smart enough to choose his battles. So, he decided as much as he wanted a dog, it wasn't an argument worth winning. He'd surely pay for such a victory with constant complaining if the dog shed its fur or slobbered on the furniture, which, of course, would happen. Having to listen to her bemoan the presence of a dog would have soured the win like vinegar does milk. For that reason, after a few heated conversations on her part—as was her way, not his—Garvin chose not mention dogs again.

Six days after his final push to convince LaDelle that a dog would fill a hole in their lives, Garvin's life was taken from him.

The conversation was over. Stubbornness of this type is often regretted, and this particular bout haunted LaDelle more than she could have ever foreseen, mostly because she never took the opportunity to apologize for it.

Tired of the hold this past mistake had on her, she finally decided she had to do something to try to release herself from it. So, a year and a half to the day after Garvin was gone and she moved from New York to Alabama to start her position at the Tuskegee Institute, LaDelle began her search for the right mutt to adopt. The search took a good while, but on the second anniversary of her husband's death, LaDelle drove to Montgomery to see a litter of Border Collie mixes—three females, one male, all as friendly and keen as they come as advertised in the paper. When she arrived, as she read off a list of questions she had for the farmer, the male pup stopped wrestling with his sisters, eyed LaDelle, then trotted over and sat at her feet.

"Well now," she said. She bent down and gathered him into her arms, looking him over from head to tail. "You, then," she whispered in his ear and paid the farmer a dollar seventy-five in quarters and carried him to her car.

Twenty minutes into the drive back to her place, the dog finally settled himself and lay down beside her. He rested his black and white head in her lap and gave a robust exhale through his nose. The warmth this brought LaDelle permeated her whole body. Her throat closed as tears slid down her cheek. She wiped them away at first with the back of her hand but then gave into them. She let them flow until her nose began to run, and she had to pull over to the side of the road for a moment to retrieve a handkerchief from the glove compartment. How she missed Garvin, and how she wished she had given in to his request for a pup when he was alive! *Why am I so stubborn sometimes? Much of the time?*

When she had collected herself enough to continue, LaDelle drove on, stroking her new companion's fur with her right hand, keeping the left on the wheel. She managed to keep her attention on the road except for stealing some glances at the pup every mile or so for the remainder of the journey home.

"Dewey," she whispered as she rubbed his soft ears. "Dewey is your name, and I'm your new mama." A peacefulness enveloped her like she hadn't experienced in years. *My goodness—I have a pup!* But then, *what have I done?*

Though the price of the mutt was fair, she had to spend another three dollars to replace the entry rug he peed on the moment he bolted through her front door. The cost of his kibble and his penchant for chewing up towels, of all things, cost her more than she had bargained for. Yet, the truth—the awful, but wonderful truth—was that Dewey was indeed a blessing. Though he didn't completely fill a hole, he made one less deep, less lonely. Of course, she was still left to deal with the much larger and profound hole which Garvin's death had made. That pit threatened to pull her down into it every day, but Dewey, in a small but significant way, helped to keep her from being swallowed up. The pup had need of her after all.

Now, as the pair faced each other in the kitchen, she gave Dewey another loving pat and accepted his warm lick on her hand in return. She stared at him for a moment as he ate, but was soon brought back to her current worry: *How is this going to work, having a twelve-year-old boy around who, no doubt, is full of trouble? Will he eat more than his share and leave a mess wherever he goes?*

LaDelle continued to ask herself these types of questions as she dumped two scoops of ground coffee into the aluminum filter in her coffee pot before setting it onto the stove to percolate. *How on God's green earth am I going to get my work done when I have to take care of a child?*

What sort of chaos will he conjure? Darn it, Ashton. Why did you have to go and have yourself a heart attack?

LaDelle and her brother Ashton's relationship had been close, but not as playmates or confidants. She was almost ten years older, and she'd practically raised Ashton and their younger brother. "Listen to your *deuxième maman*," Papa would say to the boys whenever he and Mama left LaDelle in charge—he was obsessed with all things French. LaDelle never wanted the role of second mama, but she was on duty while her mother worked as a seamstress and Papa as a pressman for two successful print shops in New York near their home in Westchester County.

When she was assigned a job, LaDelle couldn't deny her nature—she took it seriously. She was expected to keep her younger brothers safe and out of mischief, and still keep up with her studies. So, she did. She learned early on that the best way to make sure boys stayed out of trouble was to keep them busy and not give them an inch. Under her instruction and insistence, both brothers knew how to read by the time they were four, and by age five, they could fold laundry as efficiently as any housemaid.

Now, just a few days earlier, she had received a telegram from the eldest of her younger brothers, the reverend Ashton Bartley, asking her to care for his boy for the summer while he recuperated from a heart attack. She knew the request was reasonable, especially on account of him being a widower, and with his current health issues, he had a legitimate need—a hole of his own to be filled. Still, everything about the situation made her anxious and annoyed.

She stared at her watch and sighed for the fifth time that morning. Her nephew would be boarding his bus about now. He'd be present in her life in a matter of hours. LaDelle sighed for the sixth time just thinking about it.

"Okay, Lord," she prayed, "If you're not going to help me, just turn his bus around now and release me from this burden. I'll fail for sure if you don't help. I'll try to not be too hard on the child, though sometimes boys his age could do with a little knock upside the head."

CHAPTER TWO—JUBILANT

No one is useless in this world who lightens the burden.
(Charles Dickens)

"I don't want to go," Jubilant whined to Millie Hines as she drove her blue Rambler to the bus station. "Daddy needs me. I can help him!" He repeated himself several times, but knew it was no use. The more he talked, the faster she drove. He rubbed his head and held his breath—a habit that came and went.

"That's a laugh! You can't keep yourself out of trouble for ten minutes or be counted on to do darn near anything, so how in heaven's name do you expect to help the reverend?" Millie kept her eyes on the road as she lectured him, though at four foot nine, she could barely see over the steering wheel even with the thick cushion placed under her rump.

Jubilant wondered if what she said was the truth. He was tired of feeling like he couldn't do anything right. Besides, he was worn out from the nightmares that had invaded his sleep for the past week or so. He woke up trembling each night. His heart raced, and his skin was cold and clammy. Each nightmare infused a distraught feeling into Jubilant's gut because they mirrored the truth that his daddy *did* have a heart attack—right there in front of him. One minute he was standing at the pulpit in the middle of delivering his sermon to a near-full sanctuary, and the next minute, his mouth dropped opened wide but no sound came out. Jubilant saw his daddy's eyes bug out as he stared into space, then he clutched his heart and fell to the floor. *It must've been my irresponsible ways that brought Daddy to the breaking point,* Jubilant decided. Guilt and regret kept him from falling back to sleep. This routine had left him exhausted ever since.

Now, at the bus, beads of sweat formed on Jubilant's forehead as he wrestled with his overstuffed green duffel. *What was the Southeastern Greyhound Lines thinking, making their doors so narrow? How do they expect a person to fit his bag through?* The five or six people in line behind him kept to themselves, lost in their thoughts or maybe not quite awake. Some wrapped their arms around themselves and muttered out loud about the weather. In an hour or so, the folks of Huntsville, Alabama, would be fanning their faces with bus schedules and dime novels in the June heat, but this particular morning began with a surprise bite in the air.

"Boy, turn your bag lengthwise. Now tilt it to the left a tad and lead it in by the top," a white man standing two inches from Jubilant coached too loudly in his ear as he made his third attempt at fitting his duffel through the cramped space.

"Shake a leg, boy, and get on the bus," the bus driver demanded from his seat as if that wasn't exactly what Jubilant was trying to do.

"What's takin' him so long?" The line of people grew impatient outside, grumbling to each other and shifting their feet.

"The boy can't get his bag through the door," a lady sighed, rolling her eyes. "It's almost as big as he is and more than twice as wide."

Jubilant was well aware of his skinny frame, but that comment made his face grow hot. It was true his trousers were getting looser by the day. He hadn't had much of an appetite lately. Twelve-year-old boys were supposed to eat their families out of house and home, he'd been told, but Jubilant had a knack for not doing what he was supposed to. In the past week, he had lost much of his taste for food. Having to listen to everyone coax him to "eat up" had become as annoying as taking a bath or being followed around by his snot-nosed neighbor, Artie.

Jubilant took a deep breath, and then bit his bottom lip as he balanced the duffel on one knee. He concentrated on keeping his stick-thin body vertical and his cap on his head. A strap of his suspenders fell off one shoulder, but he ignored it. With one foot on the second step leading onto the bus, he steadied himself and held his breath. Jubilant was bent on keeping his bag with him and not storing it in the luggage hold at the bottom of the bus. He lowered his head like an angry bull with a mind to charge, then he gave the duffel a final, no-nonsense shove powered by determination and sheer embarrassment.

There! He sighed to himself, finally able to manipulate the overstuffed duffel and push it through the doorway. The dozen or so onlookers already settled into their seats looked on with amusement. The reverend had been worried his son had packed more than he needed, making the bag too awkward and heavy for a child to handle on his own, but Jubilant had insisted.

"I can't leave my slingshot or my new baseball behind! What about my rabbit's foot collection? My favorite pillow? You can't expect me to leave *that* at home!"

"You won't be havin' much time for toys or sleep while you're staying with your Aunt LaDelle," the reverend warned. His voice was weak, but he added, "That woman will keep you busier than a bee in springtime. You can be sure of that."

The reverend had more he wanted to say about Jubilant cramming his duffel bag with the stuff he didn't need, but he was exhausted and not in the mood to argue, so he soon gave in.

"Ah, go ahead now and pack what you want, but that better include your underclothes, an extra pair of breeches and your toothbrush," the reverend said with a dismissive wave of his hand.

Jubilant smiled to himself. It wasn't often he could change his daddy's mind and win an argument. Now, however, after such a humiliating public wrestling match with his bag, Jubilant wasn't sure he had truly won anything. The reverend had been right. Onlookers probably thought this was the skinny kid's first time on a bus.

The truth was Jubilant had traveled by bus many times before, but never all by himself. When Mama was still alive, and the family lived in Yonkers, Jubilant would sometimes travel with her and Daddy by bus to visit elderly parishioners in Westchester County. A few years after Mama went to heaven—folks said God must have need of her there, but when Jubilant heard comments like that he wanted to spit—the reverend decided to accept a position to do the Lord's work in, of all places, Alabama. When it came time to move, father and son made the long journey together from New York to the Heart of Dixie. They traveled by train, bus, and finally streetcar until they reached the two-bedroom parsonage next door to the Amazing Grace Baptist Church, a mile outside Huntsville.

Now, while traveling alone, Jubilant was sure that all eyes were staring at him—especially the eyes of the white folks—and, thanks to the spectacle with his luggage, he was right. All that he dreaded about this day seemed to happen not only in the struggle with his duffel, but in what happened in the next several, cruel moments. He grabbed his ticket from his pocket and held it out to the bus driver, but Jubilant misjudged the hand off and let go too soon. At first, the ticket stuck to his nervous, sweaty fingers, but it broke free and fluttered toward the ground. Determined to catch the ticket midair before it could land and hide itself under one of the seats, Jubilant leapt forward which caused him to trip over the accursed duffel. A split-second later, he landed face-first onto the surprised driver's lap.

"Hey, watch it, boy!" the driver barked as he pushed Jubilant's head away from his crotch.

The passengers erupted with laughter as they watched the scene unfold. The people in the growing line outside, however, grumbled louder.

As Jubilant struggled to his feet and stammered out an apology to the driver, a large Negro woman, much darker than Jubilant and heavy on her feet, approached him. She reached down, scooped up the uncooperative ticket and handed it to the bus driver. Then, without a word, she snatched up Jubilant's duffel as if it were no heavier than a shopping bag filled with goose feathers and motioned for him to follow her. He kept his eyes on the ground and walked behind the woman down the aisle to the back of the bus. His face grew hotter with each step. If he was a dog, Jubilant thought, he would be whimpering, and his pathetic tail would be between his legs.

"You sit here now, honey," the woman said with a smile as she came to a seat already occupied by a kid around Jubilant's age. "Scoot yourself," she said to the boy. She tossed the duffel in the overhead shelf and smoothed out her cotton dress.

Jubilant nodded but said nothing. He avoided eye contact with her and everyone else on the bus.

"This here," she said, motioning to the young boy already seated, "is my son Wilson, and my name is Patience Doyle, but you best call me Miss Patty—everyone does." She sat down on the seat behind her son and added, "Now will you please tell me why a child your age is travelin' all by his lonesome?"

Jubilant stayed standing in the aisle and finally looked up at Miss Patty's face. He studied it for a moment, trying to decide if he should tell her his story. The reverend had warned him not to strike up conversations with strangers on the bus, but Miss Patty had a kind look about her. Her face was as black as a shadow and round like an autumn pumpkin. She offered another reassuring smile—wide and revealing a gap between her two front teeth—while she patiently waited for an answer.

There was something about Miss Patty that Jubilant liked, and it had been a while since he'd taken much of a liking to an adult, especially in Alabama. He decided there'd be no harm in taking the seat next to Wilson, so he sat down and removed his cap. He turned to face Miss Patty. Jubilant opened his mouth to tell her his situation, but thought better of it when he saw a man in overalls looking his way. *I don't know this woman. Besides, everyone on the bus will eavesdrop on my story, and it's no one's business.* He shrugged and said to her, "Don't worry yourself about me. I'm fine."

Jubilant turned back in his seat and faced forward. He was ashamed of his rudeness and didn't want to see a disapproving look on anyone's face. He fiddled with his cap in his hands, doing his best to not touch Wilson in any way. Without moving his head, he managed to glance at the book turned over on his seat companion's lap. He liked to read and pass the time with a book and wished he had thought to bring one of his own for the bus ride.

Then, as if Wilson could read his mind, he leaned toward Jubilant and whispered, "If you tell me why ain't you with your mama or daddy, I'll let you read a chapter of my book."

Jubilant thought for a moment, trying to decide just how badly he wanted time with that book. Before he could respond, the bus driver started up the motor and closed the glass doors. They made a final, piercing shriek, and then slammed shut, sealing the passengers inside for an entire day of travel. The rumble of the motor vibrated Jubilant's body, forcing him to steady himself by holding onto the seat in front of him. The smell of the bus's exhaust stuck in his throat and tickled his nose, but he suppressed a sneeze. His uncertain journey—a long summer spent with a stranger—was underway, whether he liked it or not. The bus ride itself was sure to be a boring one without a book in hand.

Wilson grew impatient and elbowed Jubilant. "Well?" He said, patting his book, doing his best to entice Jubilant into giving up his secrets.

Jubilant sighed and turned toward Wilson. As they made eye contact, he noticed that Wilson was a couple of inches shorter than him and a good deal heavier—with a round face like his mama's. Jubilant guessed Miss Patty would be giving her boy a haircut soon since his hair stuck up rather high and was knotted and nappy in places.

"If you must know," Jubilant said matter-of-factly, "my mama is dead."

Rattled by Jubilant's bluntness, Wilson turned to his own mama for support. Miss Patty, who had been leaning forward from behind, nodded slightly to confirm she had heard. Then, she jutted her out her chin, coaching Wilson to keep asking questions.

"Gee, boy! Did she die just now or what?" he asked.

"Mama died over four years ago on the same day that Franklin Delano Roosevelt beat out Herbert Hoover for president." Jubilant answered, proud in a strange way that his mama's death shared the date of such an important event. "November 8, 1932."

"But what about your daddy?"

"The doctor says the reverend should be okay, but he needs to take it easy and recuperate." Jubilant almost added that everyone says the preacher's son ain't nothin' but trouble around town, but he decided to leave that part out. Instead, he said, "So the reverend is sendin' me to live with my aunt in Tuskegee for a while." His face cringed at the reality of his own words.

"So, you live with your preacher?" Wilson asked.

"No!" Jubilant's tone of voice made him seem more annoyed than he really was. "I mean, yes. He's a preacher, but he's also my daddy," Jubilant said, shaking his head.

"So, let me get this straight, the reverend—your daddy—is sick?" Wilson again turned to his mama for some support.

Jubilant eyed Wilson's book once again before turning to face Wilson. "He had a heart attack, okay? He fell right to the ground in front of everyone." It was the falling and the terrible sound Daddy's body made when it hit the floor that would jolt Jubilant awake as the scene appeared over again in his nightmares.

"What's your name, son?" Miss Patty asked.

"Jubilant Jeremiah Bartley," he muttered, barely turning his face toward her.

"Jubilant? Ju-bil-ant. Jubilant!" Miss Patty repeated as if she was trying to taste the sound of it. "That's a treasure of a name. Mmmm-hmm, a treasure for sure! Your name means 'joyful.' Joyful and triumphant."

Her enthusiasm for his name made Jubilant lower his head in embarrassment. He couldn't remember the last time he was joyful or triumphant.

"Well, Mr. Jubilant Bartley," Patty said, leaving the subject of his name for the time being, "I saw on your ticket you're going to Tuskegee. That's where we're goin'—that's our home—so I guess we'll be your travelin' companions. I'll be lookin' after you today."

"All right then. If it pleases you," he said with a shrug, secretly relieved to have company.

Miss Patty nodded and bit her lip to hide a smile. "Settled then."

"Hey, is that lady waving to you?" Wilson elbowed Jubilant in the ribs and pointed out the window to a petite, gray-haired black woman wearing a green sweater buttoned to her neck. Her hair was pulled tightly in a bun on the back of her head, and she stood up straight with one hand clutching her handbag to her chest and another waving without any sign of emotion as the bus was finally leaving the parking lot.

In all the commotion of boarding and getting settled, Jubilant had completely forgotten about Millie Hines, the self-appointed leader of the Busy Bodies. Vi Nelson and Endora Grey were her willing sidekicks. The trio regularly spied on folks they suspected were up to no good and passed judgment on them. Jubilant got on their bad side when he reported their gossip and busybody ways to the reverend. He was dishing out potato salad onto his plate at a church potluck when his father stood across the table from him in front of a casserole dish full of creamed corn. Jubilant's inability to speak in a whisper came through loud and clear.

"Daddy, those Busy Bodies have been at it again!"

The reverend looked at his son with stern eyes and pursed lips as if to say, "hush!" but the boy didn't notice his father's nonverbal yet firm message. Jubilant was too busy considering which slice of cornbread in the basket was the largest as he continued his discourse. His words to his father were carried on the breeze to the congregation seated at picnic tables and on blankets on the lawn.

"I heard them say that Sadie Jake's hat cost more than a week's worth of groceries, and you really ought to find yourself a new wife to be a respectable minister, and Felix Delaney's daughter stayed out past midnight last night with that new young teller from the bank, and ..."

"Jubilant!" The reverend's voice not only stopped his son from talking, but those nearby froze for a second with their forks midway between their plates and their mouths. "That's enough, son. Do *not* repeat gossip!"

In reality, Jubilant hadn't really exposed the Busy Bodies' self-righteousness to the two dozen parishioners sitting nearby eating their supper. The truth was everyone at the Amazing Grace Baptist Church was already well aware of these ladies' antics, but this scene brought fresh attention to them. The trio was embarrassed and angered, so the Busy Bodies—each one a widow and a regular if not generous tither—stormed off toward their homes, noses in the air. They didn't show up to the Wednesday Bible Meeting that week. On Thursday, Jubilant was sent to each house to apologize, but they had been on him like glue ever since. So, he knew that Millie had volunteered to take him to the station on this early chilly morning for one reason and one reason only. She wanted to be sure Jubilant boarded the bus heading out of town before he could cause any more trouble in Huntsville.

CHAPTER THREE—SPITFIRE

There is none that doeth good, no not one. (Romans 3:12)

"I can *see* your attitude, LaDelle Corinne. I see it loud and clear, and I do not like it," Mama would tell her teenage daughter. "You may be saying 'yes, ma'am,' with your lips, but your body is shouting, 'I don't want to obey you!' You best watch yourself, child!"

As this familiar scene played out in LaDelle's mind for the umpteenth time, she muttered "I'm truly sorry, Mama," and shook her head at her own childish discourtesy. As a teenager, she had offered her apologies out loud to her mama's perceived satisfaction, but she now meant them. Young LaDelle apologized with a contrite enough face and stance to keep her mother from going on and on, but sincerity came with age. *How did Mama put up with me? I was such a pill!* She chuckled to herself, shaking her head at the memory, but a pang of sadness grazed her heart, reminding her how much she missed her mother. LaDelle knew she rarely fooled Mama with her halfhearted "sorry," but she was a most forgiving woman and willing to move on from offenses committed against her. Papa less so.

Papa took longer to get in the forgiving mood, but that's not to say he would yell or come after you with his belt in hand if he was offended or angry. Instead, a certain look would fall over his countenance. Then, he would leave the room. What followed was silence—sometimes for days. In LaDelle's mind, this was a worse punishment than being hit with a belt. After his hurt or anger subsided, Papa would act as if nothing had happened. Once, when LaDelle was eighteen and full of courage, she confronted her father about this.

"I find your silent treatment to be cruel and annoying, Papa."

"Well, child, *Je suis que je suis.* I am who I am," he said, turning on his heels and leaving the room. He didn't talk to her again for two days.

LaDelle admitted only to herself that she had both of her parents' ways in her. She rarely shied away from confrontation. If she was angry, folks would hear about it. Yet, on occasion, she chose her father's form of punishment and would give someone the cold shoulder if they made her mad.

LaDelle mulled over this reality, fully aware that her attitude lacked grace and was polluted by a large dose of huffiness as she headed out to the Piggly Wiggly after work. She had to buy extra groceries for the boy she'd soon have to retrieve from the bus station on the other side of town. LaDelle had cashed her paycheck the day she received the telegram from her brother and counted out the amount she figured she'd need to stock her kitchen. So many folks in Alabama continued to suffer greatly during these Depression days, but her job and paychecks had remained steady. Also, thankfully, she knew the ways of thriftiness and practiced them daily.

"I never bother spending money on store-bought soup," she once mentioned to Henrietta upon seeing Campbell's soup cans in her neighbor's garbage. "I simply make it myself with what I have on hand and for half the price.

I'm willing to show you how I do it whenever you're ready to start saving yourself some money." LaDelle smiled to herself as she thought back to their conversation. Henrietta had yet to take her up on her offer.

As careful as she was with her money, LaDelle knew her position and income could change, and then what? She was raised to depend on the Lord and to obey him. In her heart, she wanted to do just that, but she found it near impossible not to question him and his ways as she calculated what having a summer-long houseguest would cost her.

"Give me time, Lord," she'd pray when he seemed to be asking too much of her. She knew her response would be better received if she simply offered a hearty, "Yes, Lord! Here am I, send me." Too often her immediate prayer was, "I need to think this through first. Have *you* thought this through, this thing you're telling me to do? It seems a bit much if you ask me."

Obeying God without stall or debate, being flexible and charitable without reservation or judgment, allowing herself and her schedule to be inconvenienced and remaining sincerely gracious—difficult "tasks" for anyone—but the conviction of it stung LaDelle like a hornet. She would not admit it out loud, but she wished this wasn't her way. Yet there was no denying she was like that, and she hoped she was not too old to change. A rebellious attitude was often just below the surface if not in full view.

Fear fueled this attitude. She feared what would take place would be, or *become*, messy in some sense.

"No need to be all nerves, LaDelle, just because things don't always go the way you think they should," Henrietta scolded one day. LaDelle was agitated with her friend about a last-minute change of plans.

"I just like having my ducks in a row. What's wrong with that?" LaDelle said. "I like to plan and be prepared. I hate surprises—they're rarely pleasant."

"Ah, but that's the thing. Sometimes a change of plans—something you didn't expect—does turn out to be good. Even pleasant." Henrietta spoke with childlike excitement. "I find it keeps me on my toes and makes life interesting."

"I find it annoying," LaDelle said dryly, but to herself, she admitted she would like to be more accepting and free-spirited like Henrietta.

Though Garvin had known how to bring out the tender and more tolerant side of LaDelle like no one else, on occasion, he pointed out her lack of benevolence, which bubbled up when the stresses of life invaded her. Under perfect conditions, he would allow himself to wait until she'd had a full meal or a good night's rest before confronting his wife about her attitude. Most of the time, though, he'd seize the moment when she was ripe with gripe and not delay his reproach. Then, with a parental, but playful look on his face, he would call her a spitfire, exposing her quick temper or bad attitude for what it was.

"No one will begrudge you getting riled from time to time, babe. But do you *really* want to get all up-in-arms over *this*?"

"You don't understand! You don't feel as deeply about things as I do. Do you even know how to get riled, Garvin?"

Ignoring her retort, he'd continue. "Things will work out, Spitfire. You best calm yourself. Calmness illuminates your prettier side," he'd say, offering her that beautiful smile of his.

At this, she'd sigh. The hands on her hips would be brought to her side. Her heartbeat would begin to slow.

"That's right. Settle on down and exercise some trust and you'll do better. Breathe, baby, breathe."

Everything seemed to come easy for him.

His tone of voice, his timing and confidence, and his irresistible smile would usually do the trick for LaDelle, and she'd settle down and feel better. The proverbial smoke from her ears would dissipate, at least for a time, and her face would soften. This was the magic of Garvin.

Though she never told him, her own papa used that same term with her when she was growing up. "You're a little spitfire now aren't you, *jeune fille*?" Such a comment, more often than not, would be followed by a swat on her backside by Mama for being sassy. Being called "spitfire" by two significant people in her life gave LaDelle cause to consider.

Now, at age fifty-one, she knew without a doubt they were right, so admitting that, if only to herself, was a start. She wondered if that verse hanging in her hallway was equally true as she hoped it was. Embroidered on flax linen and adorned with grapevines and, for some unknown reason, green pears and hens, the framed handiwork was a gift from Garvin's Aunt Harriet who took more of a liking to her than did his mother. The words read: "He which hath begun a good work in you will perform it until the day of Jesus Christ."

If that's the case, then it seems I should be improving with age, for goodness' sake. LaDelle vowed to give more thought to the verse and God's promise of good work in her. She drove too fast into the Piggly Wiggly dirt lot and screeched to a stop as close as she could get to the market's entrance. "We'll have to talk about this later, Lord. I need to buy food now for the boy you're having me feed."

She grabbed her purse and, armed with a grocery list in hand, marched into the store—a woman on a mission. She grabbed a basket and maneuvered through the market with focused intention. People saw her coming and parted like the Red Sea, making a clear path for her as she strode by. Somehow, they knew it would be best to stay out of her way.

Her first order of business was meat. "What do you have on sale today, Marvin?" The butcher had his back to LaDelle but turned around when he heard her voice and sauntered to the counter. His wire-rimmed eyeglasses balanced on the edge of his nose, but he didn't bother pushing them up. LaDelle noticed he looked more tired than usual. Or maybe he had aged since she was in the week before.

"The prices are marked, Mrs. Harris," Marvin replied. "But look here, now, the pork chops are twenty-three cents a pound. This chuck roast is nineteen cents a pound, but this here's my last one."

"These are *sale* prices? That's robbery, that's what that is! How is a person supposed to make do these days?" LaDelle shook her head as she perused the meat on display.

"No sense blaming me," Marvin retorted without emotion. His southern drawl was thick and slow. "Are you interested in purchasing or complaining?"

For some reason she couldn't explain, LaDelle never minded Marvin's sour disposition. In fact, she got a kick out of it and suspected he enjoyed their banter as well. There was, behind his wire-rimmed glasses, a twinkle in his eye. She also knew she could count on his sass and that their back and forth was good-natured. Each time she needed to buy meat, chicken, or fish, she and Marvin went toe to toe, but she would never even consider going to a different butcher.

Perhaps she admired old man Marvin's willingness to stand up to her. She also knew there was a heart behind his prickliness. She admired that as well. More than once, she had secretly witnessed him handing a sack of produce or a sandwich to a down-and-outer in town. She also knew

26

his wife was frequently ill. LaDelle's neighbor, Henrietta, reported Marvin grew flowers year-round, so he'd always have a fresh bouquet to put on his wife's bed stand.

"Well?" Marvin said, bringing LaDelle's mind back to the business at hand.

"What choice do I have?" She said, throwing her arms up in defeat. "I supposed I have to feed my houseguest." LaDelle sighed, and pointed to the chuck roast. "All right, then. I'll take your last roast here and just three of those pork chops. Be sure to give me the three with the smallest bones, please. No sense paying for what I won't be eating."

Marvin let out a noise that sounded like a huff and then filled his customer's order. He took his time weighing and wrapping the meat, as was his way. LaDelle tapped her foot impatiently on the ground—which was her way.

"I suppose this won't last long, so I'll be seeing you again next week if not before," she said as she grabbed her packages. "Hope you have chickens on sale by then."

"No promises," Marvin replied.

"Well, I'll be back anyway," she mumbled, studying her list for a few seconds before heading toward the bakery section, but she stopped when she remembered something. "Oh, I almost forgot," she said as she turned back to face Marvin. She set her basket down and opened her purse. "I found this little book on native flowers in my library on campus," she said, waving it above her head. "I borrowed it for your wife. Thought she might enjoy reading it."

"Hmm," Marvin said, reaching out his hand toward the book. He thumbed through the pages. "She likes this sort of thing."

"Fine. I'll pick it up from you in two weeks. Don't forget—*two weeks*! That's our borrowing policy."

"Hmm," Marvin replied, tucking the book inside his apron. A slight smile crossed his face, but he didn't give

LaDelle the satisfaction of seeing it. She smiled too but waited until her back was turned.

CHAPTER FOUR—PREACHER'S BOY

No one is born without faults ... (Horace)

For the first half hour or so of the day-long bus ride, Jubilant kept himself busy by watching the folks on the bus and imagining their situations. *I bet that one's a strict school teacher and that one is probably a burglar who hides money under his mattress. That one is nice enough but can't keep a job for nothin'.*

Off and on during this little made-up game, his mind would wander, and he'd think about the reverend. As he watched the countryside pass by his window, the reality set in he was traveling far away from his daddy. *I don't have a chance to help him now. What if God decides not to? Daddy will die, leave me all alone, and he'll go to his grave, never knowing how helpful and responsible I can be.* With that thought, Jubilant shook his head, trying to clear his mind of it, then rubbed his head for a few seconds while holding his breath. Afterward, he sat with a blank stare, scratching the mosquito bite on his elbow both because it gave him something to do and because no one told him not to.

Finally, he decided to collect on Wilson's promise. He nudged his seat companion and asked for a turn with the book. Wilson's face was buried in it at the time. Though he wasn't ready to share just then, a deal was a deal, so he handed it over to Jubilant. As he did, Jubilant's face fell.

"*Raising Chickens for Profit*? If I had known this was the title of your book, I never would have bothered telling you about my parents. You tricked me."

"I didn't trick you!" Wilson sounded hurt when he said it, and his voice cracked. "Professor Carver himself gave me this book, which is chock full of great information." He grabbed the book back from Jubilant and quickly flipped through some of the pages to prove his point.

Jubilant stuck his finger on one of the pages as Wilson fanned them and read where it landed. "Chapter Eight ... Market Day Secrets—How Not to Get Plucked!" He shook his head, "Oh, brother!" He grabbed the book from Wilson nevertheless. At least, it was something to read to pass the time.

Wilson nibbled on his fingernails. He looked around the bus, drummed his fingers on his knee, then strained his neck to get a look at the page Jubilant had open on his lap.

"Hey! We had a deal," Jubilant said and scooted over on his seat as much as he could away from Wilson and his curious eyes.

"I was just wondering what page you're on," Wilson said, pleading his case.

"Well, you're bugging me."

"Sorry," Wilson said. "I just don't have anything to do now that you have my book."

"Obviously," Jubilant shot back. "Why don't you sit over there with your mama?"

Both boys looked over their shoulders and saw that Miss Patty had moved to a seat two rows back. She was talking with a woman she'd befriended, then she put her arm around the woman's shoulders, and they both bowed their heads.

"Lord, heal this precious woman's arthritis, and send her comfort as she cares for her no-good husband. I pray by your mercy that he'll come to know you, Lord, and she'll see him in heaven someday—even though he's been a stinkin' drunk here on earth."

Miss Patty spoke with conviction and compassion, patting the woman's shoulder as she prayed. The boys turned back around, and Wilson nudged Jubilant.

"You're a preacher's kid, right?"

"I already told you that," Jubilant said, keeping his eyes in the book.

"Then, you're used to people prayin', aren't ya?"

"Sure," Jubilant said, "but not on buses."

"My mama prays everywhere," Wilson said, rolling his eyes. "Last month, I heard her prayin' in her sleep. In her sleep! She was askin' God to give my daddy a job and by ten o'clock the next morning, he had one!"

Jubilant didn't want to talk further about prayer or being a preacher's kid, so he just pointed to the book in his hand, as if to say, "I'm trying to read." The truth, though, was Wilson's words put thoughts into Jubilant's head he didn't want to think about just now. *I believe in God,* he told himself. *I'm a preacher's son, ain't I? I pray at breakfast, supper, and at bedtime most nights, don't I?* He felt bad about not praying at the noon meal, but he usually didn't remember until he had already taken a bite of food and by then, it seemed too late.

Jubilant also tried to honor and respect his daddy. He usually set out to do his chores after only two or three reminders. Ever since he was five years old, he wished he were the son of a dentist or banker or factory worker instead of a preacher. Children who had fathers with regular jobs could go on about their business without being noticed or criticized.

People had the habit of pointing and saying, "See that young colored boy over there? He's the reverend's son. He'll help you." Or "That child's the preacher's boy. He'll be happy to let you go ahead of him in line, or watch your baby, or paint your fence."

What irritated Jubilant most about being a preacher's son was the supposing folks did. They supposed, for instance, that since his daddy was the one in the pulpit, Jubilant should be one of those boys in church who sat up tall in the pews and kept quiet each Sunday and Wednesday night. The hard, wooden pews at the Amazing Grace Baptist Church and the sheer length of the reverend's sermons made this impossible for Jubilant. He didn't have much meat on his rump and the unpadded pews made his backside sore.

A few Sundays back, between partaking in communion and listening to the choir sing "What a Friend We Have in Jesus," a loud burp escaped Jubilant's lips—one of those belches you couldn't deny or try to hide by clearing your throat or faking a cough. The way some folks glared at him, you would have thought Jubilant had committed an unpardonable sin or passed gas, which everyone knows is worse than burping.

Ten minutes after his unfortunate episode, his eyes began to feel heavy. "I'll just rest my eyes for a moment," he told himself, but seconds later, he nodded off as the reverend preached from the book of Matthew and told how Jesus would come like a "thief in the night." Jubilant's breathing grew deep, and a minute after that, the snoring began.

After church, as they waited in Elder Jamison's garden for Sunday dinner to be served, Ashton Bartley leaned forward and confronted his son about his antics. He kept the tone of his voice even and steady as was his style, but Jubilant knew the reverend meant business.

"Jubilant, I can't have you actin' up like that. Today was the second time this month you drew unfavorable attention to yourself in church. People expect the preacher's son to behave."

"It was all that Cream of Wheat you made me eat for breakfast this morning." He looked down and fiddled with his suspenders to avoid his daddy's convicting stare.

Ashton Bartley was a patient man, and Jubilant gambled his daddy would be tolerant of this accusatory comment, but he knew better than to go too far. At six foot, five inches tall and two hundred seventy-five pounds, the reverend looked as though he could crush anyone who dared cross him. His large brown hands, thick neck, and full chest gave him the appearance of being John Henry in the flesh. But instead of carrying a hammer, the reverend carried his King James Bible wherever he went. Those who didn't know him were intimidated by his build and piercing eyes. Yet, once they heard him in the pulpit or sat down and had a lemon Coke with him, their fears melted away like the ice in a soda glass on a scorching summer day. Ashton Bartley was a gentle giant most times, but he had his limits.

By age twelve, Jubilant had only been given two whuppings in his lifetime, but he remembered them well and wondered if the time was growing ripe for another one.

"You listen to me, Jubilant Jeremiah Bartley," the reverend said firmly, his eyes growing serious. "I need you to blend in and let folks around here get used to us. People tend to be more forgiving of improper behavior once they've experienced the good in a person. You have to be more responsible. I know you've been acting up around town too. Millie Hines gave me a full report about it."

"Yes, sir," was all Jubilant said, though he had plenty he wanted to say about Old Millie Hines. His eyes began to wander, hoping to see Mrs. Jamison arrive with the meal.

Jubilant knew the lecture would end once the food came out. The reverend would never carry on and lecture when someone else was within earshot, but from the looks of it, father and son were still alone.

The reverend finished his subdued rant just as Elder Jamison joined them on the lawn under the sassafras tree, carrying a mound of fried chicken while whistling. He was a whistler more than a talker. In fact, he was so good at whistling that once a month or so, the choir director invited him on stage to whistle a hymn while the basket was passed. Mille Hines's face was one big smirk when Elder J. "played" the offertory because she didn't count that as real music, but Mrs. Jamison beamed with pride at her husband's bird-like talent. Now, she followed him and his mound of chicken with a bowl of collard greens and an even bigger bowl of corn pudding. Swinging from her arm was a basket bursting with sweet potato biscuits.

Here was the one good thing about being a preacher's boy—and the son of a widower—most every Sunday after church you could practically count on an invitation to supper from one of the parishioners. And, since the reverend couldn't cook a decent meal, Sunday dinner was usually the highlight of Jubilant's week.

CHAPTER FIVE—THE ROAD AHEAD

The best thing about the future is that it comes only one
day at a time. (Abraham Lincoln)

"Here now, honey, I'll share our egg salad sandwiches
with you," Miss Patty nudged Jubilant on the shoulder and
handed him a sandwich wrapped in waxed paper.

He was thankful for the interruption. Letting his mind
think back to life in Huntsville just made him feel bad. He
hadn't thought much of food during the hour or more they'd
been on the road, but his stomach was growling. Millie
Hines had scolded him on the way to the station when she
found out he had packed nothing but a few pieces of black
licorice for the long bus ride. He didn't have an appetite at
breakfast. Besides, he hadn't wanted to fumble around in
the kitchen and risk dropping something and waking the
reverend. A tray of communion glasses had slipped out of
his hands and shattered everywhere earlier in the week,
making a loud commotion and a landmine of glass all over
the church's kitchen floor. He was just trying to help. No
one told him the tray would be so heavy. Jubilant and the
reverend had said their goodbyes the night before anyway.

Now well into the journey to Tuskegee, Jubilant
unwrapped the sandwich Miss Patty gave him and surprised
himself by finishing the whole thing. He didn't notice he

had spilled some of the egg salad down the front of his shirt, and the now closed book on his lap was covered in crumbs. Wilson barely nibbled on his, complaining to his mama she used too much mayonnaise and how could she forget he doesn't like celery?

"Here, Mr. Jubilant, have another, and use this napkin. If Wilson doesn't get serious about eating, you can have his sandwich as well."

Wilson looked at Jubilant and rolled his eyes. From the look of him, it was hard to believe that Wilson was picky about mayonnaise or any other food.

Jubilant took the second sandwich offered to him but kept it wrapped up, placing it on his lap. The whole ordeal with the reverend's heart attack and being told he'd have to go to Tuskegee had taken away his appetite days ago. His stomach had shrunk as a result. Still, Jubilant took two bites of his second sandwich before handing it back to Miss Patty.

Jubilant's stomach began to sour maybe because the smell of body odor mixed with thick humidity and exhaust fumes was growing more putrid by the mile, or maybe because he ate too much. He reached into his pocket and pulled out the licorice he'd grabbed earlier that morning from his underwear drawer before he left the house. Jubilant stashed only important items in that drawer. He kept a picture of Mama there, his favorite sling shot with a broken sling, an arrowhead made of obsidian, and a carnival ticket from when they lived in Yonkers. He had carefully wrapped the licorice whips in a clean handkerchief and shoved them into his pocket, so he'd have a treat for the bus ride. He held the sweet-smelling candy up to his nose and breathed in deeply for some relief. And then, he reluctantly offered some to Wilson because he knew he should.

Wilson scrunched up his face. "Nah! I don't like black licorice, only red, but if you have any lemon drops or caramels, I'll take some."

"You're outta luck," Jubilant said, putting the licorice between his teeth and pulling off a small bite. As he chewed, he kept one hand on his stomach and lost himself in thought again. He stared out the window at the cows in the fields and pondered his destination and the fact that he was alone. Daddy was still in Huntsville, perhaps on his deathbed. He wasn't healing as fast as the doctor thought he would. *God wouldn't dare take him, too, would he?* His hand formed a fist as the thought crossed his mind. Miss Patty interrupted his fear and anger by asking another question.

"I'm not one to pry—" she leaned forward and tapped him on the shoulder.

Yes, you are.

"—but you never did tell us what you'll be doin' in Tuskegee. How long will you be there, and who will you be stayin' with?"

Wilson grabbed his book off Jubilant's lap and brushed the remaining crumbs onto the floor. He turned to Jubilant, waiting for him to answer.

Prying runs in the family, I guess.

"I'll be staying with my Aunt LaDelle," he answered.

"LaDelle Harris?" Miss Patty asked with surprise in her voice. Wilson let out a laugh, and then covered his mouth after Miss Patty shot him a look.

"Yes, I think that's her full name," Jubilant responded with hesitancy.

"Well now, Miss LaDelle lives just down the road from us. Her dog likes to do his business on our front lawn. I don't complain, though, because no one wants to get on Miss LaDelle's bad side."

"Why? Is she mean?" A whole new wave of nausea came over Jubilant. He had to take a few breaths before his stomach settled.

"Nah, honey, I wouldn't say she's *mean*." Miss Patty hesitated. "She can be a little brash sometimes, that's all. I'm sure she has a kind heart inside, though. She's at church every Sunday, same as us."

"I once heard her chew out Belly Jones, the gas station attendant, because she said he cheated her out of gasoline." Wilson offered.

"Did he cheat her?" Jubilant asked, hoping his aunt had a good reason for getting after someone.

"Nah, he just overfilled some, and when the gasoline spilled out, she hollered at him to pay attention and said she wasn't gonna pay for what he wasted. She went on and on about it. 'Every time you're at the pump you're daydreaming and get sloppy about your job. Enough is enough!'" Wilson said in a woman's voice. "Poor Belly just stood there and didn't say nothin', which I thought was smart, but it seemed to make her madder. She hopped into her car after she paid him and sped off like a bat outta hell."

With that last comment, Miss Patty shot Wilson a look letting him know she didn't approve of the word "hell," but she left it at that.

Jubilant rubbed his stomach and let out a quiet moan. He wiped sweat off his brow. What had the reverend done sending him to Aunt LaDelle's? Would she end up yelling at him like she did the gas station attendant? Was this Daddy's way of punishing him for last month when his toad Ziggy escaped and turned up in the soap dish on the edge of the tub? It's a wonder the reverend didn't have a heart attack that night instead of at the pulpit, but Jubilant told him he was sorry—twice.

"Don't you worry now, son," Miss Patty said, patting Jubilant's shoulder, sensing his apprehension. Then, she leaned back in her seat and closed her eyes, folding her arms under her bosom and resting them on her protruding belly.

"Hey, Wilson," Jubilant whispered. "Do you think I have a better chance of survival if I jumped out of the bus while it's still movin' or lived with Aunt LaDelle a while?"

"Hmmm," Wilson tapped his chin with his finger and considered the question. "I'd say either option only gives you a fifty-fifty chance of survival."

CHAPTER SIX—WHAT CHARM CAN DO

Let us be grateful to people who make us happy,
they are the charming who make our souls blossom.
(Marcel Proust)

LaDelle finished putting her basket with her meat and other grocery items onto the counter for the store clerk. As the woman unpacked it, LaDelle surveyed her haul. Her eyes grew wide as she realized how much more she was purchasing than usual and tried to tally an approximate total in her head. When she was given the actual cost of her groceries, LaDelle blew out through puckered lips the air she'd been holding in without realizing it. Her calculations were off by eighty-eight cents—not in her favor. The total cost was almost twice as much as she usually spent in one shopping trip. She shook her head. *Does Ashton think I'm made of money?*

"Good golly, Miss LaDelle, you fixin' to have yourself a party or somethin'? I ain't never seen you buy so much at once before." As the clerk stared at her customer waiting for an answer, she smacked her chewing gum. LaDelle thought, at that moment, the woman looked nearly identical to a horse chewing oats.

"No, Cherie," LaDelle said dryly, "not a party, just a houseguest." She was tempted to add, "but that's none of your business now, is it?" yet decided to let it go. Thankfully, the new box boy—who was no "boy" but more accurately a man near the age of twenty-five or so—wasn't so chatty. She also noticed his white apron was without stain and his black tie was straight. His fingernails were clean, and his shoes were shined. LaDelle nodded her approval as he carefully placed the loaf of bread in the box on top of her other purchases. *How refreshing to receive such competent service from a well-groomed and quiet worker. He'd be an asset to the library.*

She tucked her wallet inside her purse and snapped it closed for safekeeping. Then, just as she stepped away from the counter to lead the box boy out to her car so he could load her groceries, Abel Fisher appeared before her out of nowhere.

"So good to see you, Mrs. Harris. How's life treating you these days?" The sound of his voice made her heart jump.

Abel was the manager of the Piggly Wiggly, and LaDelle had to admit that what he lacked in hair, he made up for in charm. An absence of hair aside, he did possess beautiful hazel eyes and a playful grin that she was afraid to concede to herself, or anyone else, caused her to feel like a schoolgirl again. His voice was deep and velvety like molasses. *I bet he can sing like an angel.* His skin tone was much lighter than hers—his biological father or maybe grandfather was a white man, she surmised. She also noticed, for the first time, that the shape of his bald head was darn near perfect. Not pointy or too round. The shape was smooth, but not overly glossy as is often the case with men who are hair challenged.

"You okay, Mrs. Harris?" LaDelle suddenly heard him speaking again and snapped out of her thoughts.

"What? Oh, fine. I'm just fine," she managed to respond with near composure, silently praying she hadn't gazed too long at his head. "I am surprised to see you here. I heard you were transferred to the store in Bullock County." *I bet my nose is shining like the sun with all this humidity. Why didn't I think to apply a little powder before I left my car? My thighs are sticking together like flypaper in this heat. Do I look as uncomfortable as I feel?*

"Yes, I went there for a few months to ensure the new store in Fitzpatrick had a smooth opening, but now I've returned to my original store, and I'm grateful. There's nothing like being back home in Macon County—and mighty nice to see *you*."

LaDelle's chest and face grew warm, and for some reason, her eyes grew moist. She hoped he'd noticed neither. She didn't know much about Abel except that he was near her age and was a bachelor, though Henrietta had made a comment that several years ago, he was sweet on some gal from Georgia. Seems they courted for a full two years, and then one day she up and ran off to California with a cousin to pursue stardom. She was obsessed, according to Henrietta, with the starlet Nina Mae McKinney and was determined to follow in her footsteps. Abel was left heartbroken and alone, except for the calico cat his girlfriend neglected to take with her. He adopted the feline out of the goodness of his heart, though Henrietta could have been making up that part. She had a flare for embellishment.

These thoughts filled her head, but before she could open her mouth to respond to him, Abel illustrated another one of his fine qualities when he covertly reprimanded Cherie for chewing gum with a mere stern look and a finger pointing to his lips. She sheepishly took the gum out of her mouth and wrapped it up in a spare piece of waxed paper she seemed to have handy for just such an occasion. Abel nodded his satisfaction and forgiveness of her breaking the rules and then thanked the box boy for his good work before taking LaDelle's groceries from his arms.

"At your service, ma'am!" he said to LaDelle with a wink. He nodded toward the exit doors, and then followed her out to her car, loading the groceries into the back seat.

Afterward, he nonchalantly surveyed the outside of her car, then spoke with genuine concern. "Looks like your left rear tire may be a little low. You ought to have that checked very soon."

"I'll do that," she said, keeping her gaze on the tire instead of Abel's handsome face. Finally looking up, she added, "Thank you kindly, Mr. Fisher. You've gone above and beyond the call of duty today."

"My pleasure, Mrs. Harris, and please, call me Abel. We're peers after all—friends too, I hope."

LaDelle looked down at her purse. She fiddled with the handle and let out a quiet, nervous giggle over the way he said, "I hope."

"Would it sit well with you if I called you by your first name, or am I being too bold?"

"My name is LaDelle," she responded without thinking, then considered if his request was, indeed, too bold. The thought melted away when she looked upon his face. His countenance was disarming and inviting, and she found no real reason to refuse him. "I'd be fine with you addressing me by my first name."

"Then, it's official. We truly are bona fide friends now. By the way, I knew your name was LaDelle. I've known for some time. Henrietta and I grew up together. She told me your name."

Of course she did.

Abel offered another wink and smiled. "All right now. You have yourself a good evening. I'll be seeing you later, LaDelle. You stay outta trouble!"

LaDelle nodded in response as he headed back into the store. Once he was inside, she opened her car door, tossed her purse to the passenger side, and plopped her body into the driver's seat. She sat there for several minutes replaying in her head the exchange she'd just had with Abel Fisher. *What just happened?* She was exhilarated, giddy, and guilty all at the same time. Garvin had been taken from her over nine years ago, but somehow, she still belonged to him. She had removed her wedding rings a mere six months earlier, around Christmastime, and that was only because the silver bands were cutting off her circulation. She had gained a few pounds and apparently some of the weight took up residence in her ring finger.

What am I doing taking pleasure in the friendly, almost flirty way Abel interacted with me? Don't be a fool, LaDelle Harris. He probably treats every female customer that way. If not, what does he see in me? Reaching for her purse she took out her pocket mirror that had been a gift from her mother on her twenty-first birthday and looked closely at her reflection. She told herself it didn't matter, but upon inspection, she surmised that her appearance was passable—until she smiled.

"Oh, for goodness' sake!" She exclaimed out loud. Something green from lunch was lodged between two teeth. *Did I, at any point during our interaction, smile wide enough for him to see this dadgum speck?* As she thought it over, she admonished herself out loud. "LaDelle, don't be such a fool. You are entirely too old to worry about impressing a man!"

She muttered this to herself over and over as she drove toward home. Thinking about it further, she also decided he was probably charming toward everyone, especially paying customers. In a few minutes, she pulled into her driveway and reached for her groceries to take them inside before the meat and milk had a chance to spoil in her sweltering car. As she put the food away, her mind was still deep in thought. *He is mighty fine, though.* She shook her head and smiled to herself. *Abel Fisher is a disher. Oh, shut up, LaDelle. Silly jeune fille.*

LaDelle hummed as she puttered in the kitchen, making room for more canned goods, jars, and an extra sack of flour until an uneasy thought came to mind. *I wonder if Abel Fisher is aware that I am the head librarian at the Tuskegee Institute.*

"I think most men are intimidated by a woman who holds such an important position. Don't you, Dewey?" LaDelle's faithful companion looked up at her and cocked his head, encouraging her to continue. "Yes, yes, I know, Dew. I don't mean to sound prideful. Pride is a slippery slope. But truth be told, I am proud of my position, and no man is going to make me feel bad about it!" Though she had no idea what Abel thought about a woman being successful, she found herself annoyed at the prospect of him having a problem with it.

She had come to Tuskegee when she was offered the assistant librarian job, though she knew the pay wouldn't cover her expenses for long. Still, she didn't have to think long about signing the contract. Upon signing and sending it in the mail, she made her way to Alabama to start the position.

"I'm resourceful," she told her worried father. "I'll be able to supplement my income if and when the need arises."

She arrived in Alabama full of ideas and excitement for the chance to be a faculty member of the Tuskegee Institute, but once she arrived, it was obvious she was capable of more than being an assistant. The head librarian at the time lacked imagination and gumption in LaDelle's mind. Her break to move up the ranks soon came when Mr. Gottman, the former head librarian, left. He was forced to resign after his excessive drinking habit became common knowledge. The final straw for the Institute was when his lack of self-control with the bottle was fully exhibited one night when he drove his car into a tree. He escaped with only a gash on his forehead, but his auto was beyond repair, and the poor chestnut oak suffered from incurable shock.

"Instead of advertising to fill the position," LaDelle implored President Patterson after marching over to his office across campus, "I ask that you consider promoting me. I am more than capable, I assure you."

"Well," he said, seemingly unfazed by her boldness, though she had burst into his office. His secretary wasn't at her desk when LaDelle arrived, so she had taken it upon herself to knock on his door and let herself in. "The decision is not mine directly, but I do know one of the Institute's first librarians was a female, and since we have no other ready candidates, and you are eager, I'll recommend that you are given the position."

She walked out of his office in a calm, professional manner with her head held high, but inside she was jumping up and down and squealing with excitement like a child on her birthday.

As for pride, she knew there was a form that could work in one's favor. Pride can fuel a job well done to continue to be done well but taken too far can also make you self-important and arrogant, which never has a good outcome. LaDelle knew to be careful, but it wasn't easy. And since pride cometh before a fall, she could end up with a broken hip with how she felt about being head librarian if she wasn't mindful.

Dewey nudged her with his nose just then, bringing her mind back to the present and her task of putting away the remaining groceries. She let him out the back door, and then glanced at her wristwatch. *Where had the day gone? The boy's bus will be arriving soon.* She finished putting away the last of the groceries, poured herself a glass of watered-down lemonade, and took a swig. She opened the back door and called for Dewey. He obediently followed her out to the car and jumped in, his wagging tail fanning her face. "Here we go, Dew. Our 'Jubilant' summer is upon us," she said, then added, "whether we're ready or not."

CHAPTER SEVEN—NO LUCK

May good luck be your friend in whatever you do and may trouble be always a stranger to you. (An Irish blessing)

"Wake up now, boys," Miss Patty gently shook his shoulder with her large, warm hand. "We're gettin' ready to pull into the bus station."

Jubilant rubbed his eyes and tried to focus on the scenery outside. Realizing he had fallen asleep, he sat up and shook his head to wake himself more fully. Wilson, he noticed, had moved to the seat behind and had fallen asleep on his mama's shoulder. The long bus ride was coming to an end. Jubilant was thankful he had slept away some of the journey to Tuskegee. He shook his head once more and ran his hand over his face and hair a few times. Naps were always harder to wake up from than regular sleep. It seemed strange his hand glided so easily over his head. He had very little hair left since Millie Hines made him go to the barber for a near scalping before he left on his journey.

"Your aunt won't want to be pickin' bugs out of your hair all summer, and I can tell you're not one to be takin' care of your own hair, so there's no choice but to shave it off," Millie Hines said as she escorted him to Jerry's Barbershop and paid the bill.

Jubilant would never admit this to her, but he really didn't mind. The truth was he did hate washing his hair, and sometimes, the reverend made him apply some of his Murray's Pomade on it Sunday mornings before church. He hated the feel of the goo—on his hair and his hands. Besides, such fussing was a waste of a boy's free time.

"Do you think, Mr. Bartley, that you will be able to handle that duffel of yours now that you'll be leavin' the bus?" Miss Patty said, poking Jubilant and winking at him. She laughed when she said it, and her belly bounced up and down.

Jubilant's face grew warm, and he avoided eye contact but said, "Yes, ma'am."

"Good! So, we'll be comin' by to check up on you at your aunt's house in a few days. We live toward the end of LaDelle's road. Our place is the yellow one with a picket fence in front. The whole place needs paintin' and repair, but it's home."

Together, the three made their way off the bus. Jubilant held his duffel with two hands and avoided eye contact with any of the other passengers. He focused on not tripping over his own feet or the duffel. Then, his eyes half-closed as the sun, approaching dusk, hit him the moment he stepped through the doorway of the bus. The air smelled warm and dusty—not much different from Huntsville—but all the faces waiting to greet people coming off the bus were unfamiliar. Jubilant wished by some miracle the reverend would be there to collect him.

"There she is. There's your Aunt LaDelle." Wilson pointed to Jubilant's left and then snickered and patted his shoulder. "Good luck, buddy!"

Jubilant knew right away the tall woman with the serious face was the reverend's sister. She wasn't as heavy as Daddy, but she was thick like him and had his mouth and nose. Her curled black hair was peppered with gray, which Jubilant didn't expect, but he remembered she was older than the reverend. The two made eye contact.

"Goodness, there you are. It's about time your bus arrived," she said the moment she made her way over to him. She reached down and grabbed the duffel out of his hand. "I swear these bus drivers think the scheduled arrival time is merely a suggestion. Your bus was twenty-three minutes late!"

Jubilant stood frozen for a second, dumbfounded. *I haven't done anything wrong, have I?* Confident he hadn't, he told himself to be brave but responded with a quiet, "Wasn't *my* fault."

"I wasn't blaming you, now was I?" Aunt LaDelle shot back, perspiration rolling down the sides of her face. "Well, come on," she added. Then, she turned on her heels and walked away from Jubilant with his duffel in her hand.

She maneuvered her way through the crowd like a skilled halfback. Jubilant quickly followed behind her, though it wasn't easy to keep up. Finally, she stopped at an old, black, dinged up Model T parked at the back of the dirt lot and turned to face Jubilant.

"I suppose," she sighed, "I didn't introduce myself. I'm your Aunt LaDelle. We haven't seen each other since you were about four years old, I think. And this here is Dewey."

She pointed to a medium-sized, black and white mutt sitting obediently at her feet.

"Yes, ma'am," was all Jubilant thought to say. He was taken aback by her tone of voice and bluntness. He didn't remember ever meeting this woman, and if he had, he probably ran into his mother's arms crying! She seemed put out by him, and he hadn't even acted up yet. He suddenly wondered if Millie Hines had called ahead to tell her that "Jubilant is irresponsible and clumsy and you might as well be mad at him!"

As the pair stood next to LaDelle's automobile, Jubilant sensed someone looking in his direction. He turned and saw Wilson sitting in a wooden wagon, making faces, and trying to get his attention. A man, who must have been Miss Patty's husband, was loading their one suitcase onto the wagon, which was being pulled by two old, tired-looking horses. Miss Patty, carrying a young girl in her arms, offered Jubilant a reassuring nod and waved goodbye. She never mentioned she had other children, but the girl who was about four or five was obviously hers. They had the same look about them, and the child clung to Patty's neck as if she'd missed her something terrible. Wilson smiled and nodded his head in Jubilant's direction.

"You look like your mama," Aunt LaDelle announced after squinting her eyes and sizing him up and down. "Adelaide was a good woman," she added, matter-of-factly. "I was sorry I couldn't get back to New York for her funeral," she said. "I had just come back to Alabama after having attended my father's funeral when I received the news. My suitcase wasn't fully unpacked when the telegram arrived. What a cruel sense of timing death has at times."

She looked off into the distance for a few seconds, and then shook her head. "Well, life goes on, I suppose," she added softly. LaDelle surveyed the parking lot. She stuck two fingers in her mouth and gave a sharp whistle intended for Dewey, who had left them to go sniff the tires of some parked cars several feet away. The dog relieved himself on the wheel of one of them and trotted over to his owner.

Jubilant took a better look at the dog now seated at his aunt's feet. He didn't appear the least bit afraid of her. He wagged his tail and almost seemed to be smiling. *At least it doesn't look like she beats her dog. Though some folks like their dogs more than people.*

"Well, come on now. Don't just stand there. The bugs are out this evening and feasting on flesh. Get in the car. Let's go."

This seemed like a big step all of a sudden—to go off with this ill-tempered stranger and her dog. He hesitated and glanced in both directions as if looking for options.

"Are you hard of hearing, son? Hop in!" she demanded, tossing his duffel onto the backseat.

Jubilant slid into the front passenger's seat without a word. Dewey jumped into the car at the same time and stood on Aunt LaDelle's lap. She didn't seem to mind that he was wrinkling her dress, getting it dirty, and digging his paws into her legs for balance. He was too big to be a lap dog, but it was apparent his owner was used to him being there. She was tall enough to see over Dewey and thick enough to not be bothered by his weight. The dog stuck his head out the window as Aunt LaDelle looked behind her and backed out of her parking spot. She wasn't particularly concerned whether she would run someone over. Everyone scooted out of her way as if they knew better than to dawdle. Jubilant rolled his window down all the way for some extra air—it had to be ninety degrees outside and thirty degrees hotter in the car. He silently patted his leg, trying to coax Dewey to come over to his side and stick his head out the passenger window. He had always longed for a pet and the frogs he caught on occasion weren't as satisfying as he knew a dog or cat would be.

"You're in Macon County now. What do you think?" Aunt LaDelle asked, breaking the awkward silence.

"I thought you lived in Tuskegee."

"I do. Tuskegee is in Macon County."

"Oh," Jubilant said, shrugging his shoulders. He didn't care either way, really.

"I'll give you a little tour before heading home," Aunt LaDelle said. She drove with one hand on Dewey and one on the wheel. "Pay attention, boy, because there are some places in town colored folk are smart to avoid, and I'm going to point them out to you."

Jubilant nodded, and then reached down into his pocket to retrieve his lucky rabbit's foot. He kept it in his hand and rubbed it for a few minutes. Aunt LaDelle glanced in his direction and her eyes grew as wide as dinner plates.

"What in heaven's name is *that*?"

"It's my lucky rabbit's foot."

Without a word of warning, she swerved recklessly and pulled over to the side of the road. She hadn't given the driver behind her enough notice, so he swerved in the other direction and honked his horn. He yelled something out his window as he passed them on the left, but Aunt LaDelle shooed him on with her hand. She came to a screeching stop, shut off the engine and turned to face her shocked nephew.

"Boy, what are you doing with *that*? I won't have you bringing any talismans into my home, do you understand me?"

"This isn't a—what did you call it, a towels man? It's just a rabbit's foot." His hands began to sweat as he sensed he was already in trouble. He rubbed his head and held his breath. Wilson's impersonation of Aunt LaDelle yelling at the gas station attendant came to mind, and he realized how perfect it was.

"I can tell I am going to have to educate you on several levels," she said with a huff, shaking her head. "First of all, the word is 'talisman,' which means a trinket of some kind that people hold to because they think an object will protect them against evil spirits or disease. The very idea is a bunch of hogwash and directly against the Lord Almighty so don't be messing with junk like that. Do you understand me, boy?"

"Yes, ma'am, but—"

"I don't want to see any four-leaf clovers, zodiac signs, or lucky pennies anywhere near you either. You got that, boy?"

Jubilant couldn't speak. He didn't want to cry, so he barely nodded. *What was happening?*

"I said, 'do you hear me?'" She enunciated each word, and her bulging eyes kept right on bulging.

"Yes, ma'am." Jubilant made himself respond, and took note that nodding wouldn't be enough for Aunt LaDelle. He'd need to be verbal with his agreements even when he didn't really understand.

She snatched the rabbit's foot out of his sweaty palm and tossed it out the window!

"Hey! That was mine!" Jubilant shouted. He wasn't about to add he had packed eight more rabbit's feet in his duffel—his entire collection in a rainbow of colors—and he still had his lucky penny in his right pocket. His face grew hot, and he choked back angry tears.

It took me two years to collect all those rabbits' feet. This crazy lady is not going to ruin my collection. I am not stayin' with her. I don't have to stay here.

After she lobbed the rabbit's foot into the bushes, he noticed his aunt had a satisfied look on her face, which inflamed Jubilant's anger. She took a deep breath—in through the nose, out from the mouth—and patted Dewey's head to calm him. The dog had started pacing back and forth from LaDelle's lap to Jubilant's when she pulled over to the side of the road. Now both dog and owner seemed calmer. Aunt LaDelle's nose was no longer flared.

Jubilant sat silently as LaDelle pulled back onto the road as quickly as she had left it, and they were on their way through Macon County once again. He stared straight ahead with his arms folded in front of his chest, trying to keep his own heart from pounding out of his shirt, but LaDelle paid no attention. She continued driving and pointing out what she called "points of interest" along the way to her house. But nothing she showed was interesting in the slightest to Jubilant, who couldn't stop thinking about the fact his favorite purple rabbit's foot was gone forever in a bush somewhere. He also ruminated on the terrible truth that until he could get back home, he was going to have to stay at this wild, and maybe even insane, woman's house.

"On the left, over there, is our Piggly Wiggly—a fine grocery store. Very clean and well run. Next to that is Cal's Hardware. Cal is my neighbor, a good man. He barely says a word, but he's always willing to lend a hand if you need him. His wife Henrietta does hair. She thinks she's a singer," Aunt LaDelle made a quick right down another road and announced, "This here is the famous Tuskegee Institute, a stellar school. It's for Negro folks only."

Aunt LaDelle acted as if it was her job to promote the school, her voice dripping with pride. "A former slave named Mr. Louis Adams was the founding force behind this school back in 1881. His dream was to have a Normal and Industrial School, and he worked hard to make it come true. He and a board of smart men hired Booker T. Washington to be the first principal. There are other schools for Negroes, of course, but in my humble opinion, this here is the finest institution of higher learning there is in the entire state of Alabama."

I don't care about any of this, Jubilant gave a slight nod at this point to appease her and not set her off.

"George Washington Carver still works here, and his scientific research is recognized all the way over in Europe." LaDelle paused for a moment, then continued, "The papers like to call Professor Carver 'The Peanut Man' because he's come up with some amazing uses for the peanut, but there's a whole lot more to him than that, for goodness' sake. Take crop rotation for instance. It's of utmost importance. Have you heard of that?"

Jubilant had not. He shook his head.

"Well, he's a whiz about soil, and over the years, he has helped our people to farm more effectively, that's the truth. 'The Black Leonardo.' That's the nickname I prefer for him. A Renaissance man, to be sure."

Jubilant wondered if George Washington Carver was the same Professor Carver that Wilson said gave him the chicken book, but he didn't want to ask and have a conversation with Aunt LaDelle, so he just nodded again. This day seemed to have no end, and it was becoming too much for a twelve-year-old feeling misplaced and down a rabbit's foot. Jubilant fought to yawn with his mouth closed, but Aunt LaDelle saw him trying to hide it.

"Well now, you must be tired, but I'm about to show you the most important thing in all Tuskegee so stay awake a while longer, then I'll take you to the house and get you settled in." She told her nephew to look to his right as she drove down West Montgomery Road and parked her car.

"Follow me," she said as she exited the car and led Jubilant to a statue of Booker T. Washington. "Impressive, isn't it?"

Jubilant was afraid to open his mouth to respond because the only thing he could think to say would get him into trouble, so he just nodded his head and tried not to scowl.

"You'll be getting to know Tuskegee Institute pretty well during your stay, since I'm the head librarian, and you'll be coming to work with me every day."

Jubilant's tired eyes widened with disbelief. The reverend never told him that he would be spending his summer cooped up in a library. This "for a while" visit was turning into a nightmare. *I should have been more responsible and not so full of trouble in Huntsville. Maybe then, I could have stayed with Daddy.*

Finally, they walked back to the car, and LaDelle spun away from the Institute, pointing out more things and places as they drove toward home. They pulled into her dirt driveway and the tour was over. Jubilant let out a yawn big and loud at that point, which, for some reason, Aunt LaDelle chose to ignore. When the engine stopped, Dewey's tail went wild, and he barked until his owner opened the car door and let him out. He ran two circles on the lawn, and then bolted down the street. LaDelle didn't seem concerned.

"Does he always run away like that?" Jubilant asked.

"He isn't running away. He just does a quick trot to the end of the block, turns around, and comes right back home. It's a ritual of sorts—he does it every time after I take him out for a ride."

She doesn't know he stops along the way and does his business on Miss Patty's lawn. He considered telling her but decided to keep that information to himself for now. He was afraid it might start trouble somehow, and now that he was down a rabbit's foot, he didn't want to chance it.

CHAPTER EIGHT—APPLE-PIE ORDER

Rules are for the obedience of fools and the guidance of wise men. (Douglas Bader)

Jubilant carried his own duffel as they made their way inside Aunt LaDelle's house. After such a long day, the duffel seemed even heavier than it did when he brought it out to Millie Hines's Rambler before they left for the bus depot in Huntsville. He wasn't about to ask for help carrying it. Several times throughout the day, it struck him he was probably going to have to toughen up while he was away from home. The idea of that made Jubilant dread being away even more.

As he walked into Aunt LaDelle's place, he noticed it was about the same size as the parsonage he and the reverend lived in but looked completely different. It sparkled with cleanliness. As he surveyed the modest living room, he wondered if anyone actually lived in the house. Maybe it was a museum like the one Daddy took him to in Manhattan. Like the displays there, Aunt LaDelle's furniture appeared to be something to look at but not to touch. There was not a pillow on the sofa out of place, and the books in her bookcase were standing upright and straight. There were no shoes on the floor or clothing hung on doorknobs or papers piled on top of tables. No mugs half-filled with cold coffee perched on her fireplace mantle. Her home smelled like paste wax and bleach. Jubilant rubbed his head and held his breath. This place made him nervous.

"Welcome to my home, boy," she said and added a warning: "You are to treat my things carefully." She let her words soak in for a few seconds, then continued. "Well now, before I show you to your room, I want to tell you the rules I expect you to follow while you're here, so listen up, child."

Jubilant's face grew hot as it had earlier in the car when his aunt disposed of his prized possession. He wasn't used to things being so neat and tidy, and he didn't like the thought of being handed a bunch of rules to follow. He wasn't good at following rules. Although he had never thought about it before, he realized the reverend didn't have a whole lot of rules for him, and maybe he had more freedom living with him than he appreciated.

"I will write these down for you, but for now I will verbally tell you each rule, so pay attention."

Jubilant nodded and sighed loudly enough for her to hear.

"Stand up straight now, boy, and hear me with your ears *and* your body," LaDelle said, taking a sergeant's stance. "Rule number one: there is no eating in the living room or anywhere else in the house except at the kitchen table. Two, your feet belong on the floor and not on any of the furniture—ever. Three, make sure your shoes are clean before you enter my house—always and without exception. Four—are you listening?"

Jubilant nodded. He was beginning to slouch from the weight of all the rules.

"Four, you will get out of bed no later than six-thirty each morning and be in bed by nine-thirty every night. Lights out at ten. I expect you to read before you doze off.

Five, you will, of course, make your bed each morning before breakfast and complete your daily chores in a timely manner."

Chores? First, I have to go to work with her, and now I have to do chores too? I thought aunts were supposed to give you candy and money for the movies and let you do what you wanted. It dawned on him that maybe such things only applied to grandparents, and he had none. Jubilant glanced at the front door and considered how quickly he could run to it, fling it open, and escape. The bus station wasn't that far from Aunt LaDelle's and maybe he could pick up his purple rabbit's foot along the way, but with his luck, the bush she threw it into would turn out to be poison ivy.

"I guess that's enough for you to know for now. I'll give you a complete written list by morning. Come, on. I'll show you your bedroom."

Jubilant followed her to a room at the end of the hallway. The room was smaller than the one he had at home and looked too neat and tidy to be comfortable. In the room was a bed covered with a blue and white quilt, three shelves of books mounted to the wall, a chest of drawers with a lace doily and an alarm clock on top, a sewing machine with a cardboard sign taped to it that said, "Do Not Touch!" and a small writing desk and chair. On the desk was a framed photo of an older man and woman. They looked familiar to him. He bent down to take a better look.

"Do you recognize those people?" LaDelle asked.

He nodded as he continued to study them. "Yes. My daddy has a picture of them on his desk, but it's different."

"Those folks are your grandparents. God rest their souls."

"What kind of hat is he wearing?"

"It's called a 'beret.' Your grandfather loved to look French."

"Why? *Was* he French?"

"Not at all," she chuckled. "Papa thought the French language was romantic and smooth, so he studied it when he could and spoke it whenever possible. He also strived to look the part. Your grandad did not consider himself fully dressed until he put on his beret. He owned two in wool—one navy, one black—and refused to leave the house without one atop his head."

Jubilant smiled and stood up straight next to the desk. He liked hearing about his grandad and wished he had known him.

Next to the framed photo, Jubilant noticed there were a few sharpened pencils in a tin mug.

"All right now, we can talk more about Papa another time. Let me finish what I was telling you," Aunt LaDelle said without a trace of a grin. "I didn't get to this rule yet, but you'll be writing at this desk every day."

"School's not even in session and—"

"Hush! I'm not giving you a homework assignment, but I do expect you to write to your daddy each and every day." LaDelle pursed her lips giving her a face Jubilant didn't want to cross. "Each. And. Every. Day!" She repeated herself, but then her countenance softened as she continued. "You'll find everything you need—paper, envelopes, and a roll of three-cent stamps—in the top right-hand drawer. You will give me your letter each morning, and I will take it to my work and mail it."

"Every day?" He was still puzzled by the idea. He didn't think he could come up with interesting things to write every day. "Even on Sunday? That's Sabbath."

"Ev-er-y Day!" Aunt LaDelle said with her hands on her hips. "Sabbath is meant for kindness and mercy as well as rest, so you'll be thoughtful towards your daddy even on the Lord's day."

Jubilant nodded. He didn't know what to say. He wanted to tell her the reverend wouldn't want to be bothered with reading a pile of boring letters every week, but he thought it would be better to nod. At least Aunt LaDelle wasn't making him do arithmetic every day. The truth was, out of all the subjects in school, Jubilant minded writing the least. He liked to create stories, and he was good at grammar and spelling, but dealing with numbers made him feel stupid.

"As you can tell, nephew, I like things in apple-pie order—a place for everything and everything in its place." She went on to say she knew the two of them would get along just fine if he followed the house rules and obeyed her. "You'll find I'm not an unreasonable woman, but I am a no-nonsense one. Besides, I know how to handle young boys. I practically raised your father and our younger brother. God rest his soul."

"Alexander. My daddy told me about him."

"Did he tell you he collapsed outside next to our cherry tree when he was just ten years old?"

"Yes, ma'am," he said, though the reverend never told him where it had happened.

"The doctor's best guess was he had a hole in his heart no one was aware of." After adding that bit of information, LaDelle sighed and shook her head. "Makes me wonder sometimes what will be the death of me? And when? Heart troubles seem to run in the family."

Jubilant looked down at his feet and shuffled them back and forth. He wanted this conversation to be over, but at that moment he couldn't help but think it wouldn't be such a bad thing if he too had a hole in his heart. Maybe he would die in his sleep and wake up in a better place—like heaven or Yonkers.

LaDelle wasn't in the mood to dirty any dishes, but what choice did she have? "I'm fixing you a plate of food," she declared as she walked away. "Though I'm not sure what to give him," she mumbled to herself as she grabbed her apron off its hook. "How much do I feed a boy in the throes of adolescence anyway?"

Jubilant followed her and took a seat at the small round kitchen table. She watched him from the corner of her eye, but they didn't talk. She kept busy with her task of making a meal so the boy could fill his belly. He petted the dog, and Dewey wagged his tail.

LaDelle gave Jubilant a nod of satisfaction as he stuffed the last bite of food into his mouth. Convinced he'd eaten enough, she handed him a napkin and took his plate. *He'll sleep better with a full stomach, though not everyone in Alabama has the luxury of filling their child's belly these days.*

"Brush your teeth and go on to bed," she said. "I'll wash your plate this time. You get some sleep."

When Jubilant left, LaDelle helped herself to another biscuit slathered in honey and ate it leaning over the sink. Then, she hurried through the dishes, yawning several times as she scrubbed, rinsed, and set them in the strainer to dry on their own. She let Dewey out in the backyard for the night and made her way to the bathroom to wash off the sweat and stress of the day.

Before entering the bathroom, she stopped at Jubilant's door. It was closed and no light shone through the threshold. She strained her ear to listen. Nodding at the silence, she entered the bathroom.

LaDelle filled the tub with lukewarm water and soaked herself in near darkness—her only source of light was from the full moon shining through the top half of the window, just below the lace valance, and the glow of a yellow candle leftover from Christmas. As she lathered her body with soap, tears flowed down her warm cheeks. Unable to stop them, she gave in and closed her eyes to let them flow freely.

"Oh Lord," she cried out in a whisper, "why have you chosen me to care for this boy? Don't you see, I'm not up to the task. I'm so temperamental these days—more than usual. I'm afraid he'll bring disorder to my life, Lord, and I just can't handle that right now. Garvin should be here to help me. He'd calm me for sure."

A whimper escaped her lips before she could stop it. LaDelle's habit of cherishing being in control had been a lifelong struggle, but ever since Garvin's death, her desire for control had intensified. The unspeakable happened when he was killed. *What more will go wrong?* Plenty, she feared. *Life is uncertain and disappointment is a real possibility to have thrust upon you.*

And now a young boy was in her care. *Young boys have chaos infused into them. It's in their blood. Boys his age especially, question everything and are unpredictable and careless. They do stupid things! What if he brings trouble onto me?*

LaDelle could feel her heartbeat through her chest as these thoughts filled her mind. *He's sure to bring trouble, Lord. He was in town barely five minutes when he brought out that talisman of his.* Remembering her shock and anger at seeing Jubilant's rabbit's foot quickened her heartbeat even more. *Calm down, LaDelle. Don't get all riled. Breathe. Breathe.*

LaDelle remained in the tub, though now the water was too cool for comfort. She tried not to focus on the "what-if's," but fear continued to creep into her, and it only grew with every scenario she allowed her mind to conjure. She covered her mouth with her hand as her whole body shook.

She fought to stay silent, but grief and panic overtook her. *The boy must not hear you cry!* "Be anxious for nothing," she whispered several times. A moment later, she took a deep breath, exhaled, and suddenly a calmness she hadn't mustered on her own enveloped her. Then, words she had not searched for filled her mind. The words brought a feeling with them, like a protective, loving embrace covering her entire body. She wrapped her arms around her chest and leaned forward as if that would help her to absorb the words before her:

"My grace is sufficient for thee: for my strength is made perfect in weakness."

LaDelle held her breath for a few seconds, straining to listen as if the words in her mind had been audible. She recognized them. *First Corinthians? Or is it from Ephesians?* This seeing words so clearly in her mind was something new, but there they were like a gift she didn't know she needed until she received it. She couldn't deny what she saw—words so bold they were unmistakable. Tangible.

Slowly splashing her face with water, she took another deep breath. Then, she stood in the tub, grabbed her towel, and dried off—her skin cool and refreshed after bathing, her mind and spirit suddenly pacified. She covered herself with her robe, blew out the nearly used-up candle, tiptoed to her room, and closed the door behind her without a sound. After slipping her nightgown over her head, she slid into bed and turned off the lights.

Remembering the second half of the verse, LaDelle whispered out loud, "The power of Christ may rest upon me." She repeated it several more times, "The power of Christ may rest upon me ..." In a few moments, she dozed off, sound asleep before she could give thought to setting her alarm.

CHAPTER NINE—CARVER

The great pleasure of a dog is that you may make a fool
of yourself with him and not only will he not scold you,
but he will make a fool of himself too. (Samuel Butler)

Jubilant patted his stomach as he woke the next morning
and stared up at the ceiling. He stretched, yawned, and
rubbed his eyes, but kept his body horizontal, glued to
the bed. The mattress was firm and without lumps, unlike
the one he slept on at home, which had come with the
parsonage and had probably been around since the Civil
War or so he supposed. The mattress looked and smelled
ancient. The sheets on Aunt LaDelle's guest bed smelled
like lavender with a hint of bleach. After taking in a few
exaggerated whiffs of the sheets, he propped himself up
with his pillow and surveyed the room in the morning light.
Here he was—still at Aunt LaDelle's. He was in *her* house
in *her* sewing room, and had a whole summer here ahead
of him, a full day's bus ride away from the reverend. He
rubbed his head as he mulled this over. His situation was a
lot to take in. He had to admit, though, his aunt could cook,
so that was something.

The night before, she had served up a plate of mouth-
watering fried catfish, a side of collard greens that, she
informed him, were fresh from her garden out back, and
some red rice. He washed it all down with a tall glass of milk,

and his belly swelled. Although he was still worried about the reverend and hated having to be at his aunt's, the taste of her food seemed to reawaken his appetite and brought a morsel of comfort. After a long day of travel and the stress of meeting Aunt LaDelle, her food filled his shrunken stomach to near overflowing, and then he slept deeply.

A thought hit him as he rolled out of bed. This had been the first night in over a week he hadn't been visited by the nightmare of Daddy falling over at the pulpit. In fact, he couldn't remember having any dreams at all during the night. He closed his eyes for a few seconds to try to recollect more thoroughly, but nothing came to mind.

"Well, what do you know?" he muttered under his breath, and then let out an exaggerated yawn. "Not one nightmare."

That first morning, Drill Sergeant Harris wasted no time after she had walked Jubilant through his morning schedule and gave him barely enough time to complete each task. She called him to attention. Then, she checked to make sure his appearance was in order, he had made his bed, taken out the trash, fed Dewey, read the first chapter of Psalms, and said the Lord's Prayer. Once she approved—she made him remake the bed twice—she didn't say "at ease," but instead, "have a seat."

She placed in front of him a stack of pancakes that tasted like he imagined they would if they were served at a fancy restaurant where rich people dined. They were fluffy, sweet, and moist, not hard, dense, and burnt on the edges like the reverend's. To Jubilant's surprise, Aunt LaDelle didn't tell him to go easy on the maple syrup. She allowed him to help himself and offered more pancakes when his plate was empty. His stomach bulged in a most satisfying way.

"Saturdays are the only days I make pancakes, just so you know," she warned Jubilant. "And it looks like I'll have to go out and get a second job with your appetite." Though her words were sharp, Jubilant saw a softness in her eyes as she spoke.

Jubilant nodded and syrup seeped out the sides of his mouth. He knew he'd better not talk with his mouth full. Though this summer was sure to be the most awful one ever—if he lived through it—Saturday breakfast at Aunt LaDelle's could possibly see him through to fall.

LaDelle watched Jubilant swallow the last bite of pancake and wash it down with milk. She hadn't made breakfast, or any meal, for anyone in a long time. Garvin used to say her pancakes were the best he'd ever eaten. That was high praise indeed, coming from the owner of a diner.

Something about the process of preparing food—chopping, mixing, cooking—and the aroma that filled a kitchen spoke to LaDelle's soul. Here was the one place she was prone to hum without giving it a thought. Whenever she cooked and created, she cleaned as she went—rinsing, wiping, tidying, and returning each item to where it belonged. Everything had its logical place—spices in the left cupboard, spatulas and mixing spoons within reach to her right, a frying pan stored in the bottom cupboard next to the stove, large bowls next to the pans. Her broom, mop, duster, spare rags, and extra sponges were readily available in the cabinet.

Garvin had been a weekend baker, but his style in the kitchen was the exact opposite of his wife's. His style, she would say, was "willy-nilly." When he was done kneading bread and creating treats, flour could be discovered days later in various cracks and crevices of the kitchen.

LaDelle was able to tolerate Garvin's carelessness, however, for the sheer fact his rye and wheat breads—along with his shortbread cookies—were extraordinary. The man had a gift. But she firmly believed there was no good reason a kitchen in use had to look like an explosion had taken place. There was both a delight and purpose to her as she utilized what she needed for each task in her meal preparation and presentation. She possessed a certain ease of movement—a beautiful rhythm—as she labored in the kitchen.

Her finding pleasure in the kitchen had begun when she was still a teenager. She was barely able to carry a full cooking pot to the table in her youth when preparing meals for her family was part of her responsibility on the days both of her parents were busy with work. She learned the art of using the groceries she had on hand and being creative with them. She received praise from her family for what she managed to do, for example, with a chicken, some greens, potatoes, and spices. "C'est magnifique!" Papa would exclaim with his mouth full after just the first bite of their evening meal. Mama and her brothers would nod in agreement as they chewed. When there was plenty, they'd help themselves to seconds, though most nights there was just enough for one plateful each. Praise goes a long way to bring out the confidence in a young girl—in a human of any age. The family's praise fueled LaDelle's culinary sangfroid, and she flourished in the kitchen as a result.

As a wife, LaDelle especially loved cooking for Garvin, whose praise warmed her heart like none other. She also relished his affection for her. He'd enter the kitchen quietly at times, trying to sneak up on her. She was fully aware he was there but pretended to be ignorant of his presence and would continue peeling the potatoes or washing the lettuce or whatever she was busy doing. Then, he'd wrap his arms around her from behind and kiss her neck. He'd whisper in her ear how beautiful she was and tell her she was a most fine woman. "Keep on flattering me," she'd say, "and I'll cook for you the rest of your life!"

Of course, LaDelle had no idea the rest of his life would be so brief. Once he was taken from her, her cooking became simpler, and the pleasure of it was lost. Cooking and baking became a chore, a "have to." She wondered for half a second what Abel Fisher's favorite meal might be, but quickly chased the thought away. *Don't be silly*, she told herself, yet still she wondered.

Jubilant sighed with relief when, after a morning of her bossing him around and filling his day with chores, Aunt LaDelle announced after lunch she would take a pick-me-up nap next to the fan. She slipped the kitchen timer into her apron pocket.

"I've found a twenty-five-minute nap is optimum for a rejuvenating rest. Any longer than that, I wake in a bit of a fog, and struggle at bedtime to fall asleep."

Jubilant fought back a yawn just thinking of a nap, but more than needing rest, he needed fun. So far, the day had been a bore.

"While I rest," Aunt LaDelle said between yawns, "you have the option of these activities *after* you write a letter to your daddy—you may nap as well, read a book, or take Dewey for a walk. What'll it be, boy?"

None of her options seemed like any fun at all, and the heat outside could melt a bee in flight, but he chose to get outside with Dewey. Though Jubilant was in no mood to write a letter, he was in less of a mood to get a tongue lashing from his aunt, so before heading out with the dog, he went into his room and sat down at the desk. He chewed on the end of his pencil, drummed his fingers on his knee and on the desk. He rested his head in his hands, and rubbed his head several times. Ten minutes later, he wrote half a page about Aunt LaDelle being bossy. *Isn't slavery against the law? I can't believe you're making me stay here. Send me a ticket back to Huntsville*, he requested, and promised to not be any trouble. *No trouble at all. I can even take care of you*, he added before signing, "Sincerely, Jubilant."

Jubilant didn't bother to read over his letter. He quickly folded it, tucked it inside the envelope, and sealed it shut. Then, he dashed to the front door and grabbed the leash off the coat rack. Dewey went wild, spinning around with his tail wagging so fast it seemed he might propel himself up into the air. He barked and jumped, licking Jubilant as he bent down to secure the leash. When they were finally ready to leave, Jubilant quietly closed the front door to avoid disturbing Aunt LaDelle more than Dewey already had. They headed toward Wilson's house, which he knew was somewhere down the street and to the right.

He couldn't remember which house Miss Patty said was theirs. Maybe Dewey would lead him to it since he went there so often. Jubilant kept his eye out for the wagon he saw at the train station. He walked past seven houses. Two of them had cats lounging in the shade on the front porch, but thankfully, Dewey hadn't noticed. Finally, he had walked almost to the end of the block when he heard a sharp whistle from behind. He turned around and found Wilson sitting on his front porch steps holding a chicken.

"I was wondering when you'd make your way down here," Wilson called out. "Don't you remember? Mama told you ours was the one with the picket fence."

"Why didn't you just walk up the street to Aunt LaDelle's and come get me?" Jubilant gave Dewey's leash a quick tug and led him to Wilson's place. The dog went wild as soon as he spotted the chicken. Jubilant yanked his leash.

"Hush!" he commanded, making his voice sound deeper than it naturally was.

"Tie up the dog here in front and come to the back with me. I want to show you something," Wilson said, ignoring his question. When he stood up to lead the way, the chicken's wings fluttered in his arms, but Wilson held on tight. The cuffs on Wilson's faded overalls were different lengths, and his hair was just as long and nappy as it had been on the bus. What would Millie Hines say if she saw him? She would escort him to Jerry's Barber Shop by the end of the day, no doubt.

Jubilant walked through the gate of the fence that had so many slats missing, a gate seemed unnecessary. Then, he quickly wrapped Dewey's leash around the small apricot tree in the middle of Wilson's front lawn several times. He looped the end of the leash through and gave it a few tugs. *That should be tight enough.* He looked down at Dewey and told him to sit. The dog whined and barked a few times but was distracted for a moment with a sudden itch at the back of his ear. When he noticed the boys were walking away, he let out another bark as a final protest before sitting down in the shade the tree provided. The boys disappeared into the backyard without glancing back.

"So, why didn't you come find me?" Jubilant repeated as he caught up with Wilson.

"I've been busy workin' on stuff with my dad, and besides, your aunt—"

"Ah, I get it," Jubilant nodded, understanding Wilson's point without him even verbalizing it. "You're afraid of her."

"Nah, I just don't want any trouble with her."

Jubilant decided to drop the subject and followed Wilson in silence to the side of the house and into the backyard. The pair walked into a large pen with a chicken coop that housed a dozen or so chickens. A large black rooster strutted among the hens clustered together, his head in the air, ignoring the boys. Jubilant tiptoed around the pen, trying to watch where he stepped. If he tracked chicken poop into Aunt LaDelle's house, he would be plucked and cooked right along with the plumpest fowl.

Wilson gently set down the chicken he had been holding and picked up the rooster.

"This here is Duke. He's a Black Jersey Giant. A prize winner." The cocky bird looked Jubilant in the face as if to say, "Admire me." He was handsome with his full plumes, and he was strangely calm as Wilson held him up in the air like a trophy.

"He's a beauty," Jubilant remarked. He longed to have his own animal again. Louie, the feral cat that adopted him—and a few neighbors—when they were living in Yonkers was the perfect pet. He came and went as cats do, but when he was around, he was agreeable, allowing Jubilant to pet him and eating scraps out of his hand. Louie was just another thing he had to say goodbye to when they moved.

"Duke has won two prizes in two different categories, and my chickens lay the best eggs in town. The secret," Wilson leaned toward Jubilant and whispered as if someone might overhear him and steal this important information, "is keeping them in a calm environment."

And then, just like that, any calm those chickens had been basking in was history. Dewey, with his leash still attached to his collar and flailing behind him like a wild snake, bolted into the backyard and headed straight for the chicken coop. His bark echoed as he zigzagged around the pen like a balloon that suddenly lost its air. The chickens went berserk, clucking and squawking as if they were headed for the guillotine.

"Stop him!" Wilson screamed.

"I'm tryin'. He's goin' too crazy!" Jubilant cried as he made yet another failed attempt at grabbing Dewey's leash. "Help me!"

"Stop him! Stop him!" Wilson repeated over and over. Jubilant lunged at the dog, but Wilson seemed out of his mind in his turmoil. All he could do was stomp his feet, wave his arms, and scream.

"What on earth—?" Miss Patty and an old man came running out of the house from the back porch. "Is that LaDelle's dog? He's goin' get himself one of your chickens, Wilson! You'd better stop him."

"We're tryin', Ma! Can't you see we're tryin'?"

At that moment, before anyone could stop him, Dewey pinned one of the chickens under his paw. He chomped down on it, then lifted the helpless bird into the air. It flailed and squawked before falling to the ground, leaving a fan of feathers in the dog's mouth. Dewey went for it again and this time, punctured its skin with his sharp teeth. He shook the bird violently in his mouth and soon the bird's blood spilled out onto the dirt, staining the dog's mouth.

"No! Oh, no! Stop! Stop it!" Wilson begged, cupping his mouth with his hands in horror.

Miss Patty ran into the pen to help, as the old man with her let out a loud, sharp whistle. Dewey stopped for a split second and cocked his ears. With feathers still stuck to the side of his mouth, he looked as if he had a feather beard. If the whole scene weren't so upsetting, Jubilant might have had a good laugh at how silly Dewey looked, but what the dog had done was no laughing matter. Wilson had tears in his eyes, and Jubilant recognized his responsibility. He was in real need of a friend, and now he'd probably lose the only possibility of one in Tuskegee. Before Jubilant could say anything to Wilson, the old man swiftly took hold of the dog's leash and handed it to Jubilant.

"Here now, son. Hurry! Take him."

Jubilant gripped the leash, yanked on Dewey's collar, and led him quickly away from the coop.

"Stupid dog. Why couldn't you stay put?" Jubilant scolded Dewey. He looked over his shoulder and saw Wilson on his knees, holding his dead chicken. "Sorry, Wilson. I'm real sorry," he called out as he ushered the dog away from the scene of the crime.

Dewey continued barking until Jubilant was able to drag him back into the front yard. The old man followed him and Dewey to the front of the house. Wilson and Patty stayed in the pen, tending to Wilson's dead chicken as well as Duke and the dozen or so other chickens still unnerved by Dewey's surprise attack.

Sweat ran down Jubilant's face, and his heart continued to beat like a war drum. "I thought he was tied up tight enough," he said to the old man, now standing in front of him. "Wilson told me to leave him tied up in the yard. I didn't know he'd get away like that. I had no idea he could be such a killer. He's such a friendly dog towards people."

"It was an accident," the old man said with compassion. He put his hand on Jubilant's shoulder. "Give him time, son. I'm sure Wilson will understand. Animals do what they do. Your dog was simply acting on instinct, and that's a fact." The old man reached down and pulled a few feathers off Dewey's mouth. Then, he took a handkerchief from his pocket and wiped blood from the dog's mouth. "No sense advertising his killer ways," he said with a wink.

Still holding tightly to Dewey's leash, Jubilant raised his head and looked at the gentleman in front of him. He was tall, yet small for a man, and looked especially small in stature when he was next to Miss Patty. His hair was closely cropped with a sprinkling of gray, and his dark brown skin reminded Jubilant of worn leather. He wore an old, but clean-looking suit—though it was too hot to be wearing a jacket—and had a fresh flower in his lapel.

"Are you Wilson's grandpa?" Jubilant asked.

"No, son, I'm just a friend of the Doyle family," he said. His voice was gentle and high-pitched, not unlike a woman's. "Patience invited me over for some refreshments today."

"No, my dear George, I invited you for lunch a week ago, and here you finally come by today and after our noon meal is over! Lordy be!" Miss Patty approached them on the front lawn and entered the conversation. "You get so caught up with your laboratory secrets you don't even know the day or time!"

Miss Patty tried to sound mad, but even with her arm raised and her hand formed into a fist, her fondness for the man next to her was obvious. Her playfulness made it clear she didn't hold a grudge. Then, she came over to Jubilant and put her strong arm around his shoulder, her skin wet with perspiration from the heat as well as the excitement in the chicken coop.

"Don't worry yourself now, honey. Wilson knows it was an accident. These things happen."

Jubilant was about to say how sorry he was when—

"Goodness, boy! There you are!"

The sound of his aunt's voice made Jubilant cringe. He didn't look in her direction at first but kept his eyes on the old man.

"What's going on here? You get yourself in some kind of trouble?" LaDelle shoved her hands onto her hips and waited half a second before she continued. "Something told me I had better get my shoes on and come look for you. I had an uneasy feeling I couldn't ignore."

Jubilant turned toward his aunt, and saw that her face was glistening with sweat. Her eyes were wild and piercing.

"I was worried that you got yourself lost or worse," She exclaimed with labored breath after half marching, half jogging down the street in hot pursuit of her nephew.

Jubilant decided Aunt LaDelle may have been rested after her nap, but any benefits of that rest had disappeared like vapor. She stomped up to Jubilant and snatched Dewey's leash out of his hand. Only then did she notice Patty Doyle and the older man standing by her side. She immediately covered her mouth with her other hand.

"Oh, my! Professor Carver. I didn't realize it was you. I'm so sorry, sir, if my nephew has troubled you in any way. He was only supposed to take the dog for a walk."

"Not to worry, Mrs. Harris. Your nephew has given your dog a good amount of exercise, I assure you." The old man turned to Jubilant and winked.

"Well, that's nice to know," Aunt LaDelle replied more calmly, and nodding first to the old man and then to Miss Patty, she wished them both a good day and apologized again for any trouble Jubilant might have caused. "Come with me, boy," she said in a softer tone and giving Dewey's leash a yank, the three set off toward home.

Jubilant cheeks grew warm, and he bit his bottom lip. He turned and walked away with his head down and without saying goodbye. Aunt LaDelle bolted toward home so fast he was forced to take two steps to her one just to keep up. He didn't want her to get after him for going too slow.

"Oh, my goodness! Goodness me! I wasn't prepared for that." LaDelle chattered on the way home once she was out of earshot of Miss Patty and her guest. "What was Professor Carver doing at Robert and Patience Doyle's house? I had no idea they were friends."

"Miss Patty invited him over for lunch, but he came late so they were having tea together instead," Jubilant offered. He was thankful his aunt was so taken by the old man she wasn't asking him questions about Dewey and the chickens.

"I wonder if he'd come to my place for some sweet tea if I invited him?" Aunt LaDelle seemed to be asking the question more to herself than to Jubilant, so he didn't answer. "I could make some of my molasses cookies or maybe just serve some buttermilk biscuits with blackberry jam. Henrietta's blackberries are nearly ripe." LaDelle took a few silent steps before adding, "I mean, I see him whenever he comes into the library, and I'm always there ready to help him find any information he needs. Surely, he wouldn't think it strange if I invited him over for tea or—"

She stopped mid-sentence when they reached her front porch. With her hand on the handle of her screen door, she turned her attention to Jubilant and looked down at his feet.

"Take off those shoes before you enter this house!"

"Yes, ma'am."

"What in the world? Is that chicken poop I see on the top of that one?" She pointed to Jubilant's left shoe as if it was on trial. "If that's on the top, what's on the bottom? Boy, what sort of mischief have you been up to?"

Jubilant shrugged and without a word, did as he was told.

Aunt LaDelle checked Dewey over to make sure he was clean before allowing him entrance as well. "If only you could talk, I might get some answers," she said and patted his head.

With his back turned away from his aunt, Jubilant rolled his eyes. *She trusts her mutt more than she trusts me.*

"You have time now to finish pulling those weeds in my garden out back before supper. Also, you can begin thinking about what you'll write in your next letter to your daddy. You already have something exciting to tell him since arriving—you met the prestigious Professor George Washington Carver!"

And he helped me with your chicken-crazed dog, Jubilant wanted to say, but thought he'd save that information for the reverend.

After weeding the garden and eating supper, Jubilant was required to bathe. While he soaked in the tub and halfheartedly applied the washcloth to his skin, he relived the scene in his head of Dewey and the chicken. Though it was horrific, he had to admit the dog had skills. He was in awe of how quickly Dewey had annihilated that poor fowl.

From there, Jubilant's mind wandered to the next day. Sunday. He'd have to go to church and sit right next to his aunt. He'd also have to stay awake and hold in any bodily noises that might try to release themselves. Jubilant planned on praying extra hard while he sat on the pews at Aunt LaDelle's church. Maybe this time God would hear him and show mercy even though a chicken was violently killed on account of him. Maybe God would free Jubilant from Aunt LaDelle like he freed the Israelites from the Egyptians. Jubilant then remembered the rest of the story— even after they were freed, they had to wander the desert for forty years. God never seemed to make things easy. Of course, those Israelites were a pain in the neck.

Alone after Jubilant went to his room for the night, LaDelle's thoughts returned to Professor Carver. She was aware she sometimes gushed over this man she so admired, but LaDelle didn't care. His reputation, in part, is what had lured her to Tuskegee. Though it had been six years since she'd started her position, she still did not know Professor Carver personally, but her admiration of him had not waned.

The man doesn't have any blood-related family here or anywhere that I know of. Maybe he's lonely. I should have reached out to him a long time ago. He's just a man, after all—not a god. I don't know why I get so tongue-tied around him. Patty Doyle doesn't.

LaDelle thought back to the conversation she had with Jubilant that evening at supper. It began with a question.

"Why did you leave New York to move to here?" He spoke with a mouthful of food, but she let it slide. He sure seemed to enjoy her food. "I miss Yonkers. I miss everything about it. Especially my friends."

"New York will always be home, I suppose," she said, handing him a napkin, "but I pursued employment at Tuskegee because of the work which Professor Carver and the late Booker T. Washington started here. Also, I had a great burden growing inside me after my husband died. It was time for a fresh start."

Jubilant nodded. "Daddy probably needed a fresh start too."

"I imagine he did," she said and handed him another biscuit as an act of bestowing comfort. They sat in silence for a minute as she watched Jubilant wash down the last bite of food with a glass of milk.

"When I pursued employment in Tuskegee," she continued, "I was ready to move away from the two places I'd always lived: Yonkers, where your daddy and I grew up, and later Brooklyn where I lived and worked with my husband Garvin at his diner, Double Gee's."

"I wasn't ready to move," Jubilant said, "I liked where we lived and the people in my neighborhood. Most of them." He stood up and took his plate over to the sink.

"Just leave it," LaDelle said, pointing to his plate. "I'll do dishes tonight. You can go out back and toss the ball to Dewey."

She welcomed some alone time to think. Washing a sink full of dishes would give her the space to do it. As she scrubbed a pan, she muttered, "Some memories from New York I will always cherish, but others I am happy to forget."

One such memory was when Mama passed away, and Papa remarried. His new wife Tess was ten years his junior and fully capable of handling their affairs—duties LaDelle had been taking care of like banking and correspondence. She didn't want or need a *deuxième maman,* and LaDelle didn't approve of how quickly Papa seemed to move on with his life and remarry. Spending time with Papa and Tess made her uncomfortable more often than not.

"I need my own fresh start," she told her father one evening while having supper with him and Tess. "It's time for me to move on—and move away." This verbal declaration launched her into making solid plans for her future.

With Garvin gone and Papa having Tess, LaDelle gave herself permission to be released from her current position working at the diner. The truth was she had little interest in continuing her role at Double Gee's now that Garvin was gone. She only did the work originally to be a helpmate to her husband. Though she was fully capable, working as a bookkeeper and ordering the food and supplies didn't really suit her. Before Garvin was killed, LaDelle had reluctantly agreed to join him at work, and he kept her busy enough, for which she was thankful. Garvin and his younger brother Gabriel took care of everything else that had to do with the restaurant.

Over the years, LaDelle had become increasingly impressed with Gabriel's business sense. She knew he was completely qualified to be the sole owner now Garvin was gone. He possessed enough of Garvin's people skills to keep the regular customers happy and turn new customers into regulars before long.

LaDelle ended up selling her and Garvin's portion of the business to Gabriel. She was optimistic Gabriel would make the most of the establishment he and his late brother had created. That is unless he married one of the silly, overly fashionable girls he was prone to date. Such a woman could be his downfall. So, before she signed over her part of the business she inherited from Garvin, she gave Gabriel this advice by way of a well-rehearsed lecture.

"Be careful, dear brother-in-law. If you keep dating silly girls, you will eventually marry a silly girl, and she is bound to journey into dangerous places with your profits. I can practically promise you this. Eventually, her expensive high-heeled shoes will step in dog doo, so to speak, and you will be left to clean up the mess. So, be smart like your brother and choose your mate carefully."

With a playful smirk on his face, Gabriel nodded at his sister-in-law. "I hear you, LaDelle," he said as they hugged goodbye.

She wondered if he really had. Time would tell. Nevertheless, the diner and her work there must be left behind if she were to move forward. Moving forward was scary, but the thought of things staying the same amid her heartache was much more frightening.

Once she received word she'd been hired at the Tuskegee Institute, she made plans to migrate to Alabama, never expecting Ashton would move with his young son to Huntsville years later. Or, that it would take a heart attack to reconnect them. They had never been at odds with one another, just busy living their own lives.

As she dried the dishes, LaDelle thought back to a conversation she'd had with Papa before she left.

"Why are you taking a position so far from home?" he asked her for the third time.

"I told you, Papa. I want to be associated with George Washington Carver's reputation, along with Booker T. Washington's," she said, patting his shoulder. "We've been through all this. Please try to understand."

"I remember when Booker T. Washington died. I read about it in the *New York Times*," Papa said. "I'm not ignorant of the fact he was a true leader and visionary, you know."

"Don't you see, Papa? George Washington Carver is still employed by the Institute. He remains as a member of the faculty, conducting his scientific work. So, by me being employed there too, I will be a co-laborer, in a sense, with the great Professor Carver."

"The boys at the barber shop will be impressed when I tell them, won't they?"

"Yes, Papa. They certainly will." LaDelle smiled to herself knowing how her father valued status and reputation.

In the months to follow before she said her goodbyes, LaDelle's sense of purpose—along with her father's expressed approval—was helpful in soothing her sadness over leaving him. She also experienced renewed, fresh grief at the thought of being so far away from Garvin's gravesite in Brooklyn, which caused her some sleepless nights. Still, when the day came to leave, she packed her car and headed to Alabama with little fanfare or tears and enough money in her bank account to buy herself a house when she arrived. She had her mind set on a two-bedroom. A brick one with white shutters would be nice.

Before arriving at Tuskegee, LaDelle had learned a great deal about the professor through her research. Quite a bit had been written about him, and over the years his fame had grown. Known for his quiet demeanor, he was also smart as a whip as witnessed by his industrious accomplishments.

LaDelle admired these two traits. Professor Carver taught, experimented, invented, and spoke to councils of important folks—mostly white men—of influence, sharing his discoveries with them. He regularly impressed as well as surprised them all, though sometimes they'd laugh in his face. By remaining calm and inserting his playful sense of humor, he was generally able to win them over.

He, in fact, had won awards for his work, yet one would never know he was revered for it due to his humble ways. Some folks—out of jealousy most likely—reported that Professor Carver was somewhat of a prima donna, but LaDelle didn't believe it for a second. George Washington Carver never tooted his own horn. He was not a man to put on airs and even looked embarrassed whenever someone would bring up the accolades he received for his work.

A few years after LaDelle was hired at Tuskegee Institute, Professor Carver had been chosen to work with the Bureau of Plant Industry of the US Department of Agriculture. The school faculty was made aware by the president of the Institute, and they acknowledged this latest accomplishment by celebrating with a faculty potluck. LaDelle brought potato salad in her best crystal bowl—a wedding gift from Tess and Papa—to the gathering.

She congratulated the professor that night, but when she tried to say more, she became tongue-tied and flustered.

"You represent our fine institute so well, and—goodness—it's amazing that, um—you, well, good job, sir." Professor Carver gave LaDelle a warm smile in response, but that didn't stop her palms from sweating and her face from feeling flushed. She knew she must be coming across like a silly child and quickly excused herself, feigning the excuse it was getting late, and she needed to get home.

LaDelle's admiration for George Washington Carver had only grown over the years as she not only learned of his accomplishments, but of his history. On campus, his matter-of-fact faith, tenderness, and grace drew students to him like no other professor or faculty member she'd ever known. His demeanor drew her to him as well. Though he was more than twenty years her senior, she wanted to have him as a friend and not merely as her hero. Yet in the six years she'd held her position at the library on campus, she had barely managed to strike up a conversation.

Then, finally, she encountered her hero outside of the library, in her own neighborhood, and what happened? She was caught off guard and flustered, juggling a juvenile and a canine, and having the sinking feeling that chaos had ensued with the aforementioned. Chaos! How she despised it. Yet, how her life too often seemed plagued by it. *Lord, have mercy.*

CHAPTER TEN—FIELD WORK

We must go beyond textbooks, go out into the bypaths and untrodden depths of the wilderness ... (John Hope Franklin)

"You're having no problems holding onto your fork, I see, so I'd say your hand didn't suffer a serious cramp while writing this letter." LaDelle took the envelope Jubilant handed her and held it up to the light, trying to see if there was actual writing on the paper tucked inside. "Well now, it doesn't look like you wrote much, and your writing looks like chicken scratch to me. Make sure you take your time from now on and write neatly so your daddy can read it."

Jubilant shrugged. He'd had several teachers in his life. So far, Aunt LaDelle was the most demanding, and she wasn't even a teacher.

"I don't care for your silent shrugs, boy. A simple 'yes, ma'am,' is what I expect from you."

Jubilant put his fork down and looked at his aunt. A stare down ensued for a couple of seconds before he said, "Yes, ma'am," with defiance in his eyes. He wasn't in the mood for trouble so early in the morning. *Millie Hines and Aunt LaDelle would be best friends if they knew each other.* Luckily for him, his aunt didn't get all riled and whacky towards him over his attitude. Perhaps she was tired as well and hadn't the energy to charge him like a bull though she had the look of it.

"Let's make sure this is affixed nice and tight," she said as she put extra pressure on the stamp already firmly in place. Then, she took a pen out of one of the kitchen drawers and wrote "#2" in the bottom corner of the envelope. "From now on, number each letter sequentially like this. That way your daddy can tell clearly, before he even opens it, which letter it is without having to search for the date stamped on it. I'll be mailing your correspondence in order, but there's no guarantee the postman will deliver it that way."

"So, the post office doesn't do things in apple-pie order?" Jubilant hoped Aunt LaDelle would not pick up on the sarcasm of his words.

At this, she stared and squinted at her nephew before responding.

"You're teasing me, boy," she replied. "But the truth is organization is a lost art."

Jubilant ignored her as she went on and on about people not wanting to take the time to do things right these days.

"They're always in a rush!" She repeated the same sentence three times in her tirade before sitting down and finishing her coffee. "Now sit up young man, say your prayers, and eat your breakfast. We've a long day ahead of us, so shake a leg."

Thankfully, the drive to Tuskegee Institute was a short one. The two rode in silence, not out of anger but out of tiredness on Jubilant's part. He thought Aunt LaDelle was tired too. Jubilant rubbed his eyes and yawned, wishing he could crawl back into bed. Aunt LaDelle, he was sure, was already thinking through her day and organizing things in her head. Jubilant thought the library must be in the same apple-pie order as her house, and when she wasn't organizing things and people, she was thinking about it.

When they arrived at the Institute, Aunt LaDelle drove through the open wrought iron gate and made a right turn into the parking lot. She shut off the motor and, with a sigh, turned to face Jubilant.

"Now then, this is highly unusual, me bringing a child to work. My supervisor knows your situation and has graciously agreed to this arrangement, but I must warn you: I will *not* put up with any monkey business!"

LaDelle had the same look about her as many of Jubilant's teachers often had—serious and wild-eyed—when she handed out her warning. She wasn't finished.

"So many people are out of work these days—even educated people. I have worked darn hard for this position here at Tuskegee, so you best behave yourself and stay out of any and all trouble. Do I make myself clear, boy?"

Jubilant looked her in the face and nodded.

"I did not hear a word of that nod," she said through tight lips.

"Yes—I mean, yes, ma'am! You've made yourself clear. I'll be good."

As he said it, he couldn't help but feel as if he had told a lie. The truth was, he was always getting himself into trouble. That's the reason the reverend sent him to Aunt LaDelle's house in the first place. Trouble seemed to follow Jubilant just like Dewey followed him into the chicken coop or his annoying neighbor Artie acting as his shadow back in Huntsville.

Jubilant didn't have a good feeling about the day ahead, but he walked with his aunt down the campus pathway to the library, bracing himself for a long, boring day inside the library's four walls. What choice did he have? He tugged at the necktie she made him wear. He shuddered when he allowed himself to remember his dead uncle had worn the tie. *God must be punishing me for something.* Jubilant had prayed extra hard at church the morning before, but nothing came of it.

Maybe he wouldn't be stuck inside a library all day if he still had his purple lucky rabbit's foot. Aunt LaDelle had snooped around his room—no doubt trying to find other talismans, but she didn't know about the zippered pouch inside Jubilant's duffel. He'd unpacked everything but the rabbit's feet, and then stuffed the duffel under his bed. The rabbits' feet stayed safely tucked away inside the zippered pouch. His lucky penny was hidden in his underwear drawer.

LaDelle led her nephew past the stately white pillars and marched up the steps to the large brick building. As they approached the main door, she stopped and turned to face Jubilant.

"I know you must think I'm a cantankerous woman," she said looking him directly in the eyes.

"Well, I, uh—"

"You don't need to say anything," she told him. "I am aware of how I come across sometimes. I do ask the good Lord to temper me, I assure you."

"Yes, ma'am." He couldn't think of anything else to say. *Was she apologizing?*

"I suppose you could use some kindness and patience with all you've gone through."

He nodded, and then looked down at his feet. Hearing her say that he could use some kindness and patience embarrassed him, but it was also nice to know that maybe his aunt had a heart after all.

"Well now," she said, abruptly changing the subject. She gazed toward the roof and stretched her arm upward, inviting him to admire it. "Isn't this a beautiful building?"

Jubilant followed her gaze and nodded, though he wondered what she found so beautiful about it. It was just a building. Made of bricks.

"Yes, sir! This is a fine building, and it's even more impressive inside, I'd say." She took out a ring of keys, unlocked the double doors, turned on the lights, and headed straight for a large, worn mahogany desk in the middle of the room. "Follow me."

Jubilant stood by her desk and looked around the room. He smiled to himself. Everything was in apple-pie order as he knew it would be. Aunt LaDelle opened the bottom drawer of her desk and placed their sack lunches and her purse inside. She turned on the ceiling fans meant to force the still air to move through the building, though they didn't seem to be doing much. The day was sure to be a scorching one.

"How blessed am I," LaDelle said out loud but more to herself than to Jubilant. She didn't say the words as a question, but as a statement. LaDelle liked being a working woman. She liked making her own money and doing a job she had learned well, first by going to school, and then through dedicated practice as well as true instinct. She had taken the systems and procedures passed on to her after her predecessor had been fired and brought them to a higher level of excellence. When she was first promoted to head librarian, she came in an hour early and stayed an hour after work. When she wasn't at the library, she thought about it. *How might I make some improvements?*

In some not-so-subtle ways, LaDelle started letting folks in town know that she was in charge of the "fine library at the Institute." Then, one day her neighbor, Henrietta, made a seemingly innocent comment that awakened LaDelle to her pride.

"I'm so happy the Institute has such a capable librarian," Henrietta said. "The good Lord brought you there to serve him by serving others, I'm quite sure of that." As she spoke, she nodded her head enthusiastically causing her salmon-colored, daisy-shaped, dangle earrings to dance next to her chin. Henrietta believed in costume jewelry. Every day, for her, was an occasion to wear it. The two neighbors couldn't be more different, but they each found something in the other they took a liking to from the start. Henrietta had a way of getting under LaDelle's skin—in a good way.

LaDelle hadn't been thinking of her job as a higher calling. She was proud of her accomplishment and position. Absolutely! Her goal was to prove to her supervisor and everyone else she was the best person for the job and could keep a perfect library for all the world—or at least all the patrons—to admire.

Yet Henrietta's words that day cut her to the quick, convicting her of her misplaced devotion and purpose. She opened her mouth to reply, but then closed it again and simply nodded as she grinned sheepishly at her neighbor.

Henrietta responded with a smile of her own and reached out to gently squeeze LaDelle's arm and give her a wink before taking her leave. LaDelle's appreciation for her younger neighbor grew that day. She was humbled out of kindness. *That's what a friend does.* Before bed that night, LaDelle dropped to her knees and confessed her prideful attitude and gave thanks for Henrietta. *Maybe I ought to consider wearing earrings once in a while.*

The library was larger than Jubilant expected it to be. The shelves were long and tall, some crowded with books, others less full, but the smell was unmistakable. Books possess a certain smell that Jubilant liked. He brought one up to his nose, breathed in deep, and smiled. The smell of gasoline and cigar smoke in the cool of an evening had the same effect on him, but he never told anyone. He read some of the titles and fingered a few of the bindings. He noticed plenty of wooden desks and chairs throughout the room. As he walked up and down the aisles of shelves and desks, he wondered when the place would come alive with people.

"Follow me," his aunt whispered, even though nobody was yet inside the building. Her tone of voice, though hushed, sounded more like a command than an invitation.

She led Jubilant to a cart full of books.

"You're going to help me put these away this morning. See these numbers?" She went on before he could answer. "They tell you where the books are located on the shelves. It's called the Dewey Decimal System."

"Dewey?"

"That's right," she said, grinning at her own cleverness. "That's where my mutt got his name."

Jubilant was thinking how much nicer it was to see Aunt LaDelle with a smile on her face rather than a scowl when he caught a glimpse of someone walking into the library.

"I think someone's here," he said.

"Well, we don't open for another twenty minutes," she snapped as she turned around to see who dared enter *her* library before it was officially open. "Wh-why good morning, Professor Carver. What can I do for you today, sir?"

Jubilant wondered what made Aunt LaDelle so nervous whenever she saw Professor Carver. He was half her size and his voice, high-pitched and friendly, was not at all intimidating. To Jubilant, he was just a nice old man—nothing special. He read in a bulletin he'd found in Aunt LaDelle's sewing room that the professor had invented some important things like massage oil for polio patients and had made paint out of local clay. Aunt LaDelle told him

Mr. Carver had changed the way farmers grew their crops, which helped the state of Alabama and beyond.

As he walked towards them, Jubilant noticed that Professor Carver wore the same suit he had on the day they had first met each other. His lapel, however, had a different fresh flower tucked into the buttonhole. This time a pale pink bud, and Jubilant wondered if it smelled good, but he was too embarrassed to ask. The old gentleman carried some sort of cylinder with a leather strap attached. He removed his cap and smiled at Aunt LaDelle. *He seems to have all his teeth*, Jubilant thought for no good reason at all.

"I overheard you'd be bringing your nephew to work, and I had hoped maybe you'd let me borrow him for a while. My assistant Mr. Curtis is feeling under the weather today." The tone of his voice reminded Jubilant of a child's.

"You want the boy to help you with something? W-well, of course, he's available, Professor Carver. When would you like him?"

"I'll take him now and have him back before you leave for the day, Mrs. Harris. Would that find favor with you?"

Aunt LaDelle put her hand on her chest and managed a "that'll be fine," and then dashed to her desk to retrieve the lunch she had packed for her nephew.

Jubilant knew his aunt would have prepared another lunch if she had known that Professor Carver would come into the library and take Jubilant off her hands for the day, but how could she know?

"Take this and don't be any trouble to Professor Carver," LaDelle said calmly and in a friendly tone, though in her widening eyes Jubilant saw the silent threat—*Be good or you'll be sorry!*

"I have some collecting to do and thought you'd make a helpful partner," Professor Carver told Jubilant once they stepped outside. "I hope it doesn't trouble you to work outdoors today instead of inside our school's fine library."

Jubilant didn't know what to think. What would be worse? Enduring the full summer heat outside while working for a man he barely knew or working in the fan-cooled library with a demanding aunt he knew enough not to like. Neither option suited the twelve-year-old, but there was something about George Washington Carver that intrigued him. When he talked to Jubilant, he looked deep into his eyes, and he seemed to understand something, though Jubilant didn't know what. So, without a word, Jubilant followed the old man across the campus.

Jubilant tugged at his tie as the two walked in silence, past several buildings, including one with a sign that read "Milbank Hall."

"My laboratory is in this building," Professor Carver informed his new assistant, pointing to his right. "We'll go there later, but now we're headed past the field and into the forest." He acknowledged each passing student with a wave or a tip of his cap, greeting each one by name.

They smiled back at him, "Good morning, Professor Carver. I enjoyed your Bible study yesterday," a few said. "I'm almost done putting the finishing touches on that painting you helped me with, sir," one student commented. "You were right about Saint John's Wort," another called out. "The herb works like a charm!" The professor stopped, shyly accepted each person's greeting, and then continued on his way with Jubilant at his heels.

From behind, Jubilant was able to take a good look at the container strapped onto the old man's shoulder. When George looked back to be sure his young friend was keeping up, he noticed him staring at the cylinder. "It's a specimen case," he offered Jubilant without waiting to be asked. "I rarely go into the forest without it. I use it to collect things."

Jubilant wondered what sorts of "things" the old man was talking about, but he didn't ask. He figured the professor would tell him soon enough.

"You'll want to take off that fancy tie and roll up your sleeves," Professor Carver said as he stopped at a wooden cart in the field. He carefully removed his suit jacket, draped it over one side of the cart and rolled up his own sleeves. Jubilant didn't have to be told twice to remove his tie and he too hung it on the cart.

The professor bent down with a quiet groan and scooped up some dirt with his hands. He put it up to his nose and smelled it before sifting through it with his other hand. "Hmmm ... this looks better since we had that little rain last week," he muttered, then he stood up and announced, "In dirt is life." Turning toward his young companion, he asked, "Do you like dirt, Jubilant?"

"I guess," he said with a shrug. "But I'm not much for pullin' weeds or workin' in the garden." He hoped Professor Carver would get the hint and not scold him for being honest. "I just like having fun."

"Me too! I have found that work can be great fun if you are doing what the Creator has for you to do. I'm never bored."

Jubilant nodded and thought he had no idea what God wanted him to do, but he had known boredom many times, especially since arriving in Macon County. After the professor scooped up another handful of dirt, he poured it carefully into the specimen case.

"Let's continue on, son," he said. Leaving his suit jacket on the cart, he set off toward the mouth of the forest at the edge of the road.

After taking only a dozen or so steps away from the road, the pair had to be forceful with their feet to make any progress into the woods. The vines and leaves of the invasive kudzu plant covered the trees and ground giving the forest a dark and eerie feel and made walking a challenge. Jubilant took a few more steps, and then stopped. His heart was pounding.

"Is this safe?"

Professor turned around and faced his young friend. "There are no hungry lions or wild boar in here, I assure you!"

"I was thinking more of some white property owner who doesn't want us on his land," Jubilant replied, putting his hand over his heart as he was suddenly aware of how hard it was beating. A few weeks before coming to Macon County, he had read in the newspaper on the counter at Goode's General Store that some members of the Ku Klux Klan had attacked a black man. The incident happened in Georgia, but the picture in the paper showed a forest much like the one he and Professor Carver were entering. Reading the story of the attack gave Jubilant another reason for nightmares, and he had thought about the incident many times since. He told the professor what he had read.

"That's terrible," George said, shaking his head. "I'll never understand how a person born into this world can sow such grief. How can an innocent baby grow up to become such a cruel human being? Sin and ignorance, that's what does it. Pure and simple." The old man stood silent for a moment and stared at Jubilant. Finally, he added, "When I was a young boy, about fourteen or so, I witnessed an awful crime in Kansas. An angry mob grabbed a colored man out of his jail cell and destroyed him right in front of my eyes."

"They lynched him?"

"Yes, but they beat him first." Professor Carver closed his eyes and rubbed his forehead as if the memory itself brought him physical pain. "I knew I was in danger of the same fate simply because of the color of my skin, so I ran back to my room, packed my bags and hid in the forest."

"I'd have done the same thing," Jubilant said, his eyes wide and worried.

The pained look on Professor Carver's face gave Jubilant the chills.

"Words cannot express the fear that overtook me that night. The horrific scene has never left me all these years, and, I'm sure, never will." He took off his glasses and wiped his eyes. "God provided a refuge in the forest for me that night, and no doubt he will hold those men accountable for their evil actions."

Jubilant stared at the ground, unsure of what to say next. He pictured a young George running for his life through the thick woods in the dead of night, heart pounding, and sweat running down his face.

"I won't be putting either of us in harm's way," Professor Carver promised, and motioned for Jubilant to follow him into the forest. "I know these woods. The land belongs to the Institute. There's a bit of a clearing up ahead. I come here most every day to collect specimens and merely soak up the beauty. This is a perfect place for a man to come and talk with the Creator."

As they walked along the shaded forest, Professor Carver pointed out to Jubilant several plants.

"Look here, son. Do you know about jewel weed? It will soothe chigger bites in a flash. And that beauty over there is broad-leaf plantain. Crush the leaf if you get stung by a wasp or hornet and rub it on the bite. You'll get relief, I guarantee it."

Jubilant soaked up the professor's amazing plant facts and helped pluck leaves off several varieties as well as dig up a few by their roots as George instructed him. While Professor Carver and his new young assistant puttered around the forest, Jubilant noticed the old man's hands. They were wrinkled and leathery yet exact and loving as they caressed a flower petal or snipped off a leaf. Professor Carver touched the earth—soil and seed, leaves and roots—as if he were their caretaker.

After two hours of hunting for various specimens and telling each other stories, Professor Carver suddenly scrambled off the rock where he had been sitting.

"Good golly! I don't believe it. I've lost track of time yet again!" he said, checking his watch. "Class starts at eleven."

The old man was visibly shaken as he fumbled about gathering the last bits of samples. Jubilant grabbed the leaves and roots already plucked and resting on the dirt. He tried stuffing them inside the specimen case filled with other forest treasures, but some of them spilled out onto the dirt. Professor Carver noticed his companion's mistake, but he didn't say a word. He only grabbed the cylinder and, to Jubilant's amazement, galloped his way out of the woods. Jubilant followed him, barely able to keep up.

"You can be my assistant as I teach today," the Professor called back to Jubilant, between breaths.

"I just spilled some of your specimens," Jubilant yelled back, frustrated with himself.

"That's nothing to worry about, son. No harm done."

As fond of the professor as Jubilant was, he still did not want to sit in a boring classroom and listen to him lecture for an hour—or even a minute. Still, he was grateful he had rescued him from a morning spent learning the Dewey Decimal System. Jubilant enjoyed his time away from Aunt LaDelle for other reasons as well, so, as he thought about returning to her in the library or remaining with Professor Carver, he decided that listening to a lecture was the better choice. Maybe he could sit in the back and doze off for a while. He had been kept up by a new nightmare the night before—Aunt LaDelle throwing him out the car window with the rest of his rabbits' feet.

Professor Carver stopped at the cart in the field where his suit jacket was waiting for him. A handful of men and a few women—some young, others noticeably older—were gathered next to the cart. Several were talking to each other, some squatted near the dirt, letting the soil spill through their hands the way the professor had done earlier. One man was looking at his watch.

"Please forgive my tardiness," the professor said, out of breath with sweat rolling down his cheeks. He pointed to Jubilant. "This here is Jubilant. He's my assistant for the day. I hope you'll take it upon yourselves to welcome him. Now, let's get started."

The students, who turned out to be teachers themselves, nodded and smiled at the new young assistant, and then focused their attention on their professor. For an hour, Jubilant stood, like the dozen adults surrounding him, listening to and mesmerized by Professor Carver. Although the students scribbled from time to time in their notebooks marked "Agricultural Research" and wiped the sweat off their faces thanks to the summer heat, they were mostly kept busy collecting specimens and examining plants and soil. They discussed fertilizer and compost as they followed their professor through acres of crops, orchards, and even a few mazes of beehives.

"Is everyone still with me?" George would ask over his shoulder. Though he often jumped from subject to subject, no one seemed to mind. They continued to jot down notes, laugh at their professor's jokes—he laughed right along with them—and ask questions. The professor became as vibrant as a young man in his twenties while in front of his students.

After an hour or so, the men and women along with Jubilant followed the professor to a classroom, and then a laboratory. Whether they were in the classroom, laboratory, or a field—wherever he was teaching at that moment—the professor's enthusiasm permeated each place. Jubilant was surprised at how the professor was able to infect every member of his class with excitement about agriculture and science. They were enthralled with dirt—just ordinary dirt! When the reverend spoke from his pulpit, he got all riled up. He'd wave his arms, raise his voice, and would have to mop up the sweat running down his face, stinging his eyes, but Professor Carver spoke in a friendly and steady, but enthusiastic, tone, and he had each person present in the palm of his hand. *How does he do that? What makes this man so different from other adults?*

"Will you pass out those papers on my desk for me?" the professor's voice brought Jubilant's mind back to the room.

"Yes, sir." He gave each student a worksheet of some kind, and then the professor asked him to run back to Milbank Hall to retrieve some items that he needed. Jubilant remembered where the building was located and went there straight away. He didn't drop anything or trip or mess up even one time. Professor Carver's gentleness seemed to bring out the calm in Jubilant. *He trusts me*, Jubilant told himself more than once. He stood up a little taller and walked back to the classroom feeling confident and important.

"Did you learn something today?" a serious-looking student with thick glasses asked Jubilant when the class was dismissed. Crossing the field together, the teacher-turned-student balanced his notebook and his own smaller, newer specimen case.

"Uh-huh. Dirt and plants are more interesting than I thought," Jubilant replied.

The young man laughed, but then grew serious. "The truth is Professor Carver is divinely gifted to explain the wonders of such mundane matters."

"Not only that," added the tallest man in the class just before he took a swig of water from his canteen, "but he's like a father to many of us."

Father? Jubilant's thoughts went to home. Father. He already had one, and he was missing him and wondering what would happen if healing never came. The heat of the day and the heaviness of that thought weighed on Jubilant. A wave of sadness hit him. He made a fist with his hand and slugged the side of his leg. *Why was I named "Jubilant" when I know mostly sorrow and not joy?*

CHAPTER ELEVEN—LUNCH BREAK

Forgiveness is the giving, and so the receiving, of life.
(George MacDonald)

Every day, LaDelle remained seated at her desk during her lunch break. While she ate the sandwich or leftovers she'd packed, she'd read a book or the newspaper with a wooden "Do Not Disturb" sign placed in full view on the front of her desk. In between chewing and turning pages, she'd look up every few minutes to steal a subtle glance at her surroundings. No funny business had better be taking place in her library. She also wanted to be sure her assistant was, indeed, assisting in her "absence." However, on this afternoon, LaDelle decided to spend her break out of sight and enjoy some solitude while she ate.

Soon after picking up her nephew from the bus station, she realized that time alone would be rare this summer. Not only would he be her responsibility, but he'd be her shadow as well. Jubilant was just a child, and as there was no other family in town, she had no choice but to have him follow her around and go wherever she went most of the time. All summer long! *What a challenge it will be to not be alone as often as I am accustomed.* So, with that sobering thought and recognizing she had this chance to eat solo since Jubilant was with Professor Carver, she decided to leave her post at the front desk and entrust the fate of the library to her assistant. *Surely the place won't burn down in forty-five minutes.*

So, she gathered her lunch and purse and retreated to the small, empty room intended for storage but allowed for employees' breaks at the back left-hand corner of the library. Sitting alone at the wobbly table in the break room on a wooden chair that squeezed her hips and confined her rump, LaDelle stared at a spindly-legged spider hanging motionless under a shelf. *Was it dead or simply inactive? She had no qualms about killing spiders.* She leaned toward it and squinted for a better look. *Do spiders sleep? How long had this one been there? Was the janitor doing his job? How many more spiders were lurking about?*

Her thoughts continued to wander as she chewed her leftover pork chop and nibbled on a day-old biscuit and five cherry tomatoes from her garden. She wished she'd remembered to bring a thermos of coffee. *A slice of peanut pie topped off with a little bourbon whipped cream would satisfy her sweet tooth.*

At the time of the brief courtship of Garvin and LaDelle, and for many years following, LaDelle had no idea she would not be able to conceive a child. In the future, the reality of her inability to have children would prove to be a genuine disappointment for her and for Garvin, though they made a pact they would not dwell on the problem. Looking back, she knew it was a gift this news was not revealed to her until much later. By God's grace, she had been able to make peace with it.

LaDelle wiped her mouth with her napkin before standing up from her cramped chair and brushing biscuit crumbs off her pale pink dress with the tiny red roses and green dots. She realized how nice abandoning her desk and eating in solitude had been. She vowed to do so more often.

Before leaving the breakroom, LaDelle took a moment to look at herself in the smudged mirror hanging on the wall. Her reflection revealed faint creases above her lips she hadn't noticed before. Her eyelids drooped more than they used to, making her eyes appear smaller and less bright. There was no denying the truth—life, with its loves and losses, was moving quickly, and aging was a part of it. She leaned in closer to the mirror and gave an exaggerated smile for the purpose of checking her teeth for any obvious food stuck between them. Satisfied that she was "all good" this time, she sighed, then smiled again.

"Where's Abel Fisher now that my teeth are clean?" she thought with a chuckle, but immediately a twinge of guilt hit her when Abel came to mind. She didn't want to go there in her head. Not now. "Garvin loved you," she whispered to her reflection as a declaration. Her voice soft, but convincing. "He loved you fully and courageously." She left the break room and made her way into the main room of the library. *Thank you, Garvin, for loving me. I miss you, honey.*

Taking a walk around the library, hands folded behind her back, she appeared to her assistant and the handful of students sitting behind desks and standing before bookcases like a sergeant inspecting her troops. Though she looked serious and "all-business," she was making mental plans to whip up a peanut pie soon. She'd need to borrow a teaspoon or so of bourbon from Henrietta, who no doubt kept it on hand, and pick up some whipping cream at the Piggly Wiggly. She'd powder her nose this time before entering the store—not for Abel, of course. That man could bring trouble upon her. She just thought she ought to look presentable and represent the Tuskegee Institute as best as she could. *Appearance matters after all.*

"Did you know Abel Fisher has never ever married?" Henrietta told LaDelle a few weeks after he took over the manager position at the grocery store. "He came close one time that I know of, but never did take the plunge."

"Abel who?" LaDelle said, pretending not to know who Henrietta was talking about.

"Abel Fisher, that's who. You know, the manager at the PW. He was friends with my oldest brother when we were growing up in Notasulga. The two of them used to get in all sorts of trouble together, but Abel grew up to be a fine man—and an eligible bachelor." With that last comment, Henrietta flashed her eyebrows up and down. "Rather intriguing, don't you think?"

Thinking back on this conversation, LaDelle wondered what sort of trouble Henrietta was referring to, though it really didn't matter now. There did seem to be something agreeable about Abel if not special. *I wonder why he never married.*

With that thought on her mind, LaDelle continued her inspection with energy. Seizing the opportunity to be alone had refreshed her, and LaDelle wondered how long the effects would last. She'd forgotten to worry about Jubilant and whether he was behaving for Professor Carver. Thinking of him now revived a measure of anxiety. *Oh, Lord, help that boy to behave and keep his clothes clean, for goodness' sake!*

CHAPTER TWELVE—THE PHONE CALL

An amazing invention—but who would ever want to use it? (Rutherford B. Hayes speaking about the telephone)

LaDelle's day began at 4:45 when a neighbor's rooster interrupted a dream she was having. The interruption was welcomed because the dream was not. Shaking a bad dream is always hard, but this one proved more difficult.

Once awake, LaDelle's mind started racing about the day ahead. What would it be like? What trouble might fall upon her? She tried praying. She opened her Bible and picked up where she'd left off the night before in Ephesians, but her mind wouldn't calm. "Forgive me, Lord," she prayed before ending her time in the Word with a short chapter in Psalms. She liked King David. He had a knack for lamenting *and* praising. Often LaDelle could relate to what he had to say. She had done a good measure of lamenting in her own life and was sure more laments would continue to pour out of her in the future, but there was praise too.

She noticed her terra-cotta dress had a small stain on the skirt, so she would have to wear the paisley print. She had several stain removal recipes she'd try on this one, though she had no idea what could have caused the stain in the first place. *Perhaps the boy spilled something on me somehow. Twelve-year-old boys are the clumsiest, but*

Jubilant isn't nearly as awkward as I thought he'd be. My brother has done a pretty fine job with the boy.

By this time, the clock read 5:08, which she figured was as good a time as any to reorganize her kitchen. The utensil drawer needed cleaning, and she thought it would be easier to locate the canned goods in the pantry if they were lined up on the shelves in alphabetical order. Maybe bringing more order to her kitchen would, in turn, order her mind. Maybe she could feel a little more in control. *Maybe.*

Jubilant woke to the banging of pots and pans.

He tried pulling his pillow over his head but could barely muffle the noises coming from the kitchen. At times, Aunt LaDelle's enthusiasm for cleaning made the walls of her modest house almost vibrate. She was used to living alone and not having to be quiet, he supposed, but that didn't make it less annoying to wake up in this way. Jubilant pulled the pillow tighter around his ears and sank down into the blanket, but the racket from the kitchen was impossible to block.

"What is wrong with that woman?" he said out loud and gave the mattress a solid punch. Sitting up in bed, Jubilant rested his tired head in his hands for a while and rubbed his head several times, noticing his hair was already starting to grow. Trying to squeeze in a few more minutes of sleep was wishful thinking, so he gave in and slowly rolled out of bed. His day was starting whether he was ready for it or not. He might as well begin it with the reverend. He plopped into the chair at his desk and wrote letter number three.

Dear Daddy,
Did you know that you can make tea from potentilla leaves? Professor Carver said it's a remedy for die-areeah and stomach pains. It also makes your breath smell good.

I'll ask him if there is a plant remedy for people who are sick from a heart attack. He would know. When I was done working with the professor, he paid me with a chicken. A.L. complained the whole way home about having to ride with it in her car. She squawked louder than the chicken when it pooped on the floorboard of her car! Why is she so grumpy? I gave this kid Wilson the chicken. I owed him.

When can I come home? I can make you tea and help you.

Sincerely,

Jubilant

P.S. Why did you and Mama give me the name Jubilant? It don't seem to fit me much.

He reread his letter and nodded. He was impressed with himself he could write such a long one. Jubilant stuffed it inside the envelope, sealing it with several licks. He scribbled the address and remembered to write #3 in the bottom corner. He thought about how he really didn't mind writing letters, but he'd keep that to himself. After he was dressed, and his bed was made—he did mind that—he sauntered into the kitchen.

Finding the broom waiting for him in the corner, he made his way outside and half-heartedly swept the front and back porches. Jubilant would never admit this to his aunt, but he enjoyed feeling the stillness of the early morning once he was out of bed. Professor Carver said his favorite time in the forest was the early morning, and Jubilant imagined he would like it too.

As he put away the broom, he became distracted with thoughts about what the forest would be like at such an early hour until Dewey's cold nose nudged his hand. "I didn't forget you," Jubilant told him, patting the dog's head and scratching him behind each ear. He refilled Dewey's bowls with fresh food and water. Jubilant hoped

Aunt LaDelle would show the same courtesy and feed him as well. His mouth was watering for some grits, eggs, and orange juice. His appetite had been awakened in Tuskegee, in his aunt's kitchen. Aunt LaDelle's grits were even better than he remembered Mama's to be, and he had loved her grits.

"You must have spilled some of Dewey's kibble yesterday, because I found a morsel of it under the stove. Be more careful, child!"

Good morning to you too, Jubilant thought, but didn't let her see him roll his eyes.

Jubilant handed her his letter, then yawned. He wanted to ask her if she planned to make a habit of banging pots and pans and opening and closing the kitchen drawers this early every morning but thought it would be a better idea to sit at the table and wait for breakfast. LaDelle promptly placed the Bible in front of him instead of the food he wanted.

"Read out loud while I get your breakfast started," she said as she tied her apron.

Jubilant, slouched in his chair, looked at the oversized *King James* in front of him and smirked. He sat up and pulled the large black book toward him. Opening it in the middle, he knew he'd land on the book of Psalms, and then thumbing through several pages to the right, he arrived at the book of Proverbs. The reverend's son leaned in close and, with his index finger, scrolled down nine or ten verses until he came to the one he wanted. Jubilant cleared his throat and with a forced, deep tone read: "Proverbs 27:14: 'He that blesseth his friend with a loud voice, rising early in the morning, it shall be counted a curse to him'... or her." He added the last two words and held his breath. He thought to duck as he feared Aunt LaDelle might decide to hit him on the back of his head with a frying pan. But instead, with no expression at all, she quickly turned around and faced the sink.

"Well now, I see you know your Proverbs, Mr. Smarty Pants!" she said without looking at him.

Jubilant stole a glance her way, and though her back was turned, he saw something unexpected—her shoulders bounced up and down. He heard a noise that sounded like a giggle she was trying to stuff back into her mouth. And then, another one.

Well, what do you know? Aunt LaDelle found something to laugh about. He wasn't surprised she didn't laugh openly, but Jubilant breathed a sigh of relief just knowing she was capable of it. *Isn't that the way an aunt should be? Good natured? Fun to be with?*

Feeling better about the day ahead, Jubilant stood up and poured some orange juice for them both, spilling only a few drops. He set the glasses on the table, and the pair sat down across from each other.

"Tell me more about your time with Professor Carver yesterday," Aunt LaDelle said, handing him a napkin.

"I told you we went into the forest."

"Yes, I knew that. I could tell by the dirt on your trousers. What did you do there?"

"Well, I didn't get dirt on the tie you gave me. Did you notice that? I was real careful."

She nodded and took a sip of her coffee. "I did notice. Thank you."

"When we were in the forest, an orange and black butterfly perched itself on top of Professor Carver's specimen case. It just stayed there and fanned its wings like it was showing off. The professor held out his finger and the butterfly perched onto it like it wasn't the least bit scared."

LaDelle grinned at the scene Jubilant was painting with his words.

"The professor started talking to it, saying things like, 'You're a beauty, Miss Butterfly. Yes, you are. My, my aren't you just the prettiest little thing?' Jubilant spoke in a high-pitched voice like the professor's and laughed at the scene he was retelling. "I think she liked what he was saying to her because she stayed put on his finger, slowly moving her wings up and down. Finally, he told her, 'Now hurry on home,' and she flew away!"

Hearing Aunt LaDelle chuckle at his story made him feel good. He grinned from ear to ear and realized, for the first time in days, he was calm inside. His mind was free from worry for his daddy. His shoulders relaxed and the knot in his stomach wasn't as tight as it usually was when he was near his aunt.

"Well, that's a fine story," she said. "I'm glad you enjoyed your time with Professor Carver. His work is generally more serious than playing in the forest, but I suppose that's a part of it."

"Yes, ma'am. We also collected specimen, like—"

"Did he happen to tell you," she interrupted, "that he has met with some influential folks, including one of my favorites, President Franklin D. Roosevelt, and is even friends with Henry Ford?"

Jubilant shook his head. "He never said anything about that."

"Well, it's true. And he receives several mailbags of letters each week from people who admire him or need his help, but I don't suppose he would ever tell you that. He's a very humble man."

Jubilant was picturing in his mind how many letters several mail bags could hold when a loud knock came from the front door.

"Who on earth is at my door so early in the morning?" Aunt LaDelle said. She pushed her chair out, wiped her hands on a terry cloth towel within reach and left the kitchen to investigate.

Jubilant grabbed his spoon and snuck an extra bite of the leftover grits straight from the pan before he followed her into the living room. He recognized the woman on the front porch talking with Aunt LaDelle—Henrietta from next door. The woman's striped cat tormented Dewey on a daily basis, and each night Jubilant could hear music coming from her kitchen. It sounded like Billie Holiday, and more than once, he caught Aunt LaDelle tapping her foot to the sound, even though she grumbled about her neighbor's loud ways. Jubilant moved a couple of steps closer to see if he could make out what the two women were talking about.

"Don't get ahead of yourself, girl! You don't know what's gonna happen. I'm sure he'll be fine," Henrietta spoke in a reassuring tone and gave Aunt LaDelle a hug before leaving. A few seconds later, Aunt LaDelle came inside and slowly closed the door behind her. Her brow was furrowed, and her eyes were moist. She fidgeted with her apron.

"That was Henrietta, my neighbor," she said slowly, looking Jubilant in the eyes. "I don't have my own telephone yet, so I let your daddy know I could be reached at her number if there was ever an emergency." LaDelle wrung her hands as she spoke, then she wiped them several times onto her apron. "I really ought to get myself a phone, but—"

"What's the emergency?" Jubilant interrupted. But inside he thought, *I don't really want to know. Only bad news would come so early in the morning.*

"Henrietta's husband Cal bought them a fancy phone a few months ago. That man loves all types of gizmos and gadgets, but it's rather ironic now that I think about it because Cal isn't much of a talker and—"

"Aunt LaDelle! What happened?" Jubilant shouted, stomping his foot.

"All right, yes, I'm sorry. Well now, your friend Millie Hines called this morning," Aunt LaDelle said, and then sighed and shook her head.

"She's not my friend," Jubilant corrected. "She's just a busybody from church."

"Well," Aunt LaDelle spoke slower than usual, "she wanted us to know that your daddy—"

"What's happened?" Jubilant interrupted. He stood frozen and tried to stop his knees from shaking, his heart from pounding. "What did she say?" he demanded, throwing his hands in the air.

"It seems Ashton, I mean, your daddy, has come down with pneumonia." Right after saying "pneumonia," LaDelle covered her mouth with her hand, wishing it weren't true, and she didn't have to say it. "The doctor said contracting pneumonia right on the heels of having a heart attack has left him extremely weak."

"He was already weak! How much weaker could he be?" Jubilant looked at her, waiting for an answer, blinking back tears. He put his hand over where he guessed his own heart was—where he placed it each day of school when he said the Pledge of Allegiance. LaDelle crossed the room to him and put one hand on his shoulder, the other under his chin to keep his head up and his gaze on her.

"Your daddy is back in the hospital now and receiving good care. He would want you to be strong." She then dabbed her eyes and tiptoed back into the kitchen as if the sound of her heavy feet would make the situation worse.

"I need to go home! Do you hear me? I've gotta catch a bus home today," he called after her. "TO-DAY!" he repeated when he reached the kitchen.

She spun around and once again looked straight into her nephew's big brown eyes. "Listen, boy, I know you want to see him, but everyone thinks it is best that you stay here with me for now."

"*I* don't think it's best," Jubilant thundered. "I don't want to stay another minute. I should be with him. I should help him!"

"What do you think you can do about it, you're just—"

"Mama died!" He yelled the words loud enough for the neighbors to hear.

"Is that what this is about?" The volume of LaDelle's voice matched her nephew's, but then she caught herself and spoke more quietly and controlled. "You think you could have saved your mama, and if you don't help your daddy, it'll be your fault? You had no control over your mama's death, child, don't you know that?"

"Nobody trusts me!" Jubilant shouted, ignoring her question. He ran to his room, grabbing a pillow off the couch and chucking it to the floor on his way. Once inside his room, he slammed the door so hard the windows shook. He seized his duffel from under the bed and threw it on top as his heart pounded and beads of sweat dotted his forehead. "Everyone thinks I'll get myself into trouble and not be a help at all," he muttered to himself. "Maybe I *could* have helped Mama. Maybe she didn't have to die. I could have behaved better."

Aunt LaDelle flung open the door, confiscated his duffel in her right hand and stood with her left hand on her hip. Her breathing was heavy like she had just run a mile.

"If things grow worse with your daddy, you and I will head right on up to Huntsville. I do promise you that. Right now, though, he wants you here with me, so here is where you'll stay." Her face was stern. But then, a little softer and with a glimmer of sympathy in her eyes, she added, "Millie

Hines will call us again with an update tomorrow morning. Let's keep our wits about us."

When Aunt LaDelle left the room with the duffel in her hand, Jubilant expected her to slam the door, but to his surprise, she closed it quietly. Her apparent calmness after their confrontation was a surprise. Jubilant, however, wasn't nearly ready to be calm. He grabbed the handle of the top dresser drawer and pulled too hard, causing it to crash onto the floor. For a few seconds, he stared at the door, waiting to see if his aunt would fling it open and lecture him about treating her things better. When she didn't barge in, and he didn't hear any steps, he pushed aside his socks and underwear until he found his lucky penny. He stared down at it before snatching the coin. With the penny in hand, Jubilant walked over to his window, flung it wide open and chucked the useless copper coin outside into the hydrangea bushes. "There's no such thing as good luck," he said out loud. "I'm the unluckiest person in the world!"

LaDelle left Jubilant alone in his room for a full twenty minutes before knocking on the door and insisting that he come out and finish breakfast. Deep in thought and concern, she didn't have it in her to get after Jubilant when she noticed him pushing the food around his plate instead of putting it into his mouth. LaDelle ate a few bites of her own breakfast and pretended to read the *Tuskegee News*. She knew she wasn't convincing her nephew, though. She turned the pages too soon and her eyes were staring more than reading. She jiggled her legs under the table. Her mind was on her brother, and the worry showed on her wrinkled brow.

Taking a sip of her lukewarm coffee, she prayed silently. *Lord, heal my brother. I beg you. He's a good man, and I'm not up to the job of being this boy's parent. So come on, now. You're the Healer. Do some healing! Please, Lord.* After repeatedly praying the words, "please, Lord," LaDelle turned mindlessly to the sports page in section D. She didn't care one lick for sports, though baseball was an orderly and organized type of game, she conceded, which was admirable.

Finally, she gave up the charade and stood up from the table. She grabbed their lunches off the counter and announced, "It's time to leave for work now. Do not lollygag this morning."

Jubilant gave her a scowl but followed her out the front door. As they sped down the road toward the Institute, he broke the silence in the car.

"I really need to go home today, Aunt LaDelle."

LaDelle didn't respond at first. She realized something she hadn't thought about before. Jubilant had said her name for the first time since he'd arrived. Her face grew hot as she realized something else. She had yet to call him by his name. Since he arrived, she'd called him, "boy" and "child" and "son" and not in an endearing way, but never "Jubilant." Shame invaded her. *This youngin' needs some tenderness. He needs some kindness and grace, for goodness' sake.* She held the steering wheel extra tight and sighed before responding to him in a calm voice. "Jubilant, we've already been through this. There are people taking good care of your daddy. You just need to stay put and pray for God's healing hand. I'm praying too."

"So, you think God will heal him like he did my mother?" Jubilant's voice had bite to it.

"Now you just hold on there, boy. God took my husband too, you know, but that doesn't mean he won't save your daddy."

"Won't or can't?" Jubilant said, and then turned his face toward the passenger window. He kept his arms crossed tightly against his chest.

"His ways are not our ways," Aunt LaDelle said sharply. Taking a deep breath, she added with a softer tone, "I'm going to pray and hold onto hope that God heals your daddy. I suggest you do the same."

LaDelle pulled into her usual parking spot on campus and turned off the engine. "His ways are definitely *not* our ways," she muttered to herself while she gathered the lunches she had packed for the two of them. In a separate bag, she had packed some extra corn muffins to give to Professor Carver in case he came by the library looking for Jubilant.

While LaDelle led him to a fresh cart loaded down with books, she assured Jubilant that a remedy for a worried mind was good, honest, focused work. She explained the Dewey Decimal System as if Jubilant was four years old, then tested him several times to see if he understood.

"Pay attention. I don't want you to bring confusion to my library by putting the books in the wrong places."

Jubilant nodded half-heartedly.

When LaDelle was convinced that Jubilant understood the system, she turned him loose in the library to shelve books.

The system didn't seem all too complicated to him, and besides, he half expected Professor Carver would enter the library soon and rescue him from having to put the Dewey Decimal System to use. He took one book and then another off the cart and, thanks to Mr. Melvil Dewey, Jubilant was able to place each book back onto the shelves in just the right place.

After an hour passed and there was no sign of the professor, Jubilant stopped watching the door—realizing an invitation to collect specimens would not be coming. Perhaps, Jubilant thought, Professor Carver didn't like having him as an assistant after all. The sting of that possibility gave Jubilant the motivation to learn the Dewey Decimal System for a whole other reason. A plan began to form in his mind—a plan for freedom and a chance to prove himself to the reverend and even to Millie Hines and everyone in Huntsville who believed Jubilant would be more of a help if he stayed away from his own daddy for "a while."

While his Aunt LaDelle busied herself helping summer school students find books on subjects like accounting and European history, Jubilant continued his work, making his way toward the back of the library and out of his aunt's view. Coming to the back door, he looked around to be sure he hadn't been spotted, and then carefully opened it. Once through, Jubilant closed it behind him with only a slight *click* as the door latched shut. Seconds later, he was running across campus, out the entrance gates, and, as best as he could tell, toward the bus station. He smiled to himself thinking if things went his way, instead of sending the reverend another letter, he would be able to tell him whatever he wanted to by nightfall—in person. He would prove to his father and to himself that he could be a help. He could stay out of trouble and be responsible.

It was only nine-thirty in the morning by this time, but already the sun was blazing. Before making his escape, Jubilant had loosened the tie Aunt LaDelle made him wear, slipped it over his head and shoved it between two of the books on the cart. Now, he rubbed his neck, feeling relieved to be rid of the green and orange striped chokehold. He rolled up his sleeves and wished he had thought to bring water.

"I should have forced myself to eat a good breakfast," he said to himself as his stomach growled. Reaching the main road he recognized as leading to the bus station, he walked along the side of it with his head down, hoping no one driving by would recognize him as "LaDelle's nephew." People in Macon County, just like in Huntsville, liked to ask questions, and he was in no mood or position to answer them. As Jubilant continued his journey, he realized he was unprepared. If his brilliant plan of running away had occurred to him before arriving to the library, he would have done better.

If the reverend were here, Jubilant knew what he'd say: "You need to stop and think before you act. You'd find yourself getting into less trouble if you'd slow down and use the brain you were born with."

Jubilant shook his head trying to shake his father's voice out of his head. He knew, once again, he had acted without thinking, but it was too late. He had to continue with his plan. If he turned around now, the trouble he was sure to face with Aunt LaDelle was more than he could handle. Ever since Mama died, he seemed to be in trouble all the time, but he had grown up to be able to handle quite a lot— more than most kids. Much of the time. But not today.

The main thing Jubilant knew he needed was money for a one-way bus ticket, and he had none. Even his lucky penny was gone. Although he would have hated taking money out of his aunt's purse, it would have been the easiest way for him to purchase a ticket to Huntsville. *Besides, it wouldn't have been the same as stealin'—I'd have paid her back somehow. After a while.* Running at times, then falling back into a brisk walk, he continued to the bus station and racked his brain thinking about how he could get himself on that bus. *There had to be a way. This was an emergency, after all. And this must be the hottest day of summer. Of course, it was.* Just his luck.

CHAPTER THIRTEEN—THE BUS TICKET

All men should strive to learn before they die what they
are running from, and to, and why. (James Thurber)

LaDelle was born to be a librarian. Her bent toward
order and organization along with her love for books and
information made it the perfect career choice for her. Of
course, she didn't know while growing up she would end up
having a career. She assumed she'd marry young and raise
children—two girls and one boy would be nice—though the
thought of it was more of a matter-of-fact notion. *That's
what I'll do.*

Once she knew she would marry Garvin, she also
assumed she would help him with the diner in some way.
She wouldn't mind having a say in the hiring of folks. She
did have a knack for being a good judge of character, but
Garvin and his brother were in charge of all that. Her love
for cooking did not extend to the diner—it was too chaotic
in that kitchen setting for her liking. Bookkeeping and
ordering supplies and other needed tasks she took on were
a concession, not a passion she had in her, but she took her
duties seriously and did her work well, helping the place
run efficiently.

Yet being a librarian gave her deeper fulfillment.
She savored all that came with the job—the resources of

information, helping people who have an appreciation for knowledge, and the added delight of a quiet, apple-pie-order kind of atmosphere.

On this day, though troubled by the news about her brother, her beloved library seemed to work its magic on her, and she was able to lose herself and her woes while she worked. The Tuskegee Institute's library was a solace to be sure. LaDelle was the happiest while there, which is why she didn't notice Jubilant was no longer shelving books. Over an hour went by before she even thought about him. Then, an uneasy feeling crept into her being, so she left her desk and started roaming the library. After about a minute, her steps and her heart quickened. *Trouble!*

"Have you seen my nephew?" she asked one of her student helpers, doing her best to keep her voice steady.

"No, Mrs. Harris, not lately," the young man answered thoughtfully. "Last time I saw him, he was shelving books in the science section, but that was some time ago."

LaDelle glanced down at her watch. It was near lunchtime. Jubilant would be hungry soon and come to find her to fetch his lunch. She tried to convince herself, but then continued to search anyway. She scoured every inch of the library, even opened the restroom door a crack and called out his name. When no response came, she opened the door wide and peered inside, but found no trace of him. The only evidence she found indicating her nephew had ever been in the building that day was the book cart she'd assigned him. The cart stood in an aisle, still half-full of books in need of being shelved. Approaching the cart, she noticed something colorful stuffed between the books—Garvin's tie!

"I hate to give that boy a whuppin' when he's already having a bad time of it, but this is unacceptable," LaDelle told her part-time assistant when she returned to her desk, shaking her hand that held the tie. "I need you to be in charge for a short while," she said, then grabbed the packed lunches and the sack of corn muffins she had brought for Professor Carver, flung open the door and marched out the library.

She searched the grounds around the library including the fountain and down the road by Thrasher Hall. She asked several students walking by if they had seen a tall, skinny boy with a shaved head and big eyes. Everyone's answer was the same: "No, ma'am."

LaDelle's heart began to beat faster with every step. She picked up her pace. "I need you, Lord. Show me where he is, I beg of you. Open my eyes to where he is. Come on, now! I need you!"

She checked the cafeteria and the restrooms there before heading toward the one place she didn't want to look. She hated to bother Professor Carver, but she didn't know where else to search for the nephew in her charge. *Why wouldn't Jubilant tell me if he was leaving the library—I'll skin that boy alive! Does Ashton allow this type of behavior? Unacceptable!* She was winded by the time she reached the professor's laboratory door. She put her hand over her heart and took a few deep breaths before knocking softly. There was no response, but something told her to knock again, louder this time.

"Busy," came a voice from inside. LaDelle recognized it as Professor Carver's.

"Excuse me, sir, I'm terribly sorry to bother you, but I'm looking for my nephew," she called out. She kept her hand on her chest trying to slow her heartbeat and took a few more deep breaths. LaDelle had never darkened the door of his laboratory before and realized that if he opened the door, she would be approaching a kind of sacred ground, though so far nothing looked impressive. The outside of the building, she decided upon a quick glance, could use some sprucing up. *A fresh coat of paint on this door might be nice.* Just as she made herself a vow to look into this situation, she heard a shuffling of feet, and a moment later, the door opened.

"Hello, Mrs. Harris. Did I hear you say you were looking for Jubilant?"

"Yes, sir. I've looked everywhere. I thought he might be here with you."

"I've been quite busy since very early this morning. An idea came to me before sunrise, and I'm laboring over some samples to find out if—" The professor stopped himself from saying anything more about his work. He apologized. "You asked about Jubilant. I'm afraid the boy hasn't been by."

He took off his glasses and rubbed the bridge of his nose. LaDelle noticed how red his eyes were and wondered if he suffered from glaucoma, then changed her mind. Taking another glance, she decided he suffered from something else—extreme dedication to his work and to people. Sleep was not a priority, at least not when he was in the midst of something important or at least interesting. She knew he spent hour after hour in his laboratory because she sometimes overheard people on campus mention it. He worked too hard for his age, she surmised, but she understood why.

"Please follow me," the professor said and led LaDelle to another room attached to his lab. As he seemed to be lost in his thoughts for a moment, LaDelle tried to hide her disappointment by glancing around his surroundings.

A large sack of mail sat next to a desk with several letters strewn across it. A small table in the corner was cluttered with various-sized bottles and jars, some filled with powders and what looked like dirt. Shelves were crowded with dozens of flourishing plants growing out of pots, tins, and milk bottles and climbing upward, obscuring the view of some of the paintings and drawings of flowers and other plant life on the walls. For a second, all LaDelle could think about was putting the room in perfect order, but then she remembered why she had come.

"We received bad news about Jubilant's father today, and I'm afraid he has run off because it upset him so."

"I'm sorry to hear that. Will his daddy be all right?" Professor Carver's hand shook slightly as he returned his glasses to their place on his face and stared at LaDelle in anticipation of her answer.

"Well, I really can't say at this point," LaDelle's lip quivered at the grave truth of her words. She covered her mouth with her hand to calm herself.

"I see. I'm not teaching today, and my speaking engagement has been postponed until next week. Allow me to go look for the boy." Professor Carver took off his lab coat and reached for his suit jacket draped over a chair. A drooping pink flower was securely tucked into its lapel.

"I can't let you do that. He's my responsibility, and you have much to do."

"You go back to the library and give me some time to find Jubilant. I need a break anyway. Besides, I won't be able to concentrate on my work with Jubilant missing."

"But Professor Carver—"

"Please, Mrs. Harris. I must help."

Jubilant didn't remember the bus station being so far from the Institute. His tired feet throbbed as they swelled in his hand-me-down shoes. Dust and dirt from the road stuck to his sweat-soaked skin. He remembered seeing a drinking fountain outside for colored folks at the bus station when he first arrived in Macon County, and he daydreamed about how good the water would taste when he finally reached it.

As he walked along, slower now, his mind began to drift back to home and the reason he was with Aunt LaDelle in the first place. He shook his head trying to get rid of the disturbing pictures in his mind, but they wouldn't leave. Several times a day, out of the blue, the horrible scene of his daddy standing at the pulpit the morning he had his heart attack would invade his thoughts. *One minute Daddy was preaching about Lazarus walking out of the grave, and the next minute he was clutching his heart with his hand, his mouth twisted in pain, his eyes bulging.*

Jubilant wasn't paying much attention to the sermon at the time, but when he heard the woman next to him gasp and the one behind him exclaim, "He's going down!" he looked up in time to see his daddy's pained expression, and then the reverend was on the floor like a strong oak tree knocked over by some unseen force. The sound was sick, like Jubilant imagined death to be if it had a sound, and for a second, everything was silent. Then the screams came. Women threw down their fans and frantically waved their hands in the air. The elders and some choir members rushed toward the pulpit.

Llewellyn Baker yelled out, "Dear God, our preacher's dead!"

Other men and women echoed, "Good Lord, save the reverend!"

Millie Hines whipped out her paddle fan and dashed to the reverend to help cool him off.

Doctor Ezra Keyes, who sang tenor each week, moved like Flash Gordon as he jumped over his fellow choir members and flew to the reverend. He rolled him over and loosened his tie. Then he spoke to him, but from where Jubilant was standing, he couldn't hear what was being said. Jubilant stood in the middle of the aisle, unable to move. He looked at the scene before him; his invincible daddy lying on the ground like a helpless animal on the side of the road. *"Get up!"* He repeated the command to himself over and over, but the words never left his mouth. Jubilant wanted to run to his daddy and hold his hand and tell him he loved him, but his legs wouldn't move.

This shameful fact hounded Jubilant several times throughout the day and sometimes, in the middle of the night. He thought back at how some of the men in church lifted the reverend and carried him carefully and quickly down the aisle, while he just sat there frozen. Millie Hines took Jubilant's hand and led him outside where together they watched as they lay the reverend in the back of the doctor's truck. Felix Delaney took off his suit jacket, folded it like a pillow and put it under the reverend's head. Then Felix climbed in the back of the truck with the patient, and the doctor drove them to the hospital.

Sadness and regret turned to anger. "I'm not stupid. I can take care of Daddy even though no one trusts me to do it." Jubilant talked out loud, kicking at the dirt. In the same breath, he went to the negative voice in his head that sounded a lot like Millie Hines: "I'm too much to handle, too irresponsible—even Daddy thinks so."

And now, pneumonia! The reverend was alive, but would he stay that way? Mama didn't.

A bus from the Southeastern Greyhound Lines passed Jubilant along the road, stirring up dust and redirecting his thoughts. The bus looked empty, and the driver appeared to be eating a sandwich as he sped past. *Why didn't I grab the lunch Aunt LaDelle made me before I snuck out of the library?* He patted his stomach as if to soothe it. Jubilant hoped he'd sit next to someone like Patience Doyle again, and she'd share her sandwiches and Moon Pies.

Tired from the scorching temperature and the hard ground under his feet, Jubilant slowed down even more. He entertained himself by kicking an empty, rusted, Campbell's Soup can he found by the side of the road. The challenge of kicking the can straight and the sound of it skipping along the dirt road helped take his mind off the burden of the sun on his face for a brief time. It wasn't long, though, before Jubilant became careless and kicked the can too hard, causing it to tumble too far to the right and disappear into a bush.

Since the game was over, and he had nothing at his feet to focus on, he looked up in despair, and lo and behold— The Promised Land. The bus station! With renewed energy, Jubilant picked up his pace and licked his lips in anticipation of some cool water at the drinking fountain. He noticed that the parking lot had fewer cars and other vehicles—wagons, bicycles—than the day he first arrived, but there were still plenty of people coming and going. He hoped at least one person would be willing to give him the money he needed for the ticket. He had no idea how much a bus ticket to Huntsville would cost or if anyone would take pity on him. *Maybe they will let me pay at the end of the trip if I write an I.O.U. Daddy would be happy to settle accounts once I arrived back in Huntsville. Probably.*

Just before he reached the station, he glanced to his right, and then to his left. He wanted to be sure nobody was around who might recognize him. If there was somebody, that person might spill the beans about him being there, and Aunt LaDelle would find out what he'd done and where he was in no time. *How gossip travels in a small town!* Relieved at seeing no familiar faces, he headed for the outdoor water fountain designated for him and those of his color and guzzled before pushing open the door and walking inside the station.

There was a scattering of people, some sitting on benches, some in line at the ticket counter, and one man pacing back and forth while he took puffs from his cigarette, waiting to board his bus or for someone to arrive. The station was thick with people smells—tobacco, perfume that smelled like Jubilant's favorite teacher Mrs. Wiley, and sweat. With his belly full and sloshing from all the water, Jubilant wiped his mouth on his sleeve and headed for the ticket counter in the "colored only" line.

He waited behind an older man in farmer's overalls. Beside him, across the room in the line for white people, was a woman with a small strawberry blond-haired boy at her side. The toddler turned and looked at Jubilant. He held out his toy car and showed it to him without a word. Jubilant nodded. The toddler's face lit up with a wide smile, and he jumped up and down after receiving Jubilant's silent approval of his special toy. *Life is simple when you're young,* Jubilant thought. *Toy cars and your mother's hand is all you need to be happy.* Life, to him, was so hard now that he was practically a teenager.

Finally, it was Jubilant's turn at the ticket counter. "How much is a ticket to Huntsville?"

"Depends. How old are you, boy?"

"Twelve since last March."

"Then you'll need a child's ticket—two dollars and forty-five cents."

The amount was more than Jubilant expected, but he nodded and turned to leave when the man at the ticket counter gave him worse news.

"If you're travelin' alone, son, you'll be needin' a signed note from a parent—no exceptions."

Jubilant grimaced and placed his hand on his stomach as if someone had just slugged him in the gut. This running away business was harder than he thought it would be, and now he was stuck. He remembered, when he came to Tuskegee from Huntsville, Millie Hines had already purchased his bus ticket. She handed it to him, and that was that. He never thought about how much it cost or whether the reverend had to give permission for him to travel. Jubilant held his ground and stared into the ticket seller's eyes, trying to discern if the man was being truthful. *Maybe he is just trying to make things difficult for me*, he thought. The man held his expression—a lifeless one—and Jubilant moved out of the line.

Taking a seat on one of the benches inside the station, in his section, he tried to collect his thoughts as they swirled in his head. Jubilant realized sitting slouched in his seat with his head in his hands made for a sorry sight, but he couldn't help it. If he were alone, say, in the woods, he might have let himself cry. He cried after Mama died, but not long after, he stopped crying and became angry. Now, in this busy bus station, he was nauseous, overwhelmed with sadness and had no outlet.

He would've liked to go into the restroom to relieve himself and splash water on his dirty face, but this station did not provide a restroom for colored people. The facilities were only for whites. *That's dumb*, he thought, *almost everyone in Tuskegee is Negro*. With his eyes closed, he rubbed his head and held his breath. He soon felt a light touch on his arm. Startled, he opened his eyes and discovered the strawberry blonde-haired boy looking up at him, his toy car still in his hand. Jubilant cracked a half-smile. He couldn't help himself.

"Ma tar go fast," the boy said.

Jubilant sat up and wiped his eyes with the back of his hand. He nodded at the boy, and they locked eyes.

The toddler smiled and climbed up onto the bench and took a seat next to Jubilant. He held out his toy again so

Jubilant could take a closer look. A second later, his young mother approached the bench where they were sitting. Jubilant braced himself. White women, especially those who wore such fancy shoes and pressed clothing as the little boy's mother, wouldn't want a black boy playing with her child, especially a dusty and dirty black boy. Jubilant scooted over as far away from the boy as he could without falling off the bench.

"I'm sorry," the woman said kindly. "I hope my Finley isn't bothering you." She took off her white gloves and reached out for the boy.

"No!" The toddler said defiantly, leaning toward Jubilant.

"It's no problem, ma'am," Jubilant spoke up. "He can stay here, I don't mind, but don't you want to sit in the white section?"

"Thank you. He obviously likes you," she said with a winning smile. "Say, would you mind watching him for just a tad while I use the ladies' room? I'll be back in a flash."

Jubilant nodded on the outside, but inside he shook his head in disbelief this stranger would trust him with her young child. He couldn't have been more than three. She thanked him as she stood up and dashed into the restroom. As promised, she returned a few minutes later. At the sight of her, Jubilant let out his breath. He hadn't realized he began holding it once she disappeared into the ladies' room.

"Are you traveling somewhere today?" she asked as she took a seat next to Jubilant and put Finley on her lap. He immediately began to squirm.

Jubilant looked away for a second, trying to gather his thoughts as he surveyed the room. What were people thinking, seeing him carrying on a conversation with a pretty, young white woman? Why did she want to sit in the colored section? How much should he tell this stranger?

Looking at her, he knew she had money even though times were bad for most people these days. He'd heard the reverend talk about the hard times even some wealthy people were struggling to endure, yet this woman didn't seem at all affected by a shortage of money. The clothes she wore, from her yellow hat down to her fancy white shoes, were crisp and clean and new. He imagined the diamond in her wedding ring was as big as a queen's. Her skin was pale and smooth as if she never worked out in the sun a day of her life. Jubilant guessed she was twenty-two or maybe twenty-three-years-old, and he imagined she had been raised with much privilege.

Perhaps her daddy owned a plantation, and her husband was a lawyer or a successful businessman. No matter—she had the smile of an angel and seemed to be an agreeable sort of person. She was pretty like a daisy and smelled sweet like peppermint. Jubilant was careful not to stare, but he did breathe in deeply to capture all the fragrance he could fit into his nostrils. He figured her husband had probably bought her some expensive perfume from a fancy place like Paris, France, to get her to smell so good. Folks don't smell like that from Ivory soap and water. He took a deep breath, then swallowed hard and decided to test the waters.

"My daddy's very sick, and I'm tryin' to get to Huntsville so I can be with him."

"Oh, my! I'm sorry to hear that," the young woman said with sincerity. Finley wiggled off her lap and was now in between the pair making car noises and driving his toy over his mom's skirt, onto the bench, and then over Jubilant's leg.

"Trouble is, I don't have enough money for a ticket," Jubilant continued.

"Well, now. It can't be that much. What amount do you need?"

Jubilant told her the price of the ticket and without batting an eye she opened her purse and took out a wad of money. She handed Jubilant two one-dollar bills and then opened a small coin purse.

"Here's a quarter and two dimes," she said, plopping the coins into his hand. "I'm not much for blind charity, you know. I'm not one to send money to every organization who asks for it, but I like to help when I see an actual need with my own eyes." She paused then added, "My daddy's a big giver, but Mama rarely trusts people and would never think to help a colored person. No offense."

Jubilant was glad that he hadn't run into her mother, and he couldn't believe his luck. In a million years, he never would have dreamed he could have obtained the money he needed so effortlessly. He thanked the woman and stood up to buy his ticket when he remembered the other need he had.

"Um, I hate to trouble you again, ma'am."

"My name is Dorothy."

"Thank you, ma'am, but—"

"What's your name?"

"Jubilant."

"Jubilant? What a fine name! Do you like it, and are you that? Are you jubilant?"

Her question surprised him. He had been thinking a lot about his name lately, but he hadn't come to a solid opinion about it yet. Did he like it? He wasn't sure. For much of his life, starting when Mama passed on, he rarely felt jubilant at all. Maybe his name suited him when he was younger, but now no longer. *Maybe when I'm older I should change it to Jesse or Mack or Ishmael.*

"At the moment, I'm mostly just worried about my daddy, ma'am," was all he could reply.

"Why, of course," Dorothy nodded, "what a twit I am. Sorry. It's nearly impossible to feel jubilant when you're worried. I completely understand." She went on to tell him that the reason she came to Tuskegee in the first place was to visit her former mammy. "Bertha Rae took care of me from the time I was eight until I married at age eighteen. Then, she moved back to her home in Tuskegee."

Jubilant nodded, fidgeting with the money in his palm.

"I came to visit her because she's getting on in years, and she had never met Finley," Dorothy talked on, unaware of Jubilant's impatience to get on with his escape to Huntsville. "I didn't want her to up and die before I saw her again and showed off my baby to her! That would have been a shame, don't you think? Although Mama thought I was a twit to come all this way just to—"

"Ma'am, I think I'd feel jubilant if I could just buy this ticket and get to my daddy," Jubilant finally interrupted. He thought Dorothy had a beautiful voice, but he didn't have time to sit and chat! He went on to explain that to board the bus, he also needed a note of permission from a parent. "You're not *my* parent, but you are *a* parent and that's all the man at the ticket counter said I needed—'A parent's signature.'"

Dorothy pressed her lips together trying not to laugh. Then, she smiled wide, her white teeth like perfect pearls. "I like you, Jubilant. I don't know why, but I do, and maybe, I can help you."

Jubilant rubbed his sweaty hands on his pants, uncomfortable again that he was having such an easy conversation with a young white woman. He was sure, by now, others must be staring. How could they not be? Keeping his movements slow and casual, he glanced around the bus station and let out a sigh of relief. Folks were too busy buying tickets, reading newspapers and saying goodbye to loved ones to be staring at him and Dorothy—at least at that moment.

"Something tells me I shouldn't do this, and that I should ask more questions, but perhaps the less I know the better," Dorothy said quietly.

"Yes, ma'am," Jubilant agreed.

"But let me just ask you this," Dorothy leaned in closer to Jubilant and whispered. "Have you hurt anyone or stolen anything?"

"No ma'am! I swear!"

"Are you running away from the law?"

"No, ma'am, I swear!"

"Are you in any sort of trouble?"

"No, ma'am, not really."

"Hmm ... not really?" Dorothy gave him a suspicious look and then sighed. "Jubilant, do you swear on a stack of Bibles you have a sick daddy who needs you?"

"I swear."

"Then I believe you." Dorothy lifted Finley, who had crawled back onto her lap, and set the boy's feet onto the floor. She opened her purse again and took out a small notebook and one of those new, fancy ballpoint pens. Then she wrote, *I give my permission for Jubilant to ride unaccompanied from Macon County to Huntsville. Please allow him to purchase a ticket.* Then she asked, "What's your mama's name?"

"My mama is dead."

"Oh, my! I'm sorry to hear that. What bad luck you've had! But what was her name?"

"Adelaide Bartley."

Dorothy signed the letter "Sincerely, Adelaide Bartley," ripped out the page from the notebook and handed it to Jubilant.

"There," she said. "I'm now probably an accomplice to a crime. Mother would be so mad at me if she ever found out. But I don't care. I think this is exciting!"

"Birmingham! Now boarding passengers traveling to Birmingham." A man in a uniform made his announcement, and most of the folks in the depot stood up to leave. Dorothy slipped her white gloves back onto her small hands. Leaving Finley alone with Jubilant once again, she walked over to the bench she had been sitting on before she had come over to him and retrieved her suitcase. Returning, she flashed her ready smile and whispered, "Good luck, Jubilant, dear. I wish you all the best!" Then she said, "Come along, Finley, it's time to go home and see your daddy."

Jubilant sat for a moment and watched the pair walk outside. Finley turned and waved while still clutching his favorite car. Dorothy, with her yellow hat, high heels, and stylish clothes, made heads turn as she boarded the bus. Jubilant sat shaking his head, in shock from what had just happened. He opened his palm and stared at the money, now damp with sweat. He was afraid that this had all been a dream. Glancing at the ticket booth, it occurred to him, although he now had the money and the note giving him permission to board the bus, he hadn't yet purchased the ticket! There was no one in line, so he jumped up from the bench and headed straight to the ticket counter. He slapped down the dollar bills, three coins, and Dorothy's note.

"I'd like a ticket to Huntsville, please," he said in the most grown-up voice he could muster but kept his gaze downward. He thought it best he avoid eye contact with the ticket seller. The reverend often said that he could tell when Jubilant was lying just by looking him in the eyes. He didn't want to risk that the ticket seller might have the same power.

The man read the note Dorothy had written and then looked at Jubilant, then back down at the note. He smiled.

"Now, this is interesting. Yes, sir. Well, I suppose it will do," he said as he counted the money. "But there ain't no more buses travelin' to Huntsville today, I'm afraid."

"What?" Jubilant now looked the man directly in the eyes. "But I must leave today. I must! My father is sick." He wanted to add, "And I'll be whupped something awful for sure for runnin' away from my aunt if I don't leave today," but he knew better than to include that information.

"The next bus leaves at 7:10 tomorrow morning. Do you still want to buy your ticket now?"

Jubilant was stumped. He didn't know what to do. Should he buy a bus ticket to another destination and slowly make his way back to Huntsville? Getting there in that way could take days and more money than he had. There were no guarantees he'd meet another kind soul like Dorothy along the way who would be willing to give him any extra money he may need. Maybe he should just hide near the station for the rest of the day and night until he could leave in the morning.

"You be holdin' up the line, boy. What'll it be?" The ticket seller snapped.

Jubilant slowly gathered his money and the note and stepped away from the counter so he could think. He walked away, head down and mulling over his options when he bumped into somebody. The quarter and two dimes spilled out of his hands and onto the wooden floor.

"Sorry," he said without looking at the person he had run into. He kept his eyes on the coins as they rolled about the floor. He didn't dare lose track of them. He dropped to his knees and scrambled about, picking them up one at a time.

"Let me help you," said a familiar voice.

"Professor Carver!"

CHAPTER FOURTEEN—WAITING AND AN AWAKENING

And sure enough even waiting will end ... if you can just wait long enough. (William Faulkner)

LaDelle was left standing in the professor's laboratory as he took off his white coat and put on his tattered suit jacket, then his cap. He tossed the expired flower from his lapel into the trash and directed his steps to a cluttered side table that was adorned with a small bouquet of flowers displayed in a vase in need of fresh water. He reached into the drawer, pulled out scissors, snipped off a young pink gillyflower and slipped it into his lapel. The whole process took a few seconds, but LaDelle was mesmerized by it—by him. Now, apparently, he was ready to go. He turned to LaDelle, nodded to her, patted her shoulder, and asked her to lock the door on her way out. Then he was gone, on a mission to find Jubilant.

Now, after being away much longer than she had anticipated, LaDelle finally returned to her post at the library, though it wasn't easy to leave Professor Carver's lair without spending time putting it into some kind of order and state of cleanliness. The hardest thing—one of the most difficult realities in her mind in all of life—was not knowing how long a wait would be. Waiting and wondering how something would turn out was torture. If she knew she must wait an hour or a day or a full weekend to have Jubilant safely back in her care, that would be difficult enough, but the not knowing was a punch in the gut.

LaDelle shook her head as if that could help rid herself of negative thoughts. She closed her eyes, took a deep breath, and as she exhaled, opened her eyes to the library's interior. The library brought her a twinge of comfort. Her agitation and worry could be masked, she thought, by her ability to keep busy. She soon realized she was wrong. No one approached her with any questions or asked anything of her though she had been inside, standing next to her desk for nearly ten minutes. Instead, she noticed several sideways glances from a distance from co-workers and patrons alike. A few patrons hurried to the desk to have their books checked out and then made a beeline for the door. Her student helper wheeled a cart of books to the far end of the library and began to shelve each book with uncharacteristic vigor. Their actions showed LaDelle everyone thought they'd be wise to stay out of her way. She agreed.

LaDelle couldn't stand feeling so helpless as the hours passed slowly. Her already short fingernails were down to the nubs. Not even library work was enough of a diversion. After two hours, LaDelle announced to her assistant she was taking her delayed lunch break and left the library. She headed straight to the administration office.

"Phoebe, I must have use of a telephone right away, in private, please." LaDelle spoke in her direct, no nonsense way.

"Mr. Treg is on holiday, so you can use his phone. Come this way, Mrs. Harris."

LaDelle never had much of an opinion about Phoebe, but at that moment she decided the younger woman was the most competent and congenial receptionist she'd ever encountered. Phoebe did not ask questions that were none of her business. She simply provided what was requested and did so lickety-split. LaDelle followed at her heels, taking deep breaths as she walked.

Once inside Mr. Treg's office, LaDelle picked up the phone and asked the operator to ring the police station. As soon as Sergeant Baker picked up, LaDelle began to report Jubilant missing, exactly as she had rehearsed it in her head for the past hour. "He's only twelve, and he is my responsibility. He was very upset this morning, and he's been gone for several hours now. I need you to send out your finest officers to search for him right away."

Sergeant Baker listened to her report, but instead of jumping into action upon hearing her request and sending out his best man for the job, he tried to console her. "He's twelve, you say? He's all riled up? Ah, now, no need to worry. The child just needs some time to think, Mrs. Harris. Give him space. He's probably off fishin' somewhere. I'll bet you a dollar that by dinner time he'll bring you home a string of catfish as a peace offering for worryin' you to death. You know how young boys are."

LaDelle feigned patience at first and tried to explain calmly once again that someone needed to go find her nephew at once. However, when it became clear the sergeant wasn't grasping the urgency of the situation, LaDelle growled out of frustration and worry. She pounded her fist onto the desk, nearly upsetting Mr. Treg's ceramic totem pole pencil holder. She sounded so bear-like both were surprised, and for a second, neither spoke. But then, using the most lawyer-sounding, intimidating words she could think of, LaDelle lit into the man on the other end of the line.

"Let me remind you, Sergeant, that I am a taxpayer, and I've given generously to the Christmas Policeman Fund for the past three years in a row, so I expect more from the public servants of Macon County!" She then made mention of the Holy Scriptures, assuming Sergeant Baker was a God-fearing man. "Also, consider this, sir. I am a widow in need, and the Bible is clear that widows and orphans are to be helped, and if my brother dies, my nephew would become an orphan, for goodness' sake!"

Sergeant Baker, an even-keel sort of man and a father to four sons and two daughters, kept his composure and responded to LaDelle with a calm voice. "Well now, Mrs. Harris, I'll go ahead and send out an officer," but then added a friendly but firm warning not to call back to check on the situation. "When my officer locates the boy, we'll contact you, though I'd bet my best fishing pole your nephew will be back at home asking for his supper before then."

LaDelle rolled her eyes at the naïveté of the sergeant, but reluctantly agreed and mustered a half-hearted "thank you." She hung up the phone and headed back to the library, her eyes scouring the campus as she marched along. No sign of the boy.

After another hour went by, LaDelle fiddled nervously with some paperwork and straightened her desk, though there was no need. The small number of items on the surface were already in apple-pie order. Each drawer was organized as well. She stared at her desk for a moment—the kind of stare that looks to others as if you're in some sort of trance.

"Mrs. Harris, hey." Eugene the janitor was hovering behind her, his lanky body inches from her own. He was a kind man and a hard worker, but he lacked an awareness of personal space. His breath perpetually smelled of coffee and garlic, so when he opened his mouth with his face too close to whomever he was talking with, there was no escaping the odor which hovered like fog. Still, folks tended to overlook this offense because of Eugene's genuine heart for helping others and his positive attitude.

"Goodness, Eugene! You scared me."

"Forgive me, ma'am. Just checkin' to make sure you're all right there. You seem outta sorts, ma'am. Can I do anything for you?"

"I'm fine, Eugene. Thank you," she managed to say before excusing herself. She didn't want to share the whole story with him, knowing the entire school would know her business by the next morning. She made her way to the restroom and ducked inside. She splashed water on her face, forgetting to be careful not to get her dress wet. As she blotted both her face and the front of her dress with the towel hanging on the hook, she caught sight of herself in the mirror. She didn't have to lean in close. From where she stood, she could easily see the worry lines in her face and the fear in her eyes.

"I have no control over this situation," she said out loud, at first as a declaration. But then she repeated the sentence as a prayer. Upon further thought, she realized it needed to be a confession. Needing to be in control was her idol. If she felt she was in control, all was well. If it looked like things were not under her control, her stomach was in knots, and she was angry. She examined her reflection again and saw something else—fatigue. She wasn't tired from lack of sleep. She was exhausted from her labor. How hard she worked at maintaining control, which was never truly hers anyway.

She closed her eyes to ponder the truth of that thought more deeply, and without warning, words appeared to her in what could only be described as a vision—words from Scripture. Once again, they formed in her mind, and she kept her eyes closed, but instinctively leaned in to try and get a better look at them. As she took them in, they brought her to her knees.

Holding onto the sink with both hands to steady herself, she bowed her head. Shame and despair enveloped her but only for a few seconds. A warmth flowed through her body, and she recognized divinely given comfort and peace. *"In whose hand is the soul of every living thing, and the breath of all mankind."* She repeated the words in her vision over and over, out loud. The more she said them, the more she meant them. Though she kept her voice quiet, there was conviction in it. The words were from the book of Job.

After Garvin's death, she found herself spending time in the book of Job—angry over the Scripture she read but intrigued too. Tears flowed now, and she was cleansed. She took a deep breath and her shoulders relaxed.

How I wear myself out striving to maintain control of everyone and everything in my life. Enough! I'm worrying myself sick. I look like I'm eighty years old for goodness' sake. I have to change my ways. You are in control, Lord, and I am not. Take care of the boy as only you can. Help me to trust you.

She stood up then, splashed water once again over her countenance, which looked different now—void of anger and anxiety and with a covering of calmness—and breathed in deeply.

"All right then, Lord. All right. I surrender my worry. Jubilant is in your hands," she whispered and headed back out to her desk fully aware she had just experienced a second vision. The first had come while she wept in the tub. God had never spoken to her through any vision before—never in her whole life. Since Jubilant came to live with her, she'd had two within a week or so. This Jubilant summer was proving to be more than she had imagined. She wondered if another vision would follow. She wouldn't mind if it did.

CHAPTER FIFTEEN—
THE HISTORY OF GEORGE

> Anything will give up its secrets if you love it enough.
> Not only have I found that when I talk to the little flower
> or to the little peanut they will give up their secret, but
> I have found that when I silently commune with people
> they give up their secrets also—if you love them enough.
> (George Washington Carver)

After almost an hour and one bottle of lukewarm Coke, Professor Carver was finally able to convince Jubilant to come with him. Leaving the bus station together, Jubilant kicked the hard dirt as he made his way to the car. He was thankful not to have to walk back to the Institute, but defeat enveloped him. His shoulders slumped. He couldn't speak. He had failed his mission of getting on a bus to the reverend. The professor didn't insist he tell him anything, and he didn't try to compensate for the quiet by chattering. He remained as Jubilant—silent.

When they arrived back at campus, Professor Carver thanked Mr. Curtis, his friend and co-worker, for driving him to the bus station and for bringing Jubilant and him back to the Institute. Before he stepped out of the car, the professor took out a scratch pad and a pen from his coat pocket. He wrote several sentences, signed his name, folded the paper, and handed it to Mr. Curtis.

"Deliver this for me, would you?"

"Of course,"

"I'll be busy for the rest of the day, but I'll see you tomorrow bright and early."

Mr. Curtis nodded to Professor Carver, and turned to Jubilant before walking off. "Good luck to you, son."

The distinguished-looking man looked amused, though Jubilant couldn't find anything funny about the situation.

That's the second person to wish me good luck—first Dorothy and now Curtis. Don't they know when it comes to me there is no such thing?

Jubilant nodded without a word or even an expression on his face. A dread he couldn't shake came over Jubilant the moment he bumped into Professor Carver at the station and realized he had been discovered. When the professor insisted he leave with him in Mr. Curtis's car, Jubilant knew nothing he could say would change the situation, though at first, he tried in vain. The worst part was the facts of this whole ordeal were clear. He had failed. Again. He failed his daddy and caused trouble—and disobeyed his aunt.

Now, back at the parking lot of the Tuskegee Institute with the library in clear view, Jubilant let out a burp that had built up inside him—the result of nausea and nerves.

"S'cuse me," he muttered. "I feel sick."

"You'll be okay," Professor Carver said, putting his hand on his young friend's shoulder.

"I was so close to going home!" Jubilant threw his hands in the air, and then placed one on his stomach and bent over. Another belch escaped his lips. "I know how to deal with the reverend's wrath. I was even getting used to Millie Hines's temper, but what is Aunt LaDelle gonna do to me?"

Professor Carver stood quietly as Jubilant's mind raced. *My running away will surely bring on a tirade and most likely some sort of painful punishment. She might even tattle about my actions to the reverend and cause Daddy's health to fail even more. Even if he survives, he may never want me to come back home.*

"Come with me, son," Professor Carver interrupted Jubilant's thoughts. Adjusting his cap, he walked away from the parking lot.

Jubilant was about to protest when he realized that the professor was not headed toward the library. He stayed put, watching him for a few seconds. Professor Carver continued to walk in the opposite direction of the library, never turning around to see if Jubilant was following. So, partly out of curiosity and partly out of not knowing what else to do, Jubilant ran and caught up to him. After a few minutes of walking side by side in silence he asked, "How old are you anyway?"

"About seventy-two," Professor Carver replied without stopping.

"Even though you're stooped over some, you have a lot of energy for an old man."

Professor Carver chuckled at his young friend's observation. "When a person is given a task, he will also be given what is needed to complete the task at hand, no matter his age."

"What's your 'task at hand'?"

"You."

After Professor Carver's reply, the two walked in silence again until they reached the old man's dormitory located on the second floor. Jubilant followed him up the stairs and through the doorway like a tired cocker spaniel, but once inside, he perked up. His mouth fell open, and his eyes grew wide. He shook his head and whistled. Jubilant couldn't help himself—there were so many interesting things to look at!

Amongst the bottles, jars, and piles of papers, he gazed at beautiful paintings of flowers signed with "GWC" in the corner. Another whistle escaped his lips. Each painting—some the height of Jubilant, others no larger than a postcard—looked like something that ought to be in an art museum. The same picture of Booker T. Washington displayed in the school's library above Aunt LaDelle's reference desk hung amongst Professor Carver's artwork. One picture on his disheveled desk that caught Jubilant's eye was of an older white couple, and another was of the professor and a man Jubilant thought he recognized standing in front of a fancy car.

"Is that you with that car man?" He had seen him in the newspaper but couldn't remember his name.

"Henry Ford? Yes, that's Mr. Ford." The Professor looked through a stack of papers giving Jubilant a few extra minutes to take in the contents of his dormitory. Jubilant enjoyed being allowed to look at things up close and even touch stuff without being told not to. After several minutes, though, Professor Carver scooped up two paper sacks and a thermos. "Come with me, Jubilant."

He motioned for Jubilant to follow him and the pair walked out of the dormitory and down the stairs leading outside. He handed Jubilant one of the paper sacks—a sandwich wrapped in wax paper was inside. As he continued to walk next to Professor Carver, he unwrapped the sandwich and took a small bite. He wasn't sure how much of the sandwich he would be able to keep down, so he took it slow. The professor opened his own sack and pulled out a corn muffin. Before he even put the sweet muffin up to his lips, Jubilant recognized it as one of the corn muffins that Aunt LaDelle had made for this man she admired so much.

"Aunt LaDelle made you come find me, didn't she?"

"No, son. She didn't make me. She simply informed me of the situation. I wanted to come find you."

"You said you were given a task. Who gave it to you?" Jubilant wiped the crumbs off his mouth with his sleeve.

"Son, every morning I get up before dawn and take a walk in the woods. During that time, I gather samples to bring back to my laboratory, as you know. But I also spend time speaking to the Creator and listening as he speaks to me. He gives me my tasks, and I obey him."

Jubilant nodded, unsure of a proper response.

"I had a feeling about you the first time we met at the Doyles'," Professor Carver continued. "I saw pain in your eyes that went beyond a dead chicken. That's when the Lord told me to reach out to you."

Soon, the pair were at the edge of the forest. They took the trail as they had the day before and walked until they came to the same large rock in a clearing amongst the trees. There was a dragonfly on it, so Professor Carver waited until it flew away before he sat down. He dusted off the rock with his leathery hand, took a seat, and motioned for Jubilant to do the same. The rock was nice and cool in the shade, tucked away from Alabama's summer heat. They sat side by side in silence munching on the food Professor Carver had brought and drinking water from the thermos. Jubilant leaned back and breathed deeply. The woods were once again comforting to him. The food filled his belly bite by bite, and the old man's presence somehow helped him feel calm inside.

While the two sat silently chewing, Jubilant thought about his time in the bus station and all that had transpired there, including running into Professor Carver. Then something occurred to him.

"What do you mean you are 'about' seventy-two years old?" Jubilant asked between bites.

"I was born sometime around July 12, 1864."

"Well, is that your birthday, or isn't it?"

"I was born into slavery, son. They sometimes didn't keep clear records of slaves being born, but that was Aunt Sue and Uncle Mose's best guess."

"Couldn't your mama remember?"

"I'm sure she did," Professor Carver laughed. "But the three of us—Mama, my sister, and I—were kidnapped. Slave raiders grabbed us. I was just a small baby at the time." His voice grew serious as he added, "I was the only one recovered and returned to the Carver farm."

"Kidnapped? What happened to your mama and sister? Where was your daddy?" Done with his lunch and curious about Professor Carver's story, Jubilant readjusted himself on the rock. He lifted his knees up to his chest and hugged them with his arms.

"My father died in an accident before I was born, and no one ever did find out what happened to my mother and sister. I was too young to remember them."

Jubilant shook his head. "I remember my mama," he said and then he rubbed the top of his head as if trying to get the pain of the memory of her death out of it.

"I know. That's what I saw in your eyes when we met. You ache for your Mama and more. I know something about that, see?"

Jubilant looked down at the ground, embarrassed his pain was found out without him speaking it. When he looked back up at Professor Carver and saw the kindness in his eyes, he gave a slow nod and then a slight grin. "How'd you get all grow'd up without parents?"

"Well now, the Creator was lookin' out for me. He put it in Mose and Susan Carver's hearts to love me and my brother Jim. They raised us. They started out as our owners, but they most certainly became our loving parents."

"What? White folks raised you like you were their own sons?" Jubilant slapped his knee as if he had just heard the impossible. He could never imagine having white folks as his parents. Jubilant thought back to the picture he noticed in the professor's dormitory. "Is that a photo of them on your desk?"

"Yes, that's them. That's dear Aunt Sue and Uncle Mose. They were of German heritage. They helped start me out on my journey."

Jubilant wondered what exotic travels a smart man like Professor Carver must have had, especially since he knew important people like Henry Ford. "What sort of journey?"

"The journey to learn all I could and use the gifts and abilities the Creator gave me. I started out a sickly child—I nearly died—but the Lord had plans for me. He has plans for you too."

Jubilant sat quietly, trying to understand his friend's words. The professor had spoken often about 'the Creator' and what he had done for him. Jubilant didn't know faith like that, but he thought of how nice it would feel to possess it.

"The Creator hasn't given me any gifts or abilities, but I know I want to help the reverend, and I can't do that from Tuskegee." Jubilant's voice cracked as he mentioned his daddy. He found Professor Carver easy to be with. With him, he could let his guard down so when tears began to sting his eyes, he blinked and allowed them to fall down his face. They stained his dusty cheeks, and he tasted their saltiness on his lips. Professor Carver put his hand on his young friend's shoulder to comfort him, but he didn't say a word or try to get him to stop crying. Jubilant turned his head and wiped away the tears, but fresh ones continued to streak his face.

"You probably think I'm just a stupid baby," Jubilant said as he finally gained control over his emotions.

"I don't know what you're talking about," the man replied. "What I see is a tenderhearted young man who feels a call to action. You're just frustrated, that's all."

Jubilant nodded, but once again, Professor Carver's words were a bit of a mystery.

"Aunt Sue and Uncle Mose gave me their blessing to leave them to get a better education. I was younger than you—about eleven if that. The questions I had were as numerous as the stars. I needed those who knew more to help me find answers," the professor said in his gentle way.

"Did you find the answers you were lookin' for?" Jubilant blew his nose with the handkerchief handed to him.

"Many of them, yes. I knew what I was learning—inside and outside the walls of a classroom—could be put to use to help our people someday, but I didn't know what that would look like. 'How did the Creator plan on using little ole George?' I asked myself."

"When did you find out?"

"Oh, that's where the journey comes in. Along the way, I took hold of the opportunities I was given." Professor Carver looked Jubilant right in the eye as he spoke those words. "And I experienced many disappointments."

Jubilant looked away and sat in silence for a moment before blurting out, "The only opportunity I had to help my daddy and prove to him that I could stay out of trouble is gone now that you made me leave the bus station." Jubilant added more calmly, "Aunt LaDelle will surely beat me silly for runnin' away and trying to go to him after she told me not to."

Professor Carver watched a butterfly land on the flower in his lapel before he responded.

"You have the opportunity to help your daddy right here, but you don't have the eyes to see it."

"What in the name of Jehoshaphat do you mean?" Jubilant threw his hands up in the air. "He's stuck in bed with a sick heart and pneumonia, and I can't help him because I'm stuck in Tuskegee! I couldn't help Mama either." Jubilant wished the professor would make sense. Early evening was upon them, and he was tired from such a long, frustrating day.

The professor stood up from the rock and put his worn cap back on his head. "It's time to take you to Mrs. Harris now."

Jubilant was confused, but too spent to argue. As they walked out of the forest, the professor caught a toad he spotted hiding partly under a rock. He looked like a little boy, bending down and trapping the nervous hopper.

"Here," he said, lifting up the toad, inviting Jubilant to peek inside his cupped hands. "Put this little guy in your pocket and bring it to your aunt as a peace offering."

Jubilant stared at the old man. *Was he joking?* The professor winked and flashed Jubilant a mischievous smile before they both started to giggle.

"Oh, she'll *love* this," Jubilant said sarcastically.

"Who wouldn't want a toad?" Professor Carver offered. "They're very clean creatures!"

CHAPTER SIXTEEN—WHO'D HAVE THOUGHT?

The moments of happiness we enjoy take us by surprise.
It is not that we seize them, but that they seize us.
(Ashley Montagu)

Someone in an old Model T was laying a heavy hand on the horn.

"Why does that man keep honkin' his horn?" Jubilant asked in an irritated tone. They were near the parking lot closest to the library, but it was well closed by this time. Jubilant was relieved.

"That's Robert Doyle," Professor Carver said and waved. "He's come to retrieve us. Follow me."

For the third time that day, the professor told Jubilant to follow him. The twelve-year-old normally didn't take well to being told what to do, but George Washington Carver was different. He had a quiet, convincing way about him without saying much. So Jubilant, once again, followed the professor—this time without delaying or questioning—like a loyal hound. As they approached the car, he recognized it as Aunt LaDelle's. He froze in his steps.

"Get in Jubilant—your aunt let my daddy borrow her car!" Wilson said from the back seat.

Letting out a sigh of relief, Jubilant approached the automobile and bent down to see Wilson's face.

"Hey, Wilson," was all he could think of to say. He wasn't sure if he had been told about the latest trouble he'd caused.

"Busy day?" Wilson asked with a knowing smile.

Jubilant glared at him.

"Take it easy. I'm just playin' with you," Wilson said and patted the bench seat. "Sit back here so Professor Carver can sit up front with Pop."

Jubilant slipped into the back seat next to Wilson while Mr. Doyle left the driver's seat and helped the professor into the car. Jubilant studied the back of Robert Doyle's head while they drove down the road. He was a well-built man with broad shoulders and long fingers that the reverend would say were "piano-playin' fingers." He looked like a serious man and one you wouldn't want to cross, not unlike the reverend, yet it was obvious Professor Carver was perfectly comfortable with him. As the two men carried on a conversation in the front seat, Jubilant hesitated, but then cleared his throat before interrupting them.

"We're going to Aunt LaDelle's, aren't we?" Jubilant asked, rubbing his head.

"Yes, son, that's where I be takin' you," Mr. Doyle said. Wilson nodded his head and laughed. Jubilant didn't see what was so funny.

Jubilant wondered why Professor Carver was coming along, but not because he didn't want him to. The professor made him feel safe and more grown up than most adults did. Jubilant wanted to ask him more questions about his past, and he hoped to spend some time in his laboratory. Maybe the professor could teach him how to make a stink bomb or some other interesting concoction. He liked keeping company with him to be sure, but Professor Carver never mentioned coming along with him to Aunt LaDelle's when they spoke earlier in the woods. Now it seemed as if this ride to LaDelle Harris's was planned all along.

Mr. Doyle drove like he was in a race. He also hit every pothole on the road, which made Wilson and Jubilant fly up from their seats. As nervous as Jubilant was, he couldn't help but join Wilson in squealing and laughing each time it happened. Too soon for Jubilant's liking, the car rounded the corner to Aunt LaDelle's street. When her house came into view, Jubilant's stomach did flip-flops. He rubbed his head some more and told himself to breathe.

"Be a man," Wilson said as they both crawled out of the back seat.

Jubilant sighed and nodded. Facing his aunt was inevitable. He figured he might as well get it over with.

"I think everyone's out back," Mr. Doyle said as they walked toward the house.

"Everyone?" Jubilant was confused. Had Aunt LaDelle called the police? Was that music he heard? Billie Holiday?

"We're back with the boy," Mr. Doyle announced with a booming voice. He rested his large, thick hands on Jubilant's shoulders and ushered him to Aunt LaDelle. "Go on and say what you gots to say, LaDelle, and do what you gots to do. Then let's get on with supper, eh?"

Without a word, Aunt LaDelle placed the sweet potato pie she was holding onto the picnic table and stared at her nephew. She put her hands on her hips and all eyes were on her and Jubilant. Gathered in LaDelle's backyard was the Doyle family—Wilson, Robert, Patty and Wilson's little sister, Lydia—Henrietta and her husband Cal, and George Washington Carver. Dewey was tied up away from the food and from time to time he let his presence be known with a bark.

"Jubilant Jeremiah Bartley," LaDelle said slowly and in a low, stern tone.

"Yes, ma'am," Jubilant said quietly. He kept his hands in his pockets and his head down. He kicked at the grass and wished his heart would stop beating so loudly in his chest.

"Your father has entrusted me with your care, boy."

Jubilant nodded and then remembered to say, "Yes, ma'am," though he kept his eyes down low.

"Look at me, boy!" Her words were sharp. Jubilant did as she commanded.

At that moment, Henrietta approached her friend and whispered in her ear, "Easy, girl. Go easy on him. He's a good kid. He's hurtin' right now."

LaDelle took a deep breath and cleared her throat. "I may not be the best guardian in the world," she went on. "I know I can be bossy and difficult—"

Jubilant opened his mouth to speak, but Aunt LaDelle cut him off by raising her finger in the air.

"Hush! Let me finish."

Jubilant nodded and closed his mouth tight.

"What I'm trying to say is I know this isn't easy for you, but you have to honor your father and stay put with me. Understand?"

"Yes, ma'am, but—

Aunt LaDelle held up her finger again, and Jubilant knew to stop talking. "I invited all these people here tonight, so you would see, here in Tuskegee, you are surrounded by good and kindhearted folk who care about you."

Jubilant looked around. In Aunt LaDelle's backyard were familiar faces nodding their heads and smiling at him. Miss Patty and Miss Henrietta dabbed their eyes with handkerchiefs.

"Just today, I found out how much they care about me too." Aunt LaDelle took another deep breath following that declaration and wiped her own tears with the edge of her apron. Out of the corner of his eye, Jubilant could see Henrietta nodding her head, her large dangly earrings dancing back and forth. "But," his aunt added, narrowing her eyes at Jubilant, "I'm not shy about using the belt if I need to—and you can bet the world I will—if you ever pull a stunt like this again!"

"I didn't mean to—"

"Oh, yes, you did," LaDelle shot back and then added. "When I give you a tie to wear, you'd better take care of it!"

The two stared at each other for several seconds, neither one of them blinking. Jubilant could feel his heartbeat through his shirt, but he held his breath, afraid to look away. Was she going to whup him here in front of everyone?

Finally, Aunt LaDelle sighed and shook her head. She leaned toward him, pointed in his face, and whispered, "Everything's going to be okay, no matter what the Lord has up his sleeve, but you better behave yourself—for both our sakes!" She then reached and pulled him close. She wrapped her arms around him and gave him a quick motherly squeeze before releasing him.

At that moment, he was especially glad he had left the toad Professor Carver gave him back in the forest where it belonged. A toad hopping out of his pocket at that moment would have ruined any chance of getting out of a whupping. He let out his breath and heard a deep commanding voice say—

"Now let's eat!" Mr. Doyle's voice broke the silence. Miss Patty playfully slugged her husband's arm for his bluntness before handing him a plate.

"Hey," Robert Doyle said in his defense, "we all contributed to this meal, and I'm ready to eat my share, aren't you? None of this fine food is goin' to waste tonight, that's for sure!"

The crowd laughed and several folks came over to Jubilant and patted his head. Henrietta gave him a kiss on the cheek and went over to LaDelle and did the same to her. LaDelle squeezed her neighbor's hand and then disappeared through the backdoor to the kitchen to retrieve more food.

Jubilant watched as the others filled their plates. He was sure that all this fine food was a sacrifice to provide, but no one seemed concerned tonight.

Lydia wiggled her way up to the front of the table and helped herself to a bread roll and dipped it into the soft butter. Wilson passed up the dishes of pickled okra, creamed corn, and fresh tomato slices with cheese and instead stabbed one pork chop and two rolls with his fork. He slathered a mound of butter onto each roll before placing them onto his plate.

As Jubilant put a few items on his plate, Miss Henrietta ran into her house and turned up the phonograph set up on the open kitchen window's sill. The smooth voice of Billie Holiday filled the backyard.

Henrietta unabashedly sang along to "Summertime," and she and Cal danced the duration of the song on the lawn in front of everyone. They spun around and when the song ended, Cal dipped his wife like real ballroom dancers do, kissing her on the mouth after flipping her upright. Henrietta, with her sparkly gold earrings and wearing no shoes, looked part gypsy, part Hollywood starlet. Everyone clapped—except for LaDelle who rolled her eyes but couldn't hide a grin. Someone whistled, and Cal and Henrietta took a bow, then laughed at their own spectacle.

Jubilant's face grew warm with embarrassment over seeing them show such affection in public, but something inside him liked it. He wondered if Henrietta was ever a real dancer on a stage somewhere. With her movie star looks and playful way about her, she seemed the type who was born to perform for an audience. There was nothing self-conscious about her. She was free in that way—to move and sing and be who she was. Aunt LaDelle told him that she sang to her customers at the beauty parlor as she did their hair. Now, as she mingled with others throughout the evening, Jubilant saw she accepted people the way they were, though it was obvious they were different from her. In that way, Henrietta loved well, and though Jubilant didn't know how to express it, she enchanted him.

When the dance was over, Jubilant glanced over at Professor Carver who was petting Dewey. He smiled to himself. This end-of-day was the perfect definition of "unexpected" of the best kind. *I wish Daddy could be here.* He would have smiled over this evening for days. He would express the joy of it by working it into a sermon. "A time to mourn and a time to dance ..." That's probably what he'd say.

Before folks went for seconds on dessert, LaDelle and the other women began to light candles in mason jars to provide extra light and some relief from the mosquitoes. Throughout the humid night, as Billie Holiday sang on, Jubilant listened to the friends and neighbors talk about the effects of the poor economy and the weather and the St. Louis Browns. Everyone offered kind words to him. Aunt LaDelle looked over at him and grinned—twice. *Her smile is not unpleasant. And she looks younger when she smiles.*

"We're prayin' for your pa," Henrietta said. Cal, not much for words, nodded in agreement and patted Jubilant's shoulder.

"We know it ain't easy being away from home, but we're glad you're here," Miss Patty said, hugging him so tight his face nearly suffocated in her large bosom.

"I'll be your friend," said little Lydia as she hugged Jubilant's knee. She had her mama's chubby cheeks, and her dimples made him smile.

"Georgia," Wilson blurted out with a mouth full of pie.

"Georgia what?" Jubilant asked.

"Georgia *who*," Wilson corrected him. "That's what I named the chicken you gave me," Wilson smiled. "It wasn't your fault Dewey went crazy in my hen house and killed Sophie. I'm not mad."

"Thanks, Wilson."

"Sophie tasted good," Lydia added in a loud whisper. "Mama cooked her up for supper that night."

"Lydia! You're fulla beans!" Wilson yelled and chased her around the yard threatening to spank her. Lydia ran into her daddy's arms screaming, and the chase came to an end when Mr. Doyle shot a warning look at Wilson. Lydia sat smugly in her daddy's arms and stuck her tongue out at her brother.

"She's whacky," Wilson said, picking up the rest of his piece of pie with his hands and finishing it off in two bites. He knew he couldn't win against a four-year-old. "You're lucky you're an only child," he said to Jubilant.

Jubilant nodded, but glanced toward Professor Carver, who he had watched throughout the evening.

The professor had smiled often and chatted off and on with everyone, including LaDelle who told him more than once how grateful she was to him and what a gift he was to Tuskegee Institute and the entire world. She thanked him for the note he'd had Mr. Curtis give to her and for the idea of the backyard party.

Ah, so that's what the professor had given to Mr. Curtis to deliver. Knowing the professor had made the way easy for him made Jubilant happy.

Professor Carver was polite, but he mostly listened and didn't talk a whole lot. He watched others as they interacted, just as he might have sat in the forest observing a lark build its nest. He was both intrigued and delighted. But, as the evening went on, Jubilant noticed the professor's eyes grew watery and droopy. It had been a long day for him too.

"I hate to break up this party," Robert Doyle said to the group, patting his stomach after his second piece of pie, "but this here's a weeknight, and I believe we all have work in the mornin'."

Everyone agreed it was time to call it a night. Aunt LaDelle placed some leftovers in a basket for Wilson's mom to take home, and a few people brought some of the empty food dishes into the house, piling them onto LaDelle's kitchen counter. Henrietta wadded up the checkered tablecloth and offered to take it home and wash it.

Wilson walked his mother and Lydia back home while Mr. Doyle drove Professor Carver back to his place. Jubilant followed them out to the front yard, yawning as he walked. He didn't bother covering his mouth. No women were around to scold him.

The professor turned to Jubilant and smiled. "How do you feel, son, hearing all the kind words these folks spoke to you tonight?"

"I guess it makes me feel good," Jubilant admitted. "But the reverend—I wish I could help him."

"You can." Professor Carver replied. "Wise King Solomon once said, 'Pleasant words are as a honeycomb, sweet to the soul, and health to the bones.'" Then he cupped his aged hands around Jubilant's face and looked deep into his eyes. "Think about that."

Jubilant's face grew warm and a feeling of safety and peace washed over him. The professor's touch and his grandfather-like tenderness made Jubilant feel secure in a way he hadn't experienced in a long time. He nodded, and then asked, "See you tomorrow?"

"Yes, but only after you've taken care of all the books your aunt gives you to shelve," Professor Carver said with a grin. "I don't want her blaming me for you not getting things done in the library!" Mr. Doyle helped him into the Model T, and they sped off.

Jubilant stood alone at the curb and waved. When he could no longer see the car, he went into the kitchen and, without being asked, began to wash dishes. Penance.

CHAPTER SEVENTEEN—THE LETTER

And none will hear the postman's knock / Without a quickening of the heart. / For who can bear to feel himself forgotten? (W.H. Auden)

In two separate rooms, two separate minds woke up racing.

LaDelle's started in at 4:37. In the still-dark morning, she opened her eyes. The room was a shadowy blur and without glasses resting on her face, she couldn't begin to put things into focus. She left the wire-rimmed spectacles in their place on her nightstand, not wanting to greet the day in an official manner quite yet, but her mind started in with a flurry.

When would Millie Hines call Henrietta this morning? What news would she bring about Ashton? How was all this going to turn out? What If ...? What if ...? What if, Lord? Forty-five minutes later she was up, bed made, fully dressed, and busy if for no good reason but to keep her mind quiet or at least ignore its panicky chatter.

She stopped organizing the utensil drawer and fed Dewey an earlier-than-usual breakfast. As he ate, LaDelle turned her attention to her dog. She sat down on a kitchen chair and invited him over, patting her knee. He seemed to know she needed him and came over. He rested his head on LaDelle's lap, his big brown eyes looking up at her.

"Sweet Dewey," she said and rubbed his ear. "What would I do without you?" As she stared down at his face, she noticed some of his fur above his nose was gray. She stroked it thoughtfully. "Looks like you're gettin' on in years," she sighed. Then she noticed something else. Dewey looked trimmer. "You've lost some weight since the boy's been here, haven't you? All that ball chasing has been good for you." She thought about this for a few seconds. "Having the boy around has been good for me too, I suppose. His being here brought some things to my attention about myself, that's for sure."

Dewey stood up and gave his head a vigorous shake. He then trotted into the living room to have a morning snooze on the carpet next to the radio—his favorite spot.

Aunt LaDelle thrashing around the kitchen might have awakened him at 5:32, but it was Jubilant's mind that kept him awake. Wide awake. Questions filled his mind. *I still have $2.45 cents in my pocket from Dorothy, and no chance of spending it on a bus ticket home. Should I spend it on something else? What did Professor Carver mean when he said that I have the opportunity to help Daddy right here, but I don't have the eyes to see it? See what?* Jubilant rubbed his head and mulled over the questions swimming around in it. He thought about what a surprise the night before had been. Who would have thought Aunt LaDelle would have let him out of a whupping? He would never have imagined everyone gathered in her backyard like that—just for him. A real party! And how would he have survived this far in Tuskegee without Professor Carver's kindness?

Jubilant decided he'd rather get up and get his morning chores over with rather than think himself to death while lying in bed. Humming "Summertime," he reached for his trousers and slipped them on, noticing when he tried to button them they were tight around his middle. Aunt LaDelle's talent for cooking and baking was plumping him up. That was when the fine aroma of grits and leftover pork chops reached his nose. His stomach growled, motivating him to pick up his pace and grab the broom to sweep the front porch. Then he went around back to repeat the chore there before swinging open the screen door and entering the kitchen, Dewey at his heels.

"Sleep all right?" Aunt LaDelle asked, pointing to his feet to remind him to wipe them on the mat. Dewey trounced in with wet paws, but Aunt LaDelle either didn't notice or didn't care.

"I slept all right—for a while," Jubilant said.

"Hmm-mm," LaDelle nodded as if she understood.

While they sat in silence eating their breakfast, LaDelle suddenly scrambled out of her chair and disappeared into the living room. Dewey followed, and they both returned a few seconds later, Aunt LaDelle waving a stack of mail in her hand.

"In all the craziness—and that *was* a crazy stunt you tried to pull—I completely forgot to open my mail yesterday."

She picked up each envelope one at a time, looked at it, and commented out loud.

"Water bill. That will be higher now that there's two of us living here. Gas bill. I sure have been cooking more now that I'm feeding two. Life Magazine? Oh brother, this belongs to Henrietta—Harold's a nice man, but not always the best postman—and, oh! A letter from your daddy!"

Aunt LaDelle handed the letter to Jubilant. He quickly swallowed the piece of pork chop in his mouth without taking the time to chew it first and reached over to grab the letter from her hand. But before he opened it, he looked at Aunt LaDelle quizzically.

"He obviously wrote it before his pneumonia came along," she said, reading his mind. "Open it."

Jubilant tore open the envelope and unfolded the paper inside. His face fell at first. He could tell right away that his daddy had not written the letter.

"This isn't his handwriting. He didn't write this."

"Just read it," LaDelle commanded, and then added, "Aloud, if you don't mind."

Jubilant wanted to keep it to himself, but knew he didn't have a choice, so he cleared his throat and read:

> Dear Jube,
>
> I miss you already, but I do believe it is truly a blessing you're getting to know your aunt, and I'm able to rest knowing you're receiving the best of care."

Aunt LaDelle sat up tall in her seat and puffed up her chest as she heard these words. Jubilant continued.

> I know us being apart is as irritating as a mosquito bite, yet this is the best option for you under the circumstances. Believe me, Son.
>
> Be respectful of your aunt. I didn't always appreciate my older sister when I was young, but as I grew older, I realized what a gift she is. Remember your manners and don't bring a snake anywhere near her, or she'll have your head! She nearly killed me for such an offense when I was ten. If you ever do make her cross, I recommend candy. She'll forgive you, no doubt, if you make a peace offering with a chocolate bar!

Aunt LaDelle narrowed her eyes and turned her body away from Jubilant. She crossed her arms in front of her chest. Jubilant guessed she was offended by the truth.

> I have no real news from Huntsville. I'm spending my time reading in bed mostly. That is, when I don't have a visitor—and I have plenty. Mrs. Jackson from next door

continues to come over each evening to bring me supper. She's a fine cook and a good woman. Her daughter Priscilla is acting as my secretary right this very minute. She is penning this letter as I dictate it to her. What a true gift our friends and neighbors are!

Take care, my boy. Make the most of your days.

Sincerely,
Your loving father

P.S. From Priscilla: I bet you didn't know gorillas could write!

"What's that supposed to mean?" Aunt LaDelle asked.

"Priscilla's just making a joke is all." Jubilant turned the letter face down on the table. He didn't want to reread it. He was embarrassed Priscilla brought up his mean comment in the letter. He thought back to the day before he boarded the bus for Tuskegee. Upset to learn he'd be leaving for the summer; he climbed the large oak tree in their parsonage's front yard so he could be alone and think and maybe cry.

"I see you up there, Jubilant Bartley! You shouldn't climb in your good clothes like that. Can I come up too?"

It was Artie Jackson, Jubilant's neighbor and uninvited eight-year-old shadow. He stood at the tree, looking up at Jubilant. His nose, as usual, had snot running down it.

"Leave him alone now, Artie. Don't you know his daddy's been afflicted?" Priscilla Jackson was Artie's older sister and daytime babysitter while their mama was at work washing other people's clothes. Their daddy had run off right before Artie was born and was never heard from again. Priscilla came over to her brother and joined him at the tree. She leaned in close, and, in a whisper loud enough for Jubilant to hear, added, "His daddy might die. If he does pass on, we'll have to find ourselves another reverend, I guess."

Jubilant couldn't tell if she wanted him to hear her on purpose, or if she was just bad at whispering, but either way her words were matter-of-fact, and he absorbed the sting of them through his whole body.

"You shut up, Artie, and you mind your own business, Priscilla-the-Gorilla," Jubilant called down. She wasn't at all big or overweight, nor did she have any other gorilla-like features. In fact, Jubilant thought she was sort of nice looking. Kind of cute. But calling her a gorilla seemed like the appropriate mean thing to say for some reason. Anyway, she started it.

Now, reading her comment in Daddy's letter, Jubilant remembered the look on her face after his remark. She stood staring up at him, slack-jawed over his remark. Finally, she found her voice and let him have it.

"You can't talk to us like that, Jubilant Bartley!" Priscilla yelled and stomped her foot on the hard ground. She shook her finger at him, trembling with both hurt and anger. "I know your daddy's sick and all, but you can't talk to us like that. Don't you know you're a preacher's son?"

Wishing to escape further rebuke, Jubilant, standing to climb higher up the tree, grabbed hold of the branch above his head to steady himself, but he misjudged the strength of the branch, and it broke off into his hands. His long legs wobbled, and then, before he could say, "Jumpin' Jehoshaphat!" he was headed downward. It all happened so fast he couldn't think of grabbing a different branch on his way down, not even the one that caught his shirt and ripped it beyond repair. Two seconds later, the reverend's son found himself on his back looking up at the tree. Priscilla towered over him.

"Vengeance is mine, sayeth the Lord," she said with the Cheshire Cat's cruel grin.

Jubilant's mind was racing as he refolded the letter and

tucked it back into the envelope. *Priscilla came over to my house, sat next to my daddy, and helped him write a letter? The busybody ladies at church and the doctor probably love Priscilla being around and helpin', but they don't think I could handle the job. If I was home, no one would need to help him write me a letter. Daddy could just tell me himself what he wanted to say.*

Aunt LaDelle took the envelope and wrote #1 on the bottom left-hand corner.

"From the content and the postmark date, I assume this is your daddy's first letter to you. Now you'll have a clear record of it."

Jubilant rolled his eyes when she wasn't looking. His aunt's mind was constantly organizing things. He thought over the reverend's words with mixed feelings. While he was happy to hear from him, it also made Jubilant sad—sad he wasn't with his daddy ... and jealous Priscilla got to be with him instead. He wondered if Artie came by too, wandering into his room and messing with his belongings. *If he touches my carnival ticket stub collection, I'll punch him.*

LaDelle drove extra fast to work and rolled through the stop sign at the corner right before entering the school's grounds, but they still arrived three minutes late, and the agitation this produced was evident all over her face. Once she parked the car, she practically ran to the library, hollering twice at Jubilant to "shake a leg." She quickly unlocked the library doors, turned on the lights, and started up the fans.

"Do you see that?" She asked Jubilant, pointing up at the large clock on the wall. "I'm late, and I've never arrived late to work before—not at this job or any other. Ever!"

She sounded out of breath as she spoke, but it didn't keep her from continuing, hand on her chest. "Five minutes early, in my mind, borders on late, so this morning's arrival time is unacceptable." She stomped over to her desk and yanked open the bottom drawer, tossing her purse inside.

Jubilant noticed her dress was wet under her armpits. He hated when adults got all riled about things.

"Didn't you ask me to read Daddy's letter this morning?" He didn't think he should be blamed for making them late.

"Never mind that," Aunt LaDelle shot back. "This being late just can't happen again. Understand?"

"Yes, ma'am."

"Now, give me your word this time you will stay in the library and not run away to any bus station, train station, or circus that may pass through town." LaDelle said as she wheeled the cart of books over to Jubilant. Her voice was still agitated; her face dotted with sweat.

"Promise," he said without looking her in the eyes.

Jubilant then looked up at the clock next to Booker T. Washington's picture on the wall and sighed. The morning had not gone as Jubilant expected. First of all, Miss Henrietta never came over to bring news of a phone call from Millie Hines. Aunt LaDelle and Jubilant waited at the house as long as they could before she had to leave for work.

"There must not be any news, that's all," she told Jubilant. "No one called from Huntsville this morning because your daddy hasn't gotten any worse."

"Or any better," Jubilant added, hoping he was wrong.

Now at the library, Jubilant could tell the day would surely drag on. *Tick, tock, tick, tock.* The clock on the wall seemed to taunt him with its incessant noise. His day was surely doomed with nothing to do but complete the tasks his aunt had for him. He patted the two one-dollar bills, one quarter, and two dimes, and Dorothy's folded, forged permission note hidden in his trouser pocket. Between the newspaper resource section and the science section of the library, Jubilant daydreamed about how he was able to make it all the way to the bus depot the day before, and how this day's bus to Huntsville had already left the station. Without him.

While in the middle of his thoughts, Mr. Curtis found Jubilant in the library and gave him a nudge with his elbow.

"Professor Carver told me I'd find you here." Austin Curtis was a handsome man with a formal demeanor, yet his youthfulness was evident, though he probably hoped his mustache made him appear older and more seasoned than he was.

"Yes, sir." Jubilant was relieved to see Mr. Curtis. He hoped he would take him to see the professor.

"Professor Carver is extremely busy this morning, but he asked me to give you this." Mr. Curtis handed Jubilant an old round cookie tin. "He said he'll stop by later, if he can, but between you and me, I wouldn't hold my breath." As he turned to leave, he added, "Once the professor gets busy on a project, he completely loses track of time. There aren't enough hours in the day for that man."

Jubilant nodded remembering Miss Patty teasing Professor Carver for his late arrival the first day he met him at the Doyles' house. He and Dr. Carver had a couple of things in common—they'd both lost their mamas, and they both sometimes forgot to be places when they were supposed to. Jubilant thanked Mr. Curtis and placed the tin on the book cart. Then he wheeled the cart over to the corner where no students would be studying. He rubbed his head and took a deep breath before carefully opening the tin's lid. Inside he found a handwritten note—a poem—a small jar of honey, a pencil, two sheets of blank paper, and a note that read:

Jubilant,
My hope for you today is you'll discover how the Creator
wants you to help your daddy. May the items in this tin
be of inspiration to you.
Your friend,
GWC

Jubilant set Professor Carver's note on the table and picked up the other items one by one. The poem was called "Equipment" by Edgar A. Guest. The twelve-year-old, not in the mood for poetry, shook his head at the sheer length of it before finally setting his mind to reading the poem.

You've all that the greatest of men have had,
Two arms, two hands, two legs, two eyes ...

A few verses further the words grabbed hold of Jubilant. He brought the poem closer to his eyes to soak it in as he read:

You are the handicap you must face,
You are the one who must choose your place ...

Jubilant thought over the words and shook his head with a scowl on his face. *What choice is mine? I don't have a choice about anything anymore.* A few more lines down and his attention was fully grabbed. He nodded his head while he read:

With your equipment they all began,
Get hold of yourself, and say: "I can."

Jubilant glanced over the poem one more time, rereading some of the lines. As poems go, he decided that this one was more enjoyable than most. For one thing, he understood it. He wanted to say, "I can," and believe it, but what was Professor Carver trying to tell him to do? Why wouldn't he just come out and say it?

Jubilant put down the poem, unscrewed the jar of honey and dipped his finger inside. He quickly stuck his finger in his mouth so as not to drip any on Garvin Harris's tie and sucked off the honey. The sweet, gooey liquid gave his entire mouth a thrill. It was smooth as velvet as it melted off his tongue and slid down his throat. He dipped his finger in again for a second taste. This time Jubilant closed his eyes and savored the sweetness, which brought a smile to his lips as he licked off every drop of honey. Suddenly, his eyes opened as he remembered the professor's words from the night before. "King Solomon said, 'Pleasant words are as a honeycomb, sweet to the soul and health to the bones.'" He stared down at the remainder of the contents in the tin—blank paper and a pencil. Smiling to himself, he realized what Professor Carver wanted him to see. The mystery of it solved. *What a clever old man!*

Jubilant screwed the lid back onto the honey jar, checking it twice to make sure it was on good and tight. He put it back in the tin along with the poem and the professor's letter, and replaced the tin's lid. Setting the full tin onto the bottom rung, he swiftly wheeled the book cart down the aisles of books and around the library until each book was shelved in its proper place. The Dewey Decimal System was now his friend, and he patted himself on the back in his own mind for learning it so easily. Just after the last book was shelved, Jubilant strutted to the front of the library and stood in front of Aunt LaDelle's desk with a hopeful look.

"I've put the books back on the shelves where they belong," he told her. "May I take some time now to write to the reverend since I didn't do it this morning before breakfast?"

"I'm fine with that," she said, but added, "as long as you're sure you put each of my books in their rightful place."

"Yes, ma'am, I did," he said, making a salute. He wasn't sure why he did it, but Aunt LaDelle hid a grin with her hand. Taking that as a sign he could leave, he grabbed Professor Carver's tin off the cart and dashed to the corner of the library. He had seen a desk there by a window earlier and thought it would be a good place to think, if it hadn't already been taken over by one of the students. Thinking, he knew, was going to be a challenge. Jubilant didn't normally like to sit and think for too long, but to write the reverend a letter which would help bring sweetness to his soul and health to his bones, he would have to use his brain.

CHAPTER EIGHTEEN—FOR THE PRICE OF A STAMP

If you want to lift yourself up, lift up someone else.
(Booker T. Washington)

Jubilant was glad to find the desk he was hoping to use by the window was free. He sat down, took out the pencil and paper from the tin and wrote, "Dear Daddy." Five minutes later, the blank paper held the same two words, but nothing more. Jubilant rubbed his head, chewed on the end of his pencil, tapped his fingers on the desk. Nothing. His mind was as blank as the paper staring at him from the table. The latest news was that he had tried to run away from Tuskegee and head back to Huntsville with money he didn't earn. He couldn't share that news.

What would be sweet to daddy's heart and bring health to his bones? Jubilant asked himself that question over and over while he tipped his chair back, rocking it on two legs. He glanced out the window and saw two students carrying on what looked like an amusing conversation. He was unable to hear what they were saying, but he saw that one of the young men was talking to the other, and then they both threw back their heads, laughed, and slapped their knees. Jubilant couldn't help but smile as well as he watched them enjoy their joke. He wished he knew what they were talking about.

Witnessing the scene outside gave Jubilant an idea for the reverend's letter. He attempted to put his front chair legs back squarely on the ground, so he could scoot his chair in, lean into the desk and get busy writing, but his chair had other ideas. It suddenly slid out from under him and a split-second later both the chair and Jubilant crashed to the floor—the commotion echoed through the building. He heard some snickering from behind.

The library assistant dashed over to Jubilant to see if he was all right. "Good golly! Are you hurt?" He had a look of sincere concern on his face. His concern was for Jubilant, but also for what the commotion would summon.

At that moment, Aunt LaDelle arrived.

"Jubilant Bartley! Shh!" Aunt LaDelle whispered through tight lips but in full force like they were shot out of a cannon. She threw her hands up into the air. "How in heaven's name can you cause trouble writing a letter?" She reached for the chair and stood it up.

"I'm not causing trouble. I just fell, that's all." Jubilant scrambled off the ground, his face hot from embarrassment, and dusted himself off. He resisted the temptation to rub his aching rear end as he stood up. "Do you want me to write my letter outside instead?"

"Oh, no! I want you right here where I can keep my eye on you, but I don't want to hear you, understand?" Knowing her words were sharper than she intended, she added, "Just try and be careful and quiet, okay? Please."

Jubilant nodded and turned away from her and the others in the library as he sat back down at the desk. He didn't want any more of Aunt LaDelle's words in his head. He was finally inspired to write the reverend's letter and his aunt's grumpiness could spoil the whole thing. She walked away shaking her head. Several students walked by, and he was sure they stared at him as they passed. Jubilant rubbed his head and ignored them. He was on a mission. He didn't have time to let anyone bother him.

Once again, he focused on the two men outside. Before they said goodbye to one another, they shared another belly laugh. The taller man patted the shorter man's shoulder, and off they walked in different directions, each with a smile on his face.

"I need to write something amusing and make Daddy laugh," Jubilant murmured. "A funny story would make his heart glad for sure." He didn't have to think long to decide what to write. Smiling, the words flowed from his hands onto the paper.

Dear Daddy,

My new friend Wilson raises chickens. He named the chicken I gave him Georgia, and do you know why? I figured it was because he visited the state of Georgia and took a liking to it, but that's not it. He told me he named his newest fowl after his fourth-grade teacher, Miss Georgia Keller. Wilson said Miss Georgia stands up nice and tall and has the prettiest reddish-brown colored eyes he's ever seen—just like his chicken! I nearly fell over when he told me that! I told him to be smart and not let his teacher know he named a cackling hen after her.

It made me think that maybe I should name the next toad I find "Millie" after you-know-who because I wouldn't mind it if she croaked!! Get it? Croaked. Don't be mad. I'm only joking about Mrs. Hines. Mostly.

I think we should go to the picture show when I get back home. We can see one of those comedies you like. I have some money, so I will buy both of our tickets.

I stopped believing in my lucky rabbit's foot and all. I'm just asking the Creator to come through and heal you. I love you, Daddy. I hope you enjoy this letter.

Sincerely,
Jubilant

He reread the letter to himself twice before folding it into thirds. He knew the reverend would wonder where the money he mentioned in the letter came from. Jubilant decided he would tell him about Dorothy and the train station one of these days. In the meantime, he'd keep the money she gave him and use it for a good cause—to bring healing laughter to his daddy. Dorothy would be fine with that.

As Jubilant approached LaDelle's desk, so he could ask her for an envelope and a stamp, he looked up and saw Miss Henrietta bolt through the library doors. Once inside, she stood in the middle of the room gawking at the rows of shelves of books as if she had never been to a library before. Her eyes were as wide as saucers, but when she spotted LaDelle, she snapped out of her trance and made a beeline to her friend's desk. Jubilant's heart began to race, and he picked up his pace, reaching the desk at the same time as Miss Henrietta.

"Henrietta, what are you doing here?" LaDelle asked as she stood up, making her way to her friend. She squinted as if trying to see something that would give her a clue in Henrietta's face.

"I bet she got a phone call about Daddy," Jubilant interrupted.

"Hush," LaDelle batted in the air toward Jubilant. "Speak, Henrietta! Is that true?"

Henrietta looked flushed. She nodded and fanned herself with her hand and took a deep breath. "LaDelle, is there water in this place? I'm feelin' overheated."

"I'll get you some water, but first tell us what you know about Ashton!"

"Well," she sighed again and took a gulp of air, "that woman Millie Hines called and reported your brother—your daddy—" Henrietta said, turning to Jubilant as if he needed clarification, "seems to have come through the worst of it, and his heart is beatin' a might stronger now. His lungs sound better today too. He's still in the hospital, and he'll be there for a while longer because they can't be certain he's out of the woods, but it darn well seems like it. Millie Hines said it's that Prontosil drug that's doin' the trick! I read about it in *Time* magazine a while back."

Jubilant, who had barely breathed since he saw Miss Henrietta enter the library, now collapsed onto a chair. He let out a loud sigh and rubbed his head, letting the good news soak in. His hair had grown thick and would need to be picked out with a comb soon. This fact was a sign to him and everyone who saw him he had been in Tuskegee for a while now.

LaDelle handed her friend a cup of water, took a few deep breaths, and then excused herself. Jubilant figured she was going to the restroom and stared after her until she disappeared behind a shelf of books. He glanced at Miss Henrietta and saw her watching Aunt LaDelle too. He then stood up and asked her neighbor if she wanted to have a look around the library. Henrietta smiled and gestured "yes" with a silent clapping of the hands, so he ushered her to a section he knew she would find interesting—Music. As she engaged with the books, Jubilant continued to comb the library, looking for his aunt, but he didn't see her.

"I'll be back in a few minutes," he told Henrietta. Since Aunt LaDelle had not returned, he thought he'd go look for her. He still needed that envelope and stamp for the reverend's letter. As he made his way toward the back of the library, he noticed the back door was ajar, though he'd been told it was supposed to be locked at all times. Jubilant bit his lip as he thought about opening the door wide enough to peer out. He had escaped from this same door the day before, and he didn't want Aunt LaDelle to accuse him of trying to escape again. As he stepped closer to the door, he thought he heard someone sobbing. He looked to his right and to his left, making sure no one was watching, and then slowly opened the door wide enough to step out and there, with her back turned, was his aunt.

Her shoulders were slumped, and she was wiping her eyes and sniffling. Then she lifted her head to the heavens and uttered, "Thank you, Lord. Thank you." between sobs.

Without her knowing it, Jubilant stood watching her for a few seconds before trying to figure out what he should do. It always made him uncomfortable whenever he saw a grown-up cry. Returning the door to the position he found it in, he quietly returned to Miss Henrietta, who was now back at the front desk, thumbing through a book about jazz music. He sat down on the chair near her and rubbed his head.

"What's wrong with you, baby? Why you lookin' like that? You should be celebrating. Do a little dance or something. Your daddy is on the mend!" Miss Henrietta stood up as if she were about to do a dance all by herself.

"Aunt LaDelle is out there cryin', and I don't know what to do," he confessed.

"Oh, dear. I see." Miss Henrietta replied thoughtfully. "I say we leave her be and let her have a good cry. Your aunt doesn't like to be fussed over, and cryin' has a way of cleansing the soul, so we'll just let her be for now. She'll be okay, honey." She offered a reassuring smile. Her teeth were a little crooked, but they were white as snow.

Jubilant nodded and continued rubbing his head. Seeing Aunt LaDelle like that made him nervous. He frowned as he thought things over.

"Come on, now. Ain't that great news I brought you 'bout your daddy?" Miss Henrietta squeezed Jubilant's arm. She forgot to speak in a whisper, but Jubilant didn't say anything. "I know you been crazy with worry, so I come straight over to tell you. I guess I could have called the Institute and had them ring LaDelle, but I wanted you to hear it from me in person. I don't have to do anyone's hair until twelve-thirty, so I had some time on my hands."

"Thank you," Jubilant said. The two of them sat next to each other in silence. Jubilant finally cleared his throat. "Can I tell you something, Miss Henrietta?"

"Anything, honey. What's on your mind?" She nodded her head up and down, and her gold earrings danced from her lobes.

"I plan on helping the reverend's heart heal faster by writing him powerful letters."

"Ooh! What kind of power?" Miss Henrietta tilted her head and gave Jubilant a puzzled look.

"Well, I'm gonna write him things that will make him happy and give him joy. I'll make him laugh. He'll be gettin' letters from me from now on that will be as sweet to his soul as honey."

"Hmm ..." Henrietta thought over Jubilant's words. "That's what singin' does for me, don't you know it. Doesn't matter where I am—at work or church, while washing dishes, or weeding the garden. I'm telling you it fills my soul. Also," she batted her eyes, "dancing to Billie Holiday's songs. Pure joy!"

She elbowed Jubilant and raised her eyebrows causing them both to laugh at her admission. Jubilant liked Miss Henrietta. She had a wild side about her, like when she and Cal danced in public, or she turned her music up loud enough for him to hear all the way over in Aunt LaDelle's kitchen.

"Why are you friends with Aunt LaDelle?" Henrietta made Jubilant feel so easy, he wasn't afraid to ask the question swirling in his mind. "You're so ... so ... different from her."

"Oh, honey, I know. Believe me, I know! I'm sure others wonder the same thing. The truth is I am quite a bit younger than she is, and not nearly as serious. I admire your aunt, though, and I saw through her tough act right away. She needed a friend, and God put us next door to each other so that was that."

"She's such a rule maker!" Jubilant added.

"Yes, and she's a rule follower, but ..." Henrietta put her hand on her chest. "I have a soft spot for that woman. She has a good heart. She just needs me to guide her to the lighter side of life."

Henrietta admitted, when LaDelle first moved in next door, she didn't know what to think about a single, middle-aged woman buying a house all on her own, leaving for work each morning, and keeping to herself.

"Cal told me to give her space and not be a busybody, but I told him, 'No sir, that woman needs me.' So, I knocked on her door one night holding a pot of chicken and dumpling stew and carrying two bottles of cold beer—one in each of my apron pockets. LaDelle was so shocked to find me standing there on her porch she just stood there with her mouth open. So, I nudged my way in, walked right on past her, and headed straight to the kitchen table. I sat down before she could protest."

"What did she say?"

"Nothing. I had to tell her to get the bowls, so we could eat while the stew was hot. She stared at me for a good minute, and then grabbed some bowls out of her cupboard, a couple of spoons too, and took a seat without saying a word.

"Once we started on the food, I told her about myself and started pelting her with questions. Her answers weren't too detailed, but I didn't push. We've been friends ever since. I drank both beers that night 'cause, of course, she refused to imbibe. I woke up with a headache the next day, because I'm normally a one-beer gal, but I had made a friend."

Henrietta broke into laughter all over again as she told the story to Jubilant, and he couldn't help but laugh with her. Her cackle was contagious. Suddenly, the remedy showed up.

"Shh! Both of you! You're making too much noise in my library." LaDelle stood behind them, lips pursed, hands on her hips. Then she reached into her dress pocket, took out a handkerchief and casually dabbed her red and swollen eyes like nothing was wrong.

Miss Henrietta covered her mouth with her hand for a second to hide the smile on her face. Then she pretended to be put out.

"Holy mackerel! Don't go shushin' me, LaDelle Harris, you big pill!" She stood up and gave her friend a quick, playful peck on the cheek before turning to leave. "Tsk, tsk. Don't be such a grumpy old lady. I brought you good news today, so lighten up for goodness' sake." She then blew a kiss at Jubilant and was gone.

Jubilant was shocked Henrietta got away with talking to his aunt like that, but the fact she did made him like her all the more.

CHAPTER NINETEEN—HABITS

Habit is habit, and not to be flung out of the window
by any man, but coaxed downstairs a step at a time.
(Mark Twain)

As if her day hadn't been strange enough already, an
hour after Henrietta's visit to the library, the electrical
power went out in the building. LaDelle had every intention
of keeping the library open until normal closing hours, but
she was overruled. Eugene came from the administration
office to tell her several buildings on campus were having
power issues and they wanted her to close for the day. For
once, LaDelle didn't argue. While she was waiting for the
last of the patrons to gather their books and go, she quickly
jotted two lists on scraps of paper—one for the grocery store
and one for Jubilant.

"Here's your chore list for the afternoon," she told him,
waving one of the pieces of paper in his face as soon as
they drove up to her house. LaDelle kept the car running
and her foot on the brake. She told Jubilant where she hid
the front door key, adding, "Wipe your feet and let yourself
in. You may have an apple or a piece of bread with honey
if you're hungry, but then get busy on those chores. I'll be
home shortly."

Jubilant read over the list and held his breath before
letting out an exaggerated puff of air. "Yes, ma'am."

"I'm just heading to the store to buy more food—again." The truth was, she really didn't mind the chore of grocery shopping these days. She went more often than usual now that she had to feed Jubilant, but she found herself looking forward to the opportunity to run into Abel Fisher. Just seeing the Piggly Wiggly sign gave her a little lift in her day. More often than not, Abel seemed to go out of his way to interact with her, and she found herself disappointed when they weren't able to engage in a little banter. Of course, sometimes he was attending to other things, as he should be doing as manager. Still, she found herself slowing down—haggling with Marvin longer than she needed to or spending a few extra minutes examining the fruits and vegetables—to give Abel extra time to come over and say hello at least.

On the drive to the Piggly Wiggly, LaDelle thought back to earlier at the library. *What if Henrietta had brought different news today? How would I be right now if I had found out that I not only lost my brother, but, as the only living blood relative, was obliged to raise Jubilant? Would I have been able to summon my courage and do the right thing?*

The thought gnawed at her as she continued to drive. Then she prayed, *Lord, I really must learn to trust you. Even though you allowed Garvin to be killed. Even though I don't always understand what you are doing and why. You have to help me to learn to trust you because this worrying is sure to do me in and send me to an early grave.*

She pulled into the dirt lot, parked, and read over her shopping list. LaDelle did so with two opposing emotions—excitement over another trip to the Piggly Wiggly and dread over what the total bill would come out to be. She recounted the money in her wallet to be sure she'd correctly counted the night before. Then, she took out her compact to take a quick glance at her face and reapply some lipstick.

"Oh, I look terrible! There are tear streaks on my face from earlier." She took out her handkerchief and scrubbed the sides of her face with it. Then she pinched her cheeks and applied some lipstick with a light touch—the tube of Sassy Summer Rose was nearly melted from the heat of the car.

The thought occurred to her she'd better get on with her shopping and hurry back to the house. She didn't fully trust Jubilant to be home alone, yet she took this chance and left him because she was desperate for a few moments to be alone and think. She also figured after what he pulled the day before, he'd be on his best behavior—at least for a while.

"I heard the Institute is dealing with some sort of power issue."

LaDelle recognized the voice behind her as soon as she entered the store. She smoothed her hair and turned around. "Word travels fast," she said to Abel Fisher, looking fine in his crisp white shirt and green tie.

"Miss Phoebe Barnes was in a little earlier, and I heard her tell some folks about it. I believe she works in the administration building."

"Yes, that's right," LaDelle said flatly. She wondered if he talked with Phoebe very often. *She is much younger than Abel—and me. Prettier than me too. I wonder what other young women he chats with as they shop in his store.*

"Well, I'm sorry your library was affected as well, but it sure is a pleasure to see you here this afternoon."

LaDelle studied his face for moment. He flashed a handsome smile and had a playful twinkle in his eye. She forgot about the possibility of other women. Suddenly, she realized what he said as his words soaked in.

"So, you're aware that I am the librarian on campus? I wasn't sure you knew."

"Well, now, LaDelle Harris," he grinned again. "I do know a bit about you—from Henrietta mostly." Then he leaned in closer and said, just above a whisper, "But I'm hoping you might allow me the opportunity to get to know you better firsthand—in the near future."

LaDelle's face grew warm. She didn't know what to say, but a schoolgirl-like giggle escaped her lips before she could stop it. Embarrassed, she turned her gaze at the shopping list in her hand and hoped he couldn't see that her heart was nearly beating out of her chest. When she managed to look up at him, Abel was staring right at her, grinning. He winked, gave her arm a soft pat, and walked past her, leaving her standing there like a slack-jawed statue.

A few seconds later, when another shopper passed her in the aisle, LaDelle remembered where she was and why she'd come. She grabbed a basket from the corner and floated through the store, taking items from her list off the shelf. Her head was so full of ponderings about Abel Fisher she forgot to complain to Marvin about the price of pork chops. When she took the package of meat wrapped in butcher paper from him, she noticed he looked disappointed and guessed he had hoped for more of an exchange.

"You know," LaDelle said with exaggerated indignation. "I'm thinking of getting myself a pig. That way I won't have to drive all the way over here and pay these crazy prices."

"That a fact?" Marvin asked, peering down at her through his reading glasses. "You do that," Marvin shook his head and made a *hmmph* sound.

LaDelle smiled to herself and headed for the checkout line.

"You just may have to go out and find yourself a job," LaDelle announced the next morning as she stood cooking at the stove.

More work? Jubilant already had a list of chores to do at the house each day and another list of tasks to do at the library. He surprised even himself how responsible he was becoming, getting things done and doing them right. Most of the time. The reverend would say that Aunt LaDelle's military ways had whupped him into shape, though he was thankful no actual whupping had taken place. Now he was supposed to find a job and earn money? He'd seen a family digging out of a dumpster behind the Piggly Wiggly a few days before. He overheard the clerk and some lady at the checkout talking about how Alabama seems doomed. Cursed even. "Dang Depression is still hittin' us hard," they said. He wondered how it was hitting Aunt LaDelle.

"Are you joshin' me? You expect me to get a job when so many people can't hold on to the ones they have?" Jubilant said with an exaggerated look of fatigue on his face.

"I'm just saying I can't keep up with your appetite, and all your letter writing is costing me a fortune in stamps!"

He could tell she really didn't mean for him to get a job. She beamed with pride every time he cleaned his plate, and when he handed her a letter to mail to the reverend. Lately, because even Jubilant was proud of the words he thought to write on paper, he left each envelope unsealed. More than once lately, he had peeked around the corner from the hallway and witnessed Aunt LaDelle helping herself to the envelope and reading his letters to Daddy. He didn't mind though. As she read, she smiled and sometimes nodded or slapped her knee, but always silently.

As Jubilant savored every bite of his buttery grits and leftover ham, he thought over what the day might hold for him. Would he see Professor Carver today? He rubbed his head as he thought over the possibility.

"I wonder what brought on that habit of yours." Aunt LaDelle said as she leaned against the kitchen counter and sipped her coffee.

"What habit?"

"What do you mean, 'what habit'? Rubbing your head the way you do. Don't you even know you're doing it?"

"At least I don't bite my nail or cuss," Jubilant said defensively. "Don't *you* have any habits?"

"Course not," LaDelle replied, putting her hand on her hip.

Jubilant stared at her familiar stance, then threw his head back and laughed.

"What's so funny?" LaDelle demanded. She put her coffee cup down now and dug both hands further into her hips while stomping her foot on the floor.

He shook his head, unable to stop grinning. The sight of his perturbed aunt, and the fact she had no idea she possessed this habit, was comical. "Your habit is you get mad easily," he said pointing at her, and his giggles returned. "Look at you standin' that way!"

LaDelle's mouth flung open, and she was about to get after her bold nephew when she stopped herself. Her hands dropped to her side, and she cracked a smile, but it didn't last. Her face soon grew serious, and her eyes looked moist. She pulled a chair out and plopped herself down.

"Truth is, I wasn't always like this," she said with a sigh. She took another sip of coffee, and silently fingered the rim of the cup a few times. "When my husband Garvin was alive, I had my temperamental moments, to be sure, but I was better at catching myself and being more even-tempered. When he died, I suppose something inside of me died too—my sense of humor, I guess. I became more impatient and less tolerant. Henrietta has pointed out to me more than once I try to control things I can't possibly control. She keeps telling me, 'Surrender, LaDelle!' She's so silly sometimes. I hate it when she's right, but she's right about this."

"How did he die—your husband?" Jubilant asked because he truly wanted to know, though he wasn't sure if it was all right to ask. *What if it's too painful for her to talk about? What if the question upsets her more and she starts to cry?*

"Remember I told you we owned a little diner in Brooklyn with Garvin's brother?" She began.

Jubilant nodded and leaned forward with his elbows on the table.

"When we were closing up one evening, Ben, one of our dishwashers, showed up at the back door. He hadn't come in to work that day, so we were forced to work late, doing the work of his shift and getting the place ready for the next morning. And then, all of a sudden, there was Ben, barely able to stand up straight. He was drunk as a skunk." LaDelle stopped talking for a moment and looked down at the table as if she was seeing Ben's face in the tablecloth. She shook her head as she looked up again at her nephew.

Jubilant nodded, silently urging her to continue.

"Well, Garvin let him come right on in and asked me to make Ben some coffee, so we could help sober him up. Before we knew what was happening, though, he pulled a gun on us."

Jubilant's eyes grew wide. He didn't expect that detail. "A gun?"

"My Garvin tried to calm him down, but Ben was yelling and crying at the same time, waving the gun around. He was saying through slurred words he was sorry, but he needed more money, and he couldn't earn it fast enough, so we needed to give him what we had, blah, blah, blah. He went on and on, but we stayed silent, afraid to interrupt him, and preferring he keep talking and not start shooting."

"Holy Moses! I would've been too scared to do anything!"

"Finally, Garvin was able to quiet Ben and talk him out of robbing us. He kept saying, 'We can help you, Ben, we'll do what we can, buddy. You don't have to do this,' and Ben finally stopped all his yelling. He calmed down, and it seemed like he was willing to hand over the gun, but just as Garvin reached for it, Ben pulled the trigger—or the gun just went off—I'm not sure which. Garvin was shot in the chest. He lost a lot of blood. He died a few hours later."

LaDelle stopped speaking and took a handkerchief from her apron pocket. She dabbed her eyes and blew her nose. After telling her story, she sighed loudly as if just speaking about what happened wore her out. "That was nine years ago, but it still breaks me up."

"Did the cops catch Ben? Did he go to jail?"

"Yes, Ben was convicted in a court of law and sent to prison, but he died three months later in his cell. Cancer. His widow told me he knew he was dying, and he was worried about her and the kids being taken care of after he passed on. In all his pain and worry, he started drinking more and more. That's why he came to rob us that night. He was trying to store up enough money to care for his family after he passed away. Fool man. Didn't he know we would rally around his family? He should have known that."

Jubilant looked down at his feet. What could he say? The reverend never told him Aunt LaDelle's story, so how could he have known? After a few moments of thick silence, Jubilant looked up and locked eyes with his aunt's. "Mama used to rub my head and hum to me when I couldn't sleep at night."

"Oh, I see. So that's why you rub your head when something upsets you. Hmmm. Well now, we all need comforting from time to time. All of us. I suppose we never grow out of the need to be comforted when we're sad or hurting."

Jubilant reached out and laid his hand on his aunt's arm resting on the table. She put her other hand on top of his and gave his arm a tender squeeze. They nodded at each other and left their hands in place, each enjoying the warmth and affection of the other. Tears stung their eyes. Jubilant refused to blink, but LaDelle gave in and some flowed down her cheek. She pulled her handkerchief out of her pocket, wiped her eyes, and blew her nose.

"I guess I never thought of it before. Even old people need comforting sometimes," Jubilant said.

LaDelle grinned. "Yes, boy, even old people."

Jubilant then added, "That's why I'm writin' the reverend so many letters."

"Letters can be mighty comforting and writing them is the sort of habit more people should grab hold of." LaDelle smiled at her nephew in a new way. Her body was relaxed, her expression soft. "To me, you seem much happier around here, since you've taken your letter writing seriously. You're starting to live up to your name. Jubilant."

Jubilant grinned, embarrassed but pleased with his aunt's words. He had been feeling more joyful and less angry and frustrated. He just hadn't thought about it until that moment. "I'm already on letter number sixteen," he said, sitting up tall in his chair, "but I'm runnin' out of things to write about."

"Oh, that's a bunch of hogwash! Keep your ears and eyes open, and you'll get some ideas," LaDelle said. She pushed her chair back and stood up. She walked over to the hook next to the refrigerator and grabbed her keys. "It's time you and I left for work."

Pulling out of the driveway, they spotted Harold as he delivered the mail to Cal and Henrietta's house. "Can we wait a minute until he reaches your place? I want to see if a letter came today."

LaDelle glanced at her watch, and then drummed her fingers on the steering wheel. "Hurry it up, Harold," she muttered under her breath. She honked the horn, startling the aging postman as he made his way across her front lawn. He shook his head and muttered to himself. Jubilant quickly rolled down his window.

"You're early today," Jubilant commented as he received a few pieces of mail from Harold and thanked him. He quickly looked at each envelope as LaDelle drove off toward Tuskegee Institute. And then he saw it—a letter from the reverend in Priscilla's handwriting. He kept it on his lap and rubbed his head a few times. Aunt LaDelle didn't ask him to read it—she seemed to understand. As nice as it was to receive a letter, they never came with a guarantee of good news.

CHAPTER TWENTY—
GETTING IT DOWN ON PAPER

More than kisses, letters mingle souls. (John Donne)

Dear Son,

I'm home from the hospital as you by now are aware. Priscilla insisted on penning this correspondence for me, and her mama continues to keep me well fed. They are spoiling me to be sure!

I have read and reread your letters many times, because I miss you terribly. Your letters have become increasingly more interesting and enjoyable. I thank you, and I would thank the postman for delivering me such joy, but I'm still not getting out much. I find myself cooped up like a caged animal most days. I spend too many hours sleeping due to a lack of vitality. When I am awake, I am kept busy reading the Bible and coming up with sermon ideas. I long to get back to the pulpit! God has afflicted me for a reason. Perhaps my best sermons will come about as a result of this physical weakness I have endured.

As to the question of your name, I have an answer. Your mama and I had big hopes for you before you were even born. Our dreams for you weren't for riches or power. We longed for our son to simply know joy. We wanted our child to experience a joyous life and express that joy to others. You have had your challenges, so this has not been easy to live out thus far, but I'm confident you are being shaped by the Creator, as your friend says, and that your name and your life will reflect each other. Joy, by the way, often follows thankfulness.

Thank you again for your wonderful letters. I can tell you have a gift for writing.

With joy,
Your loving father

P.S. Priscilla-the-Gorilla here. Your daddy is doing much better. His favorite part of the day is when he receives one of your letters. Maybe you can write me one too?

As soon as Jubilant had finished reading the letter for the third time—twice to himself and once to Aunt LaDelle—they arrived at the Institute, and she pulled into the parking lot. After receiving his aunt's permission, he bolted out of the car and dashed over to Professor Carver's.

"That's a fine letter," Professor Carver said after Jubilant read it out loud to him. The professor had been sitting in his cushioned chair quietly listening and knitting. "So, is Priscilla sweet on you?"

"What? No! 'Course not. She's just my next-door neighbor, that's all. Gee whiz!"

Professor Carver smiled but kept his eyes on his knitting. Jubilant decided to not make too big of a fuss about his friend's comment, or it really would seem as if he did like Priscilla. The truth was he did sort of miss her and her bossy attitude. Maybe a little. He also missed hearing her sing as she hung her family's clothes on the line to dry. Her voice was soulful, like it was coming out of a grown woman and not a thirteen-year-old girl. For a few seconds he tried to hear her voice in his head, remembering how she sang "A-Tisket, A-Tasket." *Maybe I should send her a letter. Just a short one. I ought to thank her for what she is doing for the reverend.*

Jubilant stared for a moment at the letter in his hand. He was relieved when Professor Carver invited him to spend part of the day in his laboratory. The library, even though it was a large building, seemed to shrink in size some days and box him in. He and his aunt were making peace with each other, to be sure, but she still drove him crazy sometimes.

"It *is* a fine letter," Jubilant said, responding to Professor Carver's remark, "but the reverend didn't mention when I could come home. I could help him better than Priscilla any day of the week. She's a pain!"

"You are helping him. Don't you see that, son? Your father sounds like a wise man. He'll call for you when the time is right. In the meantime, keep writing your letters." Finally looking up from his knitting needles, he added, "They seem to be bringing healing to his heart."

Jubilant sat mesmerized for a moment watching Professor Carver as he added a row to whatever it was he was knitting. "I bet he still doesn't trust me to stay out of trouble, but I've been doing pretty darn good here in Tuskegee, don't you think?"

Professor Carver nodded and kept right on clicking his needles while balancing the ball of moss-colored yarn on his lap.

"I've never seen a man knit before. I thought that was just for girls," Jubilant said, cracking a smile.

"Aunt Sue taught me when I was just a boy," the old man replied. "I'm making some socks for a friend of mine. I crochet and embroider, too." He stopped to count his stitches, and then continued. "I was sickly and weak as a child, so she kept me inside the house working with her much of the time while my brother Jim was outside working with Uncle Mose."

"What else did you do when you were a child?" Jubilant removed a stack of papers from a stool and sat down as he waited for the professor's answer.

"Laundry," George laughed. "Lots of laundry!" He talked about running a laundry business when he moved away from the Carver farm. "That skill allowed me to support myself and pay for my books and even college when I grew older. But mostly, when I was a child, I did what I do now—I spent time with plants and soil and nature. That intrigued me most of all."

"That's why you teach people about rotating their crops and keeping their soil fertile and such, right? Aunt LaDelle told me that."

"That's part of it, yes."

"You should be a rich fella with all those bulletins you write and the discoveries you've made, but it doesn't seem to me you have much money at all." Jubilant looked down at the floor after he said it, hoping he hadn't offended his friend.

Professor Carver laughed at Jubilant's right conclusion. "I don't charge for information that the Creator gives me for free. Many folks have it wrong, my boy. It is not the style of clothes one wears nor the amount of money one has in the bank, that counts. Service measures success."

Listening to him talk about his life and ideas gave Jubilant an idea of his own. He turned over the reverend's letter and began taking notes on what Professor Carver was telling him. He asked questions and carefully wrote down the answers.

"Aunt LaDelle told me you're a famous artist. Are your paintings in a museum? I went to a museum once. In New York. Daddy made me go with him. We walked around for hours."

Professor Carver laughed. "No, son. I am far from being a famous artist. Some of my paintings were displayed at the World's Columbian Exhibition in Chicago, but that was ages ago."

Jubilant nodded and wrote down the professor's words.

"Are you some sort of reporter now?" the professor asked with a chuckle.

"I just want to tell the reverend some interesting facts about you, that's all." Jubilant finished writing about the professor's art and put down his pencil. He looked around the room, trying not to seem like he was snooping when a picture of a soldier caught his eye. "Is he a friend of yours?"

"I don't know him personally. A while back, I worked with the War Department to help come up with the best way to feed soldiers during the Great War."

Jubilant's eyes grew wide. "And?"

"Well, I figured out an effective way to mass-produce dehydrated fruits and vegetables and send them to the American troops. That feller there," he pointed to the photograph, "sent me his photo along with a thank you note. Wasn't that nice of him? He said he especially enjoyed the dehydrated apricots. They're my favorite too."

Jubilant shook his head, amazed at what he learned about his friend. Professor Carver never bragged, but he spoke of his thankfulness over what he was able to achieve. He also talked about his own letter writing and how important his family and friends were to him. He said when he lived in Kansas, he wasn't receiving much mail. It turns out another George Carver lived in the same town, and most of Professor Carver's mail was being delivered to the wrong George Carver. That's when he decided to add a "W" to his name.

"Someone asked me if it stood for Washington. I thought, 'why not?' so I told him 'Sure' and from that day on it did."

Jubilant soaked up the professor's stories, coaxing information out of him like a reporter for the *Tuskegee News* and wrote as fast as he could until he got a cramp in his hand. *Wouldn't the reverend get a kick out of reading about*

George Washington Carver? He would write it all down for him in a letter. There were enough interesting facts to write a book!

The soreness in Jubilant's hand soon subsided thanks to the ointment the professor insisted he try. He made the ointment out of peanuts.

"Rub some of it in your hair as well. It will restore its moisture and shine," he urged. He then handed Jubilant a few fresh pieces of paper, and the two of them spent the rest of the afternoon working side by side in the laboratory— George looking at plant samples through a microscope, and Jubilant writing what he had learned about Professor Carver in a long letter to the reverend. They worked in silence but kept each other company. They lost track of time together. It was a good day. Jubilant would review their time together in his mind when he went to bed that night. He figured thinking on it before sleep came would give him good dreams.

CHAPTER TWENTY-ONE—SURRENDER

It is wonderful what miracle God works in wills that are utterly surrendered to Him. (Hannah Whitall Smith)

"Morning, Miss Emma," LaDelle greeted the pastor's daughter as she entered the church building. "Nice to see you, Mr. Johnson. Looks like you're feeling better." She greeted the elderly man.

"I am, Mrs. Harris. Thank you for that delicious chicken soup you sent over. I'll get your pot over to you sometime this week."

"That'll be fine," LaDelle said and continued walking down the aisle. She quietly greeted a few others she passed as she made her way to her regular spot—third pew from the front, right-hand side, middle. This seat provided a clear line of vision of the minister and choir, though with her height and stature, together with her Sunday hat, LaDelle Harris's presence was sure to provide an obstruction to those seated directly behind her.

She adjusted her hat discreetly then smoothed out her dress as other church members filed past her all a-flutter, greeting one another with hugs and kisses on the cheek and admiring each other's hats and Sunday bests. The men doled out pats on the back and handshakes as if congratulating one another for living another day. They joked with each other and laughed at a volume suitable for church.

Cherie from the Piggly Wiggly came up from behind and whispered in her ear. "Good to see you, Miss LaDelle. Been seeing a lot of you lately." She gave LaDelle's shoulder a quick squeeze, giggled, smacked her gum, and left to sit at a pew across the aisle. LaDelle's face grew hot with embarrassment. *At least, she had the decency to whisper.*

LaDelle was born an introvert. She was most comfortable in settings that didn't require her to interact with others in overly demonstrative ways or could at least do so on her terms. She made a sincere effort at greeting folks each Sunday, and she inquired with genuine concern about those who were ill or injured. Then she'd excuse herself and head to her pew. Though LaDelle preferred not to engage in small talk, she was careful to put forth some effort to not be thought of as rude. She was also always careful to arrive early for the service. For one thing, she wanted to be sure to secure the seat in which she was accustomed to sitting. But another reason for her early arrival was her conviction that being late to such an important gathering was disrespectful, plain and simple. Being late might even be a sin in some indirect way. She hadn't decided.

Someone needed to convince Cal and Henrietta of that as they could be counted on to scurry in five, sometimes up to eight minutes, late each week. Even then, they never chose seats in the back, but made their way to the front of the church, filing into LaDelle's row. Henrietta would lead the way with Cal following behind her. She'd whisper "s'cuse us, pardon us" to those having to adjust their legs so they could shuffle past. Henrietta would move people over, if need be, so she could situate herself next to LaDelle on one side and Cal on the other.

Though this greatly irked and embarrassed LaDelle, she was also touched by it, admitting this solely to herself. *Only Henrietta could get away with such a thing. How did this outgoing, always affable woman—the opposite of me in almost all respects—come to be my friend?* This not only puzzled LaDelle, but most people in the congregation. Similar to her relationship with Garvin, others could tell this was an unlikely friendship, but LaDelle found herself growing more and more thankful for her relationship with Henrietta.

"If you didn't spend so much time on your hair, you'd be able to get to church on time," LaDelle once scolded Henrietta. Here was another thing she liked about Henrietta—LaDelle could speak her mind to her, and Henrietta not only took it but good-naturedly let her own mind be known as well. "You cover most of it with your hat anyway, for goodness' sake."

"Oh, hush!" Henrietta retorted. "I spend no more time on my hair than you do, though if you don't mind me saying your hair could use a little extra time and attention, honey. Anyway, you know my hair is my billboard. When people see my hair lookin' nice, they want me to take care of their own hair and just like that I drum up business."

"I suppose that's true," LaDelle conceded.

"Besides, we're late each week on account of Cal, not my hair. He gets lost in the Sunday paper, then he has to do his business on the can which seems to take him longer on Sundays than any other day of the week. After that, we dash to the car, but he drives to church like an old woman. If he'd let me drive, we'd arrive before you do, and you know that's the truth, girl!"

LaDelle never knew what was going to come out of Henrietta's mouth, but she'd learned to not be surprised by her free-spiritedness.

On this day, before the service started, LaDelle had given Jubilant permission to sit with Wilson and his family who almost always sat on the left side of the sanctuary at the end. Both boys had run up to her, making their request with pleading eyes.

"Can I sit with Wilson today?" Jubilant asked.

"*May* I," his aunt corrected him.

"My parents said he can," Wilson added, ignoring LaDelle's grammar lesson.

LaDelle studied both boys' faces. They were that—little boys. Wilson's round, chubby face made him look younger than Jubilant. She noticed for the first time they weren't so far away from becoming young men. Jubilant's face had sprouted a faint shadow of facial hair above his lips. He was markedly taller, reaching in height to her chin.

"I suppose that's fine with me," she finally offered and shooed them on, batting the air with the back of her hand. "Go directly to your seats. Service is going to start soon."

LaDelle wasn't worried about Jubilant squirming or causing mischief with Wilson. Robert Doyle would see to that. She watched them go and made sure they took their seats straight away.

She was surprised a little while later, though, at the feelings that welled up inside her as she sat between Henrietta at her right and Harold the mailman, who dozed off just minutes after he sat down, to her left. She wondered what it would be like to sit next to Abel Fisher. *Perhaps he had a rich baritone singing voice. His speaking voice is low so there's a good possibility of it. Maybe he smelled especially nice on Sundays. He seemed the type to wear cologne. Why was he a Presbyterian?*

LaDelle stole a quick glance at Jubilant sitting with the Doyles and fanned herself as a distraction from her disappointment at not having Jubilant by her side. She'd gotten used to his presence these past summer Sundays. The week before, her nephew had taken it upon himself to hold the hymnal at arm's reach, making sure she could read it along with him. She smiled to herself when his voice cracked as he sang, "He Leadeth Me," and she noticed he didn't even glance at the hymnal as they sang all four verses of "It Is Well with My Soul." *He must know it by heart. Perhaps my brother sings it to him regularly.*

She formed a picture in her mind of her younger brother, now a man, with a young man of his own to raise. *How did time fly so fast?* She regretted not spending more time with Ashton while they lived just twenty miles apart in New York, but she was busy with her life before Garvin, and then with him as his wife and partner at the diner. By the time she had become a widow, Ashton was busy with his family and congregation. Then, of course, the loss of his own wife. They had more in common now they were both adults. They shared the hole of losing someone they loved, but he also lost the mother of his child.

She remembered how their own mother would sing "Silent Night" as a bedtime song not just at Christmas, but all year long. "It's the perfect lullaby," she'd say. As LaDelle grew up she had to agree. "Sleep in heavenly peace, sleep in heavenly peace ..." *Such soothing lyrics.* If she had been blessed with a child of her own, she would have sung it to him or her each night as her mother had done. She tried singing it to Dewey once, but he practically galloped to the back door and scratched on it until she let him out. Singing was not her gift.

Funny how a mind can wander—bouncing from one thought to another—while waiting for church to begin. At that thought, Wilma Blaucher, the minister's wife as well as the organist, pianist, and trumpet player all in one, began to play the organ, signaling the start of service.

As she tried to reel in her mind and focus on worship, LaDelle suddenly realized the feelings that had formed in her heart for her nephew revealed she no longer feared his presence—perhaps even appreciated it. She no longer resented the responsibility of him and the threat of possible chaos he could incite. In fact, she was beginning to embrace and enjoy his presence.

Recently one morning, he expressed his own appreciation for her and how she cared for him.

"I haven't tasted much of other folks' food around here, but I say you must be the best cook in all of Tuskegee, Aunt LaDelle."

"Well, thank you very much, Jubilant. That's kind of you to say."

"And you give generous portions," he added with a smile as he held out his plate for more bread pudding.

Of course, she couldn't refuse him a second helping after that compliment, so she loaded him up with another hearty spoonful. "Last night, you had seconds of the chipped beef on toast. You're going to bust out of those britches before we know it." Her voice was scolding, but they both smiled at each other. She had awakened his appetite, and he looked healthier and happier than when he had arrived.

These thoughts had grazed her mind days before, just after she had told him about Garvin's death. The tenderness he showed her by placing his hand on hers touched her heart. This display of attentive thoughtfulness was quite different from the child she'd picked up at the train station in June. *He's family. I have a family to invest in. To love. But this could get complicated.* As she pondered these things, the choir director instructed the congregation to stand and turn to page 397 in the hymnal. "I Surrender All."

"We'll sing all five verses." Surrender. LaDelle was learning. With surrender to the Lord come peace and blessing. *Help me, Lord. I want to do better in this area.*

After church, Jubilant was invited to spend the afternoon with Wilson. The Doyles extended the invitation to LaDelle, but she politely declined. God was calling her to think on some things, and she couldn't do that around a dining room table full of folks. This was an opportunity to have time alone and think. A nagging, internal urgency caused a sense of restlessness, compelling her not to put this pondering off any longer. She needed to get home, be alone, and do business with her Maker. Though she gave no explanation other than to say, "I could use some time by my lonesome, if you don't mind." Patty took no offense, and though she couldn't understand completely, she was smart enough to figure LaDelle, a single widow who was not used to having a child around, could use a break—a Sabbath alone.

"Take the time you need, LaDelle. Keeping Wilson busy with a friend is a help to us," she said, but then added, "I'll come by later with Jubilant. Maybe we can visit a while."

"Sure," LaDelle responded flatly, thinking, *Since when is 'by my lonesome' an invitation for company?*

CHAPTER TWENTY-TWO— IT HAPPENED ON A SUNDAY

Surprise is the greatest gift life can grant us.
(Boris Pasternak)

"You're looking shabby, boy. Like a ragamuffin." As usual Aunt LaDelle spoke her mind, but over the past two months, Jubilant had learned to accept it with no hard feelings. "Give me those breeches tonight and let me patch the knees. I think I'd better take them out some at the waist as well. You truly are starting to bust out of them."

"Yes, ma'am," he agreed. He secretly wished he could buy some new clothes like Miss Patty bought Wilson a few days before. He looked like a real proper human with his fresh clothes and his hair buzzed off. Wilson said his mama inherited five acres of land somewhere over in Troy and some money from an uncle who died—and she barely knew him! She used some of the money to purchase a pair of new shoes, trousers, and two shirts for Wilson. She bought fabric to make two dresses for Lydia and one for herself. Mr. Doyle was given the radio he'd had his eye on since spring. She also bought him new suspenders, though he said he didn't want them and told her not to waste her money.

Wilson passed all this important news on to Jubilant, but added, "Don't let Mama know I told you all this. She won't like it. She said folks don't need to know of our good fortune when they're hurtin' so bad, but I figured I could tell you. Besides, Mama's been tellin' all sorts of people herself!"

"This windfall of good fortune came just in the nick, I'll tell you that," Patty told LaDelle and Henrietta as they chattered together on the back patio over sweet tea. She lifted her head and waved her fan under her neck to try and cool off on this sweltering late August afternoon.

LaDelle realized ever since the backyard dinner, and due to Wilson and Jubilant's friendship, she and Patty began spending more time together. They'd been neighbors for years, but they'd never shared a meal or much of a conversation prior to this summer.

"My Wilson would have been walkin' around town naked as a jaybird if some money hadn't come in and soon. That boy seems to be growing an inch a day."

"Mama! Don't use that word. You're embarrassing me," Wilson scowled as he scolded his mother.

"What word? Naked?"

Wilson let out a growl and plugged his ears with his fingers. He shook his head in disgust.

The women cackled like hens at this exchange and fanned themselves. They took sips of their tea and laughed some more.

"You know what else seems to be growing?" Henrietta had a mischievous look on her face as she asked the question.

"What?" the two other women said in unison.

"LaDelle and Abel Fisher's fondness for each other!"

"What? You hush, now! You don't know what you're talking about." LaDelle sat up straight, shocked by her friend's outburst, and then shot Henrietta a stern look, which she ignored. LaDelle batted her hand in the air toward her, and then added, "You're ridiculous."

"Is that true?" Patty asked. "You and Abel Fisher? He's a handsome one."

"Of course, it's true!" Henrietta said. "He never carries *my* groceries out to *my* car. Whenever he sees me at the PW, though, he asks about my neighbor, LaDelle. Those two are being brought together by a divine force, you just watch."

"Henrietta, I don't know what possesses you to blurt out such things. I think you are plum crazy."

"We'll just see," Henrietta said, and then blew a playful kiss in LaDelle's direction. "We'll just see."

LaDelle didn't want to egg her on, though she was curious if what she said about Abel was true. Had he been inquiring about her?

"I did hear," Patty weighed in, "that he drives to Notulsaga early each Sunday morning to attend church with his mama and sister."

"Yes, I know that to be a fact," Henrietta chimed in. "They go to the Presbyterian church over there. Abel teaches the adult Sunday School class. After church, he and his family have Sunday supper together."

LaDelle nodded but kept silent. *I could tell somehow he was a God-fearing man, but a Sunday School teacher? For adults? He must be a Bible scholar. How attractive.* She was careful to keep a neutral look on her face, but inside she was smiling. "Well, aren't you two in the know about everything."

"You know it, LaDelle," Henrietta said proudly. "I'm just looking out for you. I want to make sure your man is a good one."

"Henrietta!" LaDelle sounded mad, but she couldn't hide a smile. She liked the sound of that—'your man.'

"To make him darn near perfect for you, I heard he's a big-time reader, and no one could deny he's a top-notch manager. We have the best run Piggly Wiggly in Tuskegee."

With that last comment, all three women laughed since it was the only PW in Tuskegee.

"All right now, you've said enough," LaDelle told her friend. "Aren't you just full of trouble and sass today."

Henrietta gave a playful wink to LaDelle. "Every day, honey. *Every day*."

LaDelle decided to change the subject to spare herself any more embarrassment, but part of her wanted to keep talking about Abel. He'd been on her mind a lot lately. *I ought to stop at the Piggly Wiggly tomorrow for some fruit. For the boy. To keep him healthy.*

LaDelle glanced over at Henrietta as the women enjoyed each other's company and continued sipping on their tea. Something about her made LaDelle stare a while. Henrietta looked different somehow, but LaDelle couldn't identify what it was.

"Henrietta, what's going on with you?"

"S'cuse me?" Henrietta replied, then raised her chin so she could fan her moist neck.

"Something about you is different. I thought so the other day as well. I just didn't say anything, but I'm seeing it again. What is it?"

"Now you're the one who's crazy, LaDelle. I'm the same as I always been—young and beautiful!" She said, fluffing her hair and batting her eyes at her neighbor.

"I'll figure it out," LaDelle said, narrowing her own eyes as if she were a sleuth on an assignment. "Give me time. I'll figure it out."

"You do that, honey," Henrietta smirked. "I'm just a little tired is all. Ain't you ever tired? I think it's been a full moon. I never sleep right during a full moon."

"You do look a bit fatigued, but there's something more ..."

"I think Henrietta looks the same as always. No wonder Mr. Cal can't take his eyes—and hands—off her," Patty chimed in.

LaDelle decided to drop it for the time being, but she couldn't dismiss a feeling brewing in her mind regarding her friend.

"Changing the subject, what do you plan on doin' with Jubilant?" Patty asked LaDelle. "School will be starting soon. S'pose you ought to register the boy? His daddy may not be ready to receive him in time to get him back to school in Huntsville."

LaDelle had been thinking about that, often in the middle of the night. "I'm sure Jubilant will be able to go back to his own school by the time it starts," she told Patty, loud enough for her nephew to hear. But the truth was, she wasn't sure at all. She planned to call the school superintendent early in the week to register him just in case.

Wilson and Jubilant played fetch with Dewey in the backyard, mostly out of earshot of the women on the porch, though Jubilant heard every word about school. He knew she didn't want him to take on the added worry of having to fit in at a new school. As the boys played with the dog, Lydia sat on a blanket Miss Patty laid out for her in the shade.

"Why are you feedin' your doll a stick?" Jubilant called out to Lydia who was holding her dolly in her arms and put a twig up to the baby's mouth.

"I'm pretendin' it's her bottle. Can't you tell?" Lydia rolled her eyes, and then looked down and whispered something to the doll. It had only one leg and wore a stained pink dress, but Lydia didn't seem to mind. "And her name's not 'baby,' it's 'Crystal Rose'," she said as if she'd been insulted. "She may not be the prettiest, but she should still have a pretty name. That's what Mama said."

The boys laughed at the indignation in her voice. Their making fun sent the little girl running to her mother for support and comfort.

Dewey wagged his tail and seemed to enjoy sharing his backyard with the children and the activity they brought with them. He was fetching the ball one of the boys had thrown when Jubilant noticed the dog stop short. Dewey cocked his ears and began to bark.

Aunt LaDelle hushed him a few times, but Dewey ignored her and kept his gaze at the back door. His barking seemed to grow louder as if he were shouting an announcement of great importance.

"Maybe he hears the doorbell. Go see if someone's at the front door, would you, Jubilant?" Aunt LaDelle said, fanning herself and shooting her dog a curious look.

"Yes, ma'am," he said and told Dewey more than once to "hush" as they made their way through the kitchen and into the living room to the front door. Dewey's tail wagged with force as his barking continued. Jubilant swung open the door with one hand while keeping the other one holding on tightly to Dewey's collar.

"Hello, Jube," a voice said from the other side of the screen door. The reverend's eyes beamed at the sight of his son.

"Daddy? What are you doin' here? How did you get here?" Without thinking, Jubilant let go of Dewey's collar as the reverend pulled open the screen and stepped into the house. Dewey sniffed the reverend's leg and let out another bark. Father and son looked each other over and then embraced. Then, to prove he was once again healthy, the reverend lifted Jubilant off the floor as they continued to hug. The reverend laughed, and tears filled Jubilant's eyes at the sound of it.

"Oh, you've grown so big, Son!"

Dewey leapt at both and his nonstop barking alerted LaDelle.

"Dewey, stop that barking right now, you hear me?" LaDelle called out in a stern voice as she entered the room. She froze at the sight of her brother standing in the middle of her living room just as sure as day. "Ashton!"

"LaDelle Harris, you don't look a day over twenty-nine!"

"Oh, shut up! You may be a preacher now, but you're still a liar!" LaDelle laughed and held out her arms. The reverend left Jubilant's side and rushed to embrace his sister.

"Well, from the look of things, I'd say the boy needs a haircut and bigger breeches, but it's obvious you did a pretty good job of looking after him."

"Watch your mouth now! I did a great job, I'll have you know." she said and pulled him in close. The two hugged again, and then stepped back and stared at each other, shaking their heads and grinning. "Why didn't you call and tell us you were coming?"

"I wanted to surprise you. Been a long time since we've seen each other, LaDelle."

"You know darn good and well that I'm not one for surprises, but I'm so happy to see you. I suppose your scaring us to death, and having a heart attack and pneumonia on top of that, caused this reconnection." She placed her hand on his cheek and said tenderly, "How are you feeling, Ashton?"

"I'm as strong as a mule, and yes, just as stubborn," the reverend added, anticipating his sister's next words.

Daddy was leaner than Jubilant had ever seen him before, though he remembered looking at pictures of him as a younger man and marveling at his thinness. He didn't seem as commanding as before, though his voice remained strong, almost booming.

While Daddy and Aunt LaDelle talked, Jubilant took a closer look at the reverend's appearance. His face was thinner, and his shirt collar was loose around his neck. He needed a shave. He looked a bit worn out. The long bus ride probably caused that. Daddy looked a little older.

In the two months father and son had been apart, changes had happened to them. Jubilant didn't mind having to loosen his belt. Gaining some weight and nearly an inch in height suited him, but something in him had changed beyond his physical appearance. He felt different inside, older and better. He'd become a real writer. Aunt LaDelle said he would make a fine reporter. With Daddy here now, Jubilant wondered if he'd go back to being just a kid. *Will I forget my responsible, helpful ways and fall back into my old habits that always bring on trouble? I better be careful, but no one's perfect. Professor Carver says, "There's grace for mistakes."*

"I've come to take my boy home. I hope he hasn't been much trouble."

"Trouble? This boy?" LaDelle put her hands on her hips and stared at her nephew and winked. "He has been no trouble at all, not at all."

Jubilant sighed with relief. He wasn't quite sure what Aunt LaDelle would say to the reverend, but her smile told him they had made peace with one another and had become family in the truest sense of the word.

"Take me home, and I'll prove it to you," Jubilant added. "I'll prove to you I can stay out of trouble and be responsible. I even make my bed now. As good as any soldier in the army."

After a few minutes of preliminary catching-up, and after Henrietta and Patty were introduced, the neighbors left for their own homes. LaDelle went into the kitchen and fixed a large bowl of collard greens and some sweet potato biscuits for her brother. She warmed up the last of the leftover fried chicken because she remembered he didn't care for chicken cold. The three sat at the table together talking and eating and telling each other some of what had transpired since they had been together last. The two siblings reminisced about their childhood and teased each other. Jubilant sat quietly chewing, soaking up their stories. A few times he reached out and placed his hand on his daddy's shoulder for a moment as if he needed to make sure he was real.

"We'll spend tonight and tomorrow here if that's fine by you, but then Jubilant and I will be boarding the bus back to Huntsville. The Amazing Grace Baptist Church has been mighty gracious to me, but they're ready to have their pastor back, and I'm ready to start fulfilling my role as their shepherd again."

The reverend paused long enough to eat another biscuit. "The good Lord has a way of getting your attention when you're lying in bed for days on end," he told them.

LaDelle hung on her brother's every word, nodding her head, and patting his hand from time to time.

Jubilant listened too as his daddy talked on about his heart attack and the changes his doctor told him he'd have to make to stay healthy.

"My doctor said I must have more exercise and eat less fried food." He grinned. "All my favorite foods, of course."

LaDelle soaked up these moments with her brother sitting at her kitchen table. Just days before she never could have imagined it. In addition to her surprise and relief, there was a sense of sadness in her as she realized how much she'd missed out on by not maintaining a relationship with her remaining sibling. He was a peer now, not a baby brother, and had been for many years. He could have been a friend, a support, and she could have been that to him as well.

An overwhelming sense of gratitude filled her, chasing away regrets as they talked and listened to one another. God was full of surprises bringing the two of them together again at this stage of their lives. She was both convicted and comforted. God was at work in her, and it was hard but good. LaDelle was different inside and wanted her outside actions to reflect the refining the good Lord had been doing in her heart during this summer with Jubilant. He'd been filling holes, talking to her straight, and providing for her in every way.

Ashton Bartley savored his sister's cooking with each bite from his full plate and surveyed her kitchen. They continued to exchange smiles and stories as he chewed. Her home was orderly and clean, tastefully adorned, and modest—just like her, he thought. He didn't realize until that moment he had missed her no-nonsense ways, but he also sensed a softness in her now that made her more attractive than he remembered her being when she was younger. Her countenance was different—older, yes, but gentler.

He'd always known she loved him, but her being a tough *deuxieme maman* who was harder on him than his own mama, caused him to not pursue much of a relationship with her once he'd grown up and left the house. Their reunion now brought further healing to him beyond the physical, as he had entertained anxious thoughts about his relationship with her over the years. During this summer, in particular. He hadn't been comfortable asking his sister to care for Jubilant, but Millie Hines pressed him to give her the name of a family member who could handle the job. LaDelle fit the bill for two reasons—she was experienced in handling boys and the chaos they could muster, and she was his only living relative.

He had dropped the ball keeping up a relationship with his sister, and as he sat at her kitchen table, that realization hit him afresh. A wave of sadness came over him. Before their visit was over, he told himself, he would confess his regret to her and ask her pardon. This reuniting of the two of them had turned out to be a welcome surprise for him. Who would have thought that so much good could come from a heart attack?

"Yes," he responded to LaDelle's offer of another biscuit, "I'll take one more, but no butter this time, please. I have to be careful now with what I eat. I'll tell you what, though—your cookin' is still *trés bonne*," he said with a wink, mimicking what their father would say after she'd fix the family a meal.

"*Merci, mon frère.*"

CHAPTER TWENTY-THREE—THE WAY A SEED GROWS

Start where you are with what you have. Make something
of it and never be satisfied. (George Washington Carver)

The next morning, Aunt LaDelle drove Jubilant and the
reverend to the Institute. "Look here to your left. That's Mr.
Booker T. Washington's former home called 'The Oaks'."

She played the role of tour guide with the reverend just as
she had done the first day Jubilant arrived in town. Jubilant
drummed his fingers on his lap and let out several loud
sighs. He wiggled in his seat. He wished his aunt would stop
talking and drive faster. He wanted to talk with Professor
Carver and let him know he would be leaving soon.

When they finally pulled into Tuskegee Institute's dirt
parking lot, Jubilant urged the reverend to walk faster as
they headed to the library. He quickly ushered his daddy
around the rows of bookshelves and demonstrated his
expertise in using the Dewey Decimal System. Feeling as
if he had done his duty, he left the reverend in the history
section.

"I have to go find Professor Carver, and then I'll bring
him here so he can meet you."

The reverend looked up from the book he had chosen
from the shelf, but before he could answer. Jubilant was

out the library doors and heading down the path leading past the cafeteria toward the other school buildings. He ran down the main campus road and went first to the professor's dorm. He knocked softly at first. *I don't want to startle him in case he's deep in thought.* After waiting a few seconds, Jubilant knocked with more force and called the professor's name. Nothing. Clearly, he wasn't in.

Realizing the time of day, Jubilant went back to the cafeteria, this time searching inside, thinking the professor would be having an early lunch since he had his breakfast before sunup. Jubilant surveyed the dining area, including the few tables set off in the back for those seeking solitude as they ate. No sign of Professor Carver. He asked Leon, one of the servers, but he hadn't seen the professor eat a meal yet that day.

Jubilant then dashed over to Milbanks Hall to Professor Carver's laboratory. *He must have lost himself in discovery.* No sight of him there either. The twelve-year-old had to catch his breath—he was wheezing like an old man by this time—then ran directly into the forest, to the professor's favorite spot. He stood on the rock they often used as a bench and hollered his name, but his friend seemed to have disappeared.

"How's it going, Jubilant?" Mr. Curtis called out when he saw Jubilant walking down University Avenue all alone, his shoulders drooped. The boy's right shoe was untied, and a kudzu leaf was in his hair. Dirt and sweat smudged his face.

"Mr. Curtis!" Jubilant's face lit up for the first time that morning. "Man, am I glad to see you! I need to talk with Professor Carver, but I can't find him anywhere."

"I'm afraid he left yesterday for Georgia."

"Georgia? But he never told me—"

"Professor Carver doesn't travel much anymore, but he agreed to a last-minute speaking engagement outside of Atlanta. Don't worry—he'll be home on Wednesday."

"Wednesday? But I'm leaving tomorrow! How could he just go to Georgia? I need to introduce him to the reverend, and I want to say good-bye."

"I'm afraid he didn't know you were leaving, otherwise he would have surely come by your aunt's to wish you well."

"I didn't know I was leaving until yesterday. I'll be on the 7:10 bus to Huntsville tomorrow morning!" Jubilant's heart beat double-time. He wiped the sweat off his forehead with the back of his hand, then rubbed his head.

Mr. Curtis laid his hand on Jubilant's shoulder. "I'm sorry, son. If you want, you could give me a letter, and I'll be sure to give it to Professor Carver when he returns."

A letter? Jubilant's posture as he continued walking back to the library revealed his distress. He shook his head in disbelief and muttered to himself. *I don't want to write him a letter. I want to say goodbye face-to-face.*

LaDelle didn't have to entertain her brother in Jubilant's absence. She knew he would be like a kid in a candy store at the Institute's well-stocked library. Too many university and public libraries were closed to negro patrons or provided only a small section of books for colored folks to enjoy. Here, at the Tuskegee Institute, in the stately brick library with its white columns outside and shelves filled with books inside, Ashton Bartley lost himself in the delight of it all. Though Jubilant had been gone longer than LaDelle expected, she remained calm, trusting, finally, that he would be responsible. Besides, she knew the likelihood of Professor Carver being a challenge to find.

Later that evening, Jubilant paid Aunt LaDelle's neighbor a visit. He'd wandered around Cal's shed a week or so before when Henrietta sent him out there to look for a bag of rags. When Jubilant opened the shed doors, he discovered a treasure trove of usable junk within those four walls.

"You need a sturdy pot, huh? I'm sure I have an extra one around here somewhere and some decent soil too. I saved some that Henrietta had mixed for her daisies a while back," Cal said, rummaging through his shed, steadying piles of this and that as he made his way toward the back. Jubilant had never seen so many bicycle tires and tools, car parts, and paint cans stuffed into such a small space. Cal had stacks of canned goods in one corner and a pile of nuts and bolts spilled out of an old coffee can onto the middle of the floor.

"Do you even know what all's in here?" Jubilant asked, wide-eyed with disbelief at what all he was finding.

"Eureka! I think I've unearthed what you're needing, son," Cal declared as a Christmas wreath balancing on a mountain of boxes toppled over, hitting the man on the head. The glittered fake pine needles left a slight dusting of shimmer in Cal's hair, but he didn't seem to care. "I'm gonna organize this stuff someday," he said, shaking his head to rid himself of at least some of the glitter.

Jubilant wondered when that day would come as Cal promptly followed him outside and shut the shed doors behind them. Clearly, like Professor Carver, Henrietta's husband didn't see the need for things to be in apple-pie order, and Jubilant admired him for it.

Jubilant thanked Mr. Cal for the terracotta pot and soil, then walked over to Aunt LaDelle's porch and sat down, straddling the pot between his knees as he filled it with dirt. A moment later as if she had some sort of radar, she threw open the screen door and stood hovering over him.

"What are you up to now? You'll be cleaning up any mess you make," she warned, eyeing the soil with her hands on her hips.

"You can watch me if you want," he said, unaffected by his aunt's henpecking.

Then he set the pot on the top step, leaned over it, and carefully poked his finger into the warm dirt several times. Jubilant took some flower seeds out of his pocket and dropped them inside the holes. He covered them over with dirt, then held the pot up for her to see.

"The holes will house those seeds until they take root and sprout beautiful flowers for Professor Carver," he announced, obviously proud of his newly discovered horticulture skills, as simple as they were.

LaDelle stood silently but nodded her approval. She spoke thoughtfully. "Holes aren't always bad. Some house seeds, helping them take root and later producing something bonnie and inviting."

Jubilant nodded not knowing how to answer her. "Mmm-hmm," he finally said before bringing up the subject of Professor Carver.

As the pair talked a while about the professor—Aunt LaDelle referring to him as "the gem of the Tuskegee Institute"—she interrupted her own train of thought when she noticed some spilled dirt on the steps and demanded Jubilant fetch a broom from the garage. He let his sigh be heard, but promptly stood up and obeyed.

"I'll let that attitude slide this time," she said and playfully slapped his rear end with the kitchen towel in her hand as he passed by.

When he returned with the broom, he heard the reverend call out. "Jube, come on in the house now. It's getting dark, and you haven't finished packing."

"It's just my luck Professor Carver won't be here to say goodbye to me. It's just my rotten luck," Jubilant lamented as he scooped up the last of the spilled soil with the dustpan and emptied it into the bushes.

"Son, you lean too much on luck. Do you still have those rabbits' feet? You'll learn soon, I hope, that God has his hands on things, and luck—good or bad—doesn't mean a hill of beans."

The reverend stepped outside onto the porch and sat down on the first step, patting it with his hand and inviting Jubilant to sit. He held up the pot with fresh soil and seeds and complemented Jubilant on his thoughtful gift for the professor. Then he blessed it out loud, "Lord, please cause this seed to grow as you intend and may it produce beautiful flowers with a sweet fragrance for George Washington Carver, a man to whom I owe many thanks. In the name of our Savior Jesus Christ. Amen."

People said the reverend had a way with words and Jubilant had grown old enough now to recognize and appreciate it. "Amen," he said in agreement.

"I didn't mean to say that stuff about luck, it's just that Professor Carver is like a grandfather to me. He's my friend. I wanted to say goodbye to him. I wanted to say thanks," Jubilant whined, fingering the rim of the pot with his finger. "He's old on the outside, but on the inside he's full of fresh ideas. And mischief! He's *full* of mischief!"

Jubilant smiled to himself as he remembered the time he saw the professor sneak a live grasshopper into Mr. Curtis's salad.

The bug hopped off the plate just as Mr. Curtis put his fork near the greens to take a bite. He screamed and jumped out of his seat yelling, "Carver, what are you trying to do, kill me?"

Professor Carver broke into such a fit of laughter that a crowd gathered around the lunch table. Even Mr. Curtis had to laugh at the sight of the professor enjoying his prank. The old man had tears rolling down his cheeks, and he continued to shake his head and giggle off and on throughout the rest of the meal. The professor bought Mr. Curtis a slice of rhubarb pie as a peace offering. Curtis dissected it with his fork before he ate it to make sure no beetles had been slipped inside. This made Professor Carver laugh all the harder.

"I was hoping to meet the professor, I truly was, but we must return home tomorrow. I promised the congregation I would teach Wednesday Bible Study." The reverend stood up slowly and looked down at his son. "I'm sorry, Jube. I'm sure the professor would appreciate receiving regular letters from you. Your letters brightened my day every time one came in the mail. They will bring joy to Professor Carver as well."

Jubilant nodded but didn't say a word. After a few minutes of further brooding, he followed the reverend into the house and finished his packing. It was no use. He'd have to be on that bus tomorrow. How strange that now it was time to leave, his desire to go back home wasn't nearly as strong. Home was here too, he'd decided.

LaDelle retreated into her room after she knew her brother and nephew were settled for the night. Jubilant was given a cot to sleep on she borrowed from Cal and Henrietta, and his bed was turned over to Ashton. *If I had myself a covered porch I could have slept there and given up my bed for the night.* She would have welcomed the cooler air, but without the screened walls in place, it would be death by mosquito, no doubt.

As LaDelle lay in her bed, her mind and hormones kept her wide awake. A sadness had come over her. She knew she would miss having Jubilant around. *When he leaves, the house will seem too big for just me and Dewey.* She liked cooking for him, knowing he loved every bite. She didn't mind doing his laundry or dealing with him leaving the toilet seat up, though once it happened in the middle of the night and proved to be annoyingly problematic. She'd miss listening to radio shows in the evenings together. She liked watching his face as he'd listen intently and throw his head back and laugh when he understood a joke and it tickled his funny bone.

Now she'd be alone again in the evenings. *You're fine, LaDelle,* she reminded herself. *You're a big girl and can handle solitary living—you've coped well so far. Besides, Dewey still needs you.* Forcing herself to dwell on that truth, which is almost impossible after midnight when the mind is difficult to tame, she finally nodded off at 2:00 a.m.

Early the next morning, after two cups of coffee and a healthy breakfast, LaDelle and Dewey drove the reverend and a sleepy Jubilant to the bus station. It was a quiet ride for a while as no one knew what to say. There was an unspoken sadness in the car. Ashton tried to get his sister to take the money he brought to pay her for all she'd paid for on account of his son. She refused.

"Get your money out of my face," she snapped, batting it away.

"I'll tell you what," Ashton said after they'd gone toe to toe over the issue for a mile or so. "How 'bout the boy and I come back sometime next spring, and we build you a covered porch. We'll pay for the materials and provide the labor."

"All right then, fine, fine," she responded, but inside her heart was dancing. She was thrilled to know she'd be with her brother and nephew again in less than a year. It pleased her even more than having a covered porch, though she was excited at that thought. She would count the days.

Dewey sat on Jubilant's lap and panted in his face while the boy scratched him behind the ears as they neared the bus station.

"He's going to miss you," LaDelle said, watching boy and dog interact.

"I'll miss him, too—even his hot, smelly breath." He kissed the top of Dewey's nose.

"You're the best dog, Dewey. Maybe soon Daddy will get me my own mutt."

LaDelle smiled and nudged her brother, but the reverend didn't comment.

When they pulled into the dirt lot and parked the car, Jubilant carried his own overstuffed duffel and followed his aunt and daddy through the terminal doors. They were twenty-eight minutes early, which was Aunt LaDelle's idea. Jubilant had become used to her obsession with punctuality, but he wished he could have stolen a few extra minutes of sleep and arrived on time instead of getting to the station well before seven. He plopped down on the hard bench— the same one he sat on when he met Dorothy—while the reverend purchased the tickets. A minute later, he heard a girl squeal.

"We came to say goodbye," Lydia announced as she ran toward Jubilant, holding a dirty Crystal Rose, and jumped onto his lap. Jubilant looked up to find Miss Patty, Wilson, Cal, and Henrietta standing in front of him with big smiles on their faces. The women kissed his cheeks and the men shook hands with him and the reverend. Wilson handed him a book called *Bows Against the Barons*. Tucked inside was a drawing he did of his rooster, Duke. Miss Patty put a paper sack in his hand. "Moon pies. Homemade," she said, holding back the tears. "We'll miss you around here, boy."

"Please, Miss Patty, make sure Aunt LaDelle gives Professor Carver the plant and letter I wrote him as soon as he gets back in town," Jubilant whispered in her ear after she hugged him so hard and long, he was nearly smothered in her bosom.

"I promise now, so don't you worry," Miss Patty assured him in a hushed tone so as not to offend LaDelle.

"You be sure to come back and visit us," Henrietta told Jubilant. "I want my baby to meet you," she added, patting her stomach.

LaDelle looked at her neighbor with wide eyes and clapped her hands together. "I knew something was different about you! I knew it!"

"Can you believe it, LaDelle? Cal and I have always wanted a child. "We've lost five of them in the early stages, but this one seems to have stuck! And I'm feelin' sick as a dog. Glory be to God!"

More hugs, more handshakes, more laughter.

"Does your family need to be so loud?" The ticket seller called out from behind the booth with a scowl on his face.

LaDelle was about to correct him in that way of hers but decided not to. Instead, her face beamed at his assumption all of them gathered there were family. She realized at that moment they had, indeed, become a family. God had used Jubilant to bring them together in such a way. To fill a hole. How clever of him. How kind.

LaDelle, along with the friends and neighbors—family now—continued saying their goodbyes and what needed to be said as they remained in the middle of the bus station, but their chatter stopped suddenly when an announcement was made that the "7:10 to Huntsville will be boarding in five minutes."

Miss Patty picked up Jubilant's duffel with a wink, and as a group, they made their way to the bus waiting for its passengers outside. After another round of hugs and handshakes, the reverend and Jubilant boarded the bus.

"Thank you, Aunt LaDelle," Jubilant said, facing his aunt. "I left a letter for you on your sewing desk."

LaDelle, overcome with emotion, hugged Jubilant and kissed his forehead. "Thank you, Jubilant. Thank you, dear boy," she whispered in his ear. Then, turning to Ashton, she gave him a final hug. "We'll do better to be in each other's lives now, won't we?" she said, admonishing him as well as herself.

A little stronger and a little taller, Jubilant was relieved that he was able to shove his duffel, without incident, through the bus doors and carry it down the narrow aisle to their seats. As they settled into their seats and waited for other passengers to board, he heard the rapid, loud honking of a car from behind the bus. He looked out the window in time to see Aunt LaDelle frantically waving her arms and mouthing something to Jubilant from the parking lot. He shook his head and shrugged his shoulders to let her know he didn't understand, and then he saw what she was trying to tell him. There was Mr. Curtis helping Professor Carver out of his car!

"Professor Carver!" Jubilant jumped over his daddy and flew down the aisle, stepping on seats when necessary to get around oncoming passengers. "S'cuse me! Let me pass, I need to get through!" Seconds later he was off the bus and standing in front of a very weary-looking Professor Carver. "You made it!"

"Curtis sent me a wire you were leaving today. I had to come back early and say goodbye."

Jubilant hugged his friend—his honorary grandfather and mentor. The old man's high-pitched voice, leathery skin, kind smile, and his old suit with the flower in its lapel would forever be etched in Jubilant's mind. But even more so, the professor's gentleness and the way he inspired and loved people. Jubilant knew a part of George Washington Carver would follow him for the rest of his life.

"I'll keep writing, I promise," Jubilant said. "In fact, I can't seem to stop! And I'm gettin' better at it. I may even write a book someday and get it published. If I do, Aunt LaDelle said she'd make sure it was in the Tuskegee Institute's fine library!"

The reverend joined the pair outside and shook Professor Carver's hand. They talked for a few minutes before the bus driver announced it was time to pull out. Just before Jubilant walked away, the professor, with tears in his eyes, reached out and put his hand on Jubilant's head. He gave it a quick rub, and they both smiled. "Your letters mattered," the old man said. "And you ought to feel really good about that. You used your 'equipment'," he added.

"Daddy says I have a gift for words."

"I don't doubt it."

"I'll write you a letter from Huntsville real soon," Jubilant promised.

Father and son waved to the group outside as the bus pulled out. Jubilant wiped away his own tears as they traveled out of Tuskegee and headed toward Huntsville.

"Looks like you found a home away from home, Jube. You feelin' a bit sad about leaving, aren't you?" the reverend asked, patting his son's knee.

"Yes, Daddy," Jubilant admitted solemnly. "I'll miss the family I have here. And Aunt LaDelle's cookin' for sure. It makes me sad to leave." He then looked up and smiled at the reverend who appeared even stronger and healthier than the day before. He patted his daddy's shoulder and sighed. "But I'm also feeling mighty jubilant."

EPILOGUE

In the days that followed Jubilant and the reverend's departure, LaDelle took back her sewing room—but first she read Jubilant's letter, which made her both laugh and cry—and started on a quilt for Henrietta and Cal's little one. The baby was due to arrive late March but would come eleven days late on April first—April Fool's Day—which Henrietta thought was hilarious. In addition to making a quilt, LaDelle put together an entire layette, praying prayers of blessing for the unborn child as she cut, measured, and sewed. She embroidered some pink flowers along some of the collars and sleeves.

"Oh, thank you, LaDelle! You've supplied my sweet Billie Louise with more linen and clothing than she could ever possibly use," Henrietta said when LaDelle brought over a basket filled with gifts. "Though on second thought, we probably will use everything. This baby girl soils everything quicker than a set of twins, and that's a fact. At ten pounds two ounces, the newborn gowns won't fit her for long, I'm afraid."

"I told you not to eat so much starch when you were pregnant—it would make the baby too big I said—but you wouldn't listen," she reminded Henrietta days later when she was complaining about her stretch marks. Henrietta responded to her friend by asking LaDelle to be her Billie Louise's godmother. True grace lived in Henrietta.

LaDelle continued to enjoy her work at the Tuskegee Institute, but instead of spending her evenings home alone, she often had Henrietta, Cal, and Billie over for supper or she'd go over to their home or the Doyles would ask her over.

Once every few weeks, she and George would share a meal which she looked forward to with such fervor that, when it was to be at her house, she'd plan the meal as if it were Thanksgiving. She'd grown more comfortable talking with George after all they'd experienced together with Jubilant, though she was still in awe of him. *He's just a human, same as me, though he's quite special.* They'd share any letters they'd received from Jubilant and read them out loud as they ate their supper together. Most of the time he'd show up late, but she'd bite her tongue. After a couple of late arrivals, she secretly planned for the meal to begin thirty minutes after the time she told him to arrive.

One of their "dates" in the early fall was to take place at lunchtime. LaDelle entered the cafeteria at the Tuskegee Institute where she had agreed to meet George. What she discovered as she approached the table took her off guard and left her weak in the knees. There was the professor with a huge smile on his face and next to him sat Abel Fisher! George had invited Abel to join them without asking her first, and from the look on his face he was rather proud of himself.

Though for a full two seconds, she was angry at George for pulling such a stunt, LaDelle took one look at Abel's hazel eyes and quickly softened. She sat down but avoided eye contact with the handsome grocery store manager for as long as she could. Her heartbeat quickened, being with him like that, outside the Piggly Wiggly, but soon the conversation flowed, and LaDelle relaxed. A sense of home and ease filled her.

After the trio ate and laughed and solved the problems of the world together, George excused himself to retreat to his laboratory. Abel seized the moment and invited LaDelle to join him at the Fall Fair the following Saturday. His invitation was humble, but confident, like Abel himself.

This man could be trouble for me. He's making his way into my heart, and I can't seem to stop it from happening.

Within two months of that night at the fair, LaDelle had lost four pounds, sewed a new dress—a cheerful red one patterned with small, playful umbrellas—began a new ritual of slathering cold cream on her face and neck at night and, to Henrietta's great pleasure, allowed her friend to give her a fresh, new hair style.

LaDelle decided whatever was happening was rather nice, like she was a young woman again and had her whole life ahead of her. Abel's charming ways kept on. The man was consistent which gave her a sense of anticipation and stability. So even though she didn't need to go to the market as often once Jubilant had gone back to Huntsville, LaDelle would find herself popping into the Piggly Wiggly for an onion or some lard or a jar of molasses, knowing full well she had an unopened one in the cupboard at home.

When Abel would encounter her—and she made sure he did—he'd come up to her and whistle quietly through his teeth and say, "Now there's a nice sight to see!" Followed by, "Mind if I stop by after work?"

After sharing a pot of stew together one Friday evening, Abel took a seat on the couch next to LaDelle instead of on the chair across the room, as he had done the half a dozen times during prior visits. They talked about their childhood, and in the middle of her describing what it was like growing up in New York, Abel Fisher reached out and took her hand in his.

LaDelle fought back tears. *What does all this mean? Is this okay by you, Garvin? It's all a little wonderful and a lot petrifying.* LaDelle decided a few days later to allow herself the pleasure of dating Abel. She added him to her life but told him she needed to take things slow. He nodded and said, "Will do." So, they did.

And when Billie Louise caught a ferocious flu and had the adults in her life worried sick, LaDelle forced herself to sing, "I Surrender All." Then, when a pipe broke in LaDelle's bathroom and flooded it pretty bad, and Ashton postponed his and Jubilant's visit until mid-summer because of a "delicate issue at hand"—which turned out to be his engagement to Priscilla and Artie's mother—so her screened in porch was late in coming, LaDelle reminded herself to sing, "I Surrender All." And when menopause threatened to be her undoing, and she found herself ruminating far too often over where her relationship with Abel might lead, LaDelle found herself singing "I Surrender All." The more she sang the song, the more she meant the words. Whenever she sang, Dewey would scratch on the door, begging to be let outside, but if she was with Billie Louise at the time, the little girl would smile up at her *deuxiéme maman* as if each word being sung made her feel jubilant.

A NOTE FROM THE AUTHOR

I enjoy reading several genres, but I tend to lose myself in historical fiction. When written well, it's both entertaining and educational—a perfect combination to me. While engaged in a work of historical fiction, I spend time intermittently doing my own research as I want to know what within the story actually took place in history and what was fabricated in the mind of the author. This sleuthing, discovery, and traveling back in time makes reading and writing historical fiction my favorite.

As for this book, you might be surprised to learn with all the research I conducted to make my story historically accurate and plausible, I was nearly done writing it when I had this thought: "I wonder if there was ever a female librarian in the early days of the Tuskegee Institute, or, as it was originally named, the Tuskegee Normal School for Teachers?" Some basic research quickly revealed Tuskegee's first librarian—in the late 1800s—was indeed female. I was thrilled with this discovery as it gave further credibility to the fact a person like LaDelle could have very well been employed as a campus librarian.

What truly amazed, if not shocked me, was learning the first librarian's name was so similar to that of my fictional character's. Her name was Adella Logan Hunt. *Adella!* I had made up the name "LaDelle" so I couldn't believe the similarity between the two names! As I learned more about Adella Logan Hunt, I discovered, however, that what these two women—one real, the other fictional—shared in common ended with their names and librarian roles on campus.

Adella's impressively accomplished life was cut short at age fifty-two when she committed suicide by jumping out of a window from a building on the Tuskegee campus. The variety of articles I read each suggest her struggles with personal heartache regarding her marriage, her discouragement over the lack of progress she experienced while serving as an activist for the suffrage movement, and the death of her good friend, Booker T. Washington, as well as probable mental illness—led to her tragic end.

The fictional life of LaDelle Harris, though met with its own brand of heartache and tragedy, progresses much differently. While in her early fifties, her life is significantly enhanced and met with great hope by her renewed family ties, the benefits of genuine friendship, and a deeper trust in God's loving and sovereign control. I had great fun creating a life on paper and bringing LaDelle into the world through my story. This meant I could dictate her every move, situation, and emotion. Even if I had known about Adella and the way her life ended prior to writing my book, I would have never incorporated her circumstances into my character's. My vision for LaDelle was set on a path when I first dove into this project, and my desire from the get-go was to promote hope and trust, among other positive virtues.

The impetus, however, of me first embarking on this long, detailed journey to Tuskegee was my fascination with George Washington Carver. His history, demeanor, convictions, and accomplishments added a true-life character of great substance to my story I could never have made up on my own. If I could go back in time and visit someone in history, he would top the list—right under Moses. He's *that* fascinating to me.

I had known about "The Peanut Man" from when I was a kid in school, but I grew to appreciate him on a whole other level when I began homeschooling my youngest two sons. We adopted the boys from birth, and both are biracial—Black and White. I wanted them to learn about male and female heroes of color in history and thought of Professor Carver and the accomplishments I knew he made in the areas of botany and chemistry. I read several picture books on his life to my kindergartner and second grader and promptly went back to the library for more books for me.

I read everything I could get my hands on regarding "young George" and "Professor Carver" and honorary "Dr. Carver." I became completely enthralled by this man, not only because of his beginnings and accomplishments, but also his humility, heart, and faith.

When I'd exhausted the library system and all that I could find online, I hopped on a plane with my friend, Ruth, and we flew from the Bay Area of California to Alabama. We stayed at the Kellogg Hotel and Conference Center on the Tuskegee University campus to learn all I could about Professor Carver and better understand "his" world.

While staying there, I had my first plate of catfish and devoured the best grits I've ever eaten. I drank too much sweet tea as I tried to cool off in the southern muggy weather in October. I shopped at a Piggly Wiggly and stood out as "a white woman from out of town" as I explored Professor Carver's historical environment, though of course it was much different from back when he was a part of it.

I visited and revisited the George Washington Carver Museum which is filled with all things George—from his paintings and bulletins, crocheted doilies and homemade paint, to a recording of his voice I couldn't listen to long enough. I wasn't ready to leave Tuskegee when the time came to catch my flight home.

Years after that visit, and as my story progressed and I wove George into it, I came across more reliable resources, including those provided by Mr. Dana Chandler who has served as the University Archivist at Tuskegee since 2007. He provided me with further insight and dispelled some common myths that have spread throughout the years regarding Professor Carver—his history, life, and accomplishments. I'm beyond grateful to Mr. Chandler and the official letter of endorsement he granted me for *LaDelle & Jubilant*.

How thankful I am for the years I invested in LaDelle, Jubilant, George, and the gang. I hope you've benefited from reading my story as much as I have in writing it.

ABOUT THE AUTHOR

Cathy McIlvoy was born and raised in Southern California, where she lived in the same neighborhood in the same house for twenty-two years. She married Rob, and adventure ensued! They had two boys, moved to the San Francisco Bay Area, where they served on staff at a church, and added to their family with two more sons through adoption. After some time, they moved again, this time overseas to Germany with their four kids in tow to serve at a Christian international boarding school in the beautiful Black Forest. Later, they moved to the Dominican Republic to work with a mission organization empowering national leaders to reach their communities for Christ. From there, they resettled back in California and unpacked ... again.

In the middle of all that packing, moving, and serving, Cathy wrote as often as she could, and some of her nonfiction work was featured in magazines and other publications. She began ghostwriting memoirs and self-help books for clients from all walks of life while writing *LaDelle & Jubilant*, her passion project.

LaDelle & Jubilant is her first published work of fiction and was initially inspired by her admiration for George Washington Carver. Her interest in him and Tuskegee grew as she taught her sons about this genuine man of faith. She especially wanted her two biracial sons to know about this scientist with his impressive accomplishments and commendable character, who looked like them.

Today, Cathy and her husband make their home near one of their sons in Louisville, Kentucky, where they minister to pastors, leaders, and missionaries through Standing Stone Ministries. (She named her Kentucky home *Evermore* because after fourteen moves in thirty-six years, she plans to stay put.) In addition to having four grown sons, Cathy and her husband are blessed with amazing daughters-in-law, a growing brood of grandchildren, and—though calling them a blessing is a matter of debate between her and family members—two persnickety cats.

QUESTIONS FOR DISCUSSION AND REFLECTION

1. Regarding taking care of Jubilant, LaDelle tells God in chapter one, *"I'll fail for sure if you don't help."* Though LaDelle was never a parent herself, she practically raised her younger brothers. So why is she so hesitant to care for Jubilant? Has there ever been a time in your life when God was asking something of you that seemed overly burdensome? How did you respond? What was the outcome?

2. We're told in chapter three that LaDelle's *"... rebellious attitude was often just below the surface if not in full view. And it was fueled by fear."* Give some examples of how her fear plays out in the story. How does fear manifest itself in your life?

3. After Jubilant lets out a loud burp during a Sunday sermon and then nods off, the reverend lectures his son about not acting out but blending in more and letting folks get used to him. He says in chapter four: *"People tend to be more forgiving of improper behavior once they've experienced the good in a person ..."* Do you think this is a true statement in our world today? How might it have been different in the 1930s?

4. We see a different side to LaDelle in chapter six when she encounters Abel Fisher at the Piggly Wiggly. In what way does she feel conflicted over him? What draws her to him? Does a budding relationship look different when someone is of middle-age and older? If so, why and in what way(s)?

5. In chapter eight, after Jubilant settles in for the night, LaDelle attempts to calm herself before she heads to bed by soaking in the tub. But, as she focuses on some "what-ifs," fear invades her. A few minutes later, she sees a vision which has an instant calming effect. Do you think God uses visions to speak to people today? Is there a specific time when you have "heard" from the Lord in a special way? What effect did it have on you?

6. In chapter nine we learn that, after Garvin's unexpected death, LaDelle decides she must move forward with her life and sets her sights on being employed at the Tuskegee Institute. What fuels her desire to work at this school and what steps does she take to make her dream a reality? What character traits does it reveal in LaDelle? What is a current dream of yours? What steps can you take toward it?

7. When Professor Carver comes to the library to get Jubilant in chapter ten, the two head to the forest together to collect specimens. What role does the forest play in George's life—at this time in the story and before that? Is there a specific place that plays a special role in your life? Where is it and how is it a help to you?

8. In chapter thirteen, in what ways does Dorothy ignore the cultural racist norms of the day when

she meets Jubilant at the bus station? Some of her actions make Jubilant uncomfortable—not because of Dorothy, but because of what others may presume or accuse him of. How has this type of oppression changed since the 1930s, and what changes still need to be made today? How can you participate in the needed change you've identified? Or, share about a time when racial inequality affected you personally.

9. As George and Jubilant retreat to the forest together in chapter fifteen for the second time, Jubilant comments to George that he has a lot of energy for someone his age. George responds: *"When a person is given a task, he will also be given what is needed to complete the task at hand, no matter his age."* Given some facts you know about George Washington Carver, what evidence do you have that this was true in his life? How have you experienced God fueling you with what you needed to complete a task of some kind?

10. After some vulnerable conversation on both their parts, we see LaDelle and Jubilant making peace with each other one morning in chapter nineteen: *"Jubilant reached out and laid his hand on his aunt's arm resting on the table. She put her other hand on top of his and gave his arm a tender squeeze."* What had to take place before they could come to this point? What did they come to understand/realize about the other person? If you've experienced a reconciliation of some sort in your life, how did it come about?

www.ingramcontent.com/pod-product-compliance
Lightning Source LLC
Chambersburg PA
CBHW070508030726
47503CB00004B/1204